Review request

As an author, there's nothing I like more than hearing how people enjoy my books. Your reviews are not only welcome but also really helpful to others who are seeking good books to read. Please consider taking just a few minutes to leave a brief review.

Draft copy.
Hugh Macnab

Further reading

Sammy Greyfox series

No Way Back
Head of the Snake
Lost Souls

Eli Ross series

Dark Matter
Final Act
Tears of Joy

Crime thriller with a supernatural twist

Seminole killer

This work is entirely fictional, and any similarity to people or places is purely coincidental.

No part of this publication should be reproduced in any form or by any means, without explicit permission from the author.

Copyright © 2021 Hugh Macnab

Crossing the line

Hugh Macnab

Copyright © 2021 Hugh Macnab

All rights reserved.

ISBN: **9798594992405**

1

The early alarm has gone off, but still, I lay in bed thinking about the recent past and the significance of the day ahead. That the past nine months have been tough would be no understatement. Responsible for the deaths of two children in very different circumstances.

A two-year-old caught in a crossfire. A death the Department had investigated and found no reprimand necessary. An outcome that didn't help me sleep at night.

Recently, I met with the mother of the child I shot and killed. It was the most challenging thing I've ever had to do. She accepted my apology with a grace that embarrassed me. That moment was one of those that changed me. With her dignity, she has shown me something I could aspire to. A better version of myself. Where I thought I would come away sad and feeling worse about myself. The opposite was true.

The other child whose death I'm responsible for was my unborn child, whom I named Bossy-boots and had terminated. A decision made without consulting the father left me guilty on many levels. I prioritized my role as a homicide detective over my unborn child's life and any rights of the father. It still hurts to think I can be so selfish and cruel. It doesn't fit my self-image. Yet, I can't deny it. I *am* selfish, and I *am* cruel. Something I must learn to accept.

* * *

Then, there's the last struggle I've been having, which is recommitting to being a detective. To do this, I've had to cross two bridges.

First, I refused an excellent life-changing job offer I'd received to head up security at the Seminole Casino and Legalized Brothel. This was a tough decision, as the package on offer was tremendous. But I would have to give up my detective badge, and I don't want to do that.

Second, I had to accept I could be responsible for further loss of life because it comes with the job. When I'm honest with myself, I've accepted this, but I know there's still doubt. Maybe the uncertainty is something that will live with me.

Aware that I'm having the same internal dialogue I've been having for nine months, I swing my legs out of bed and head for the shower.

While the water cascades over me, I force my mind to consider the more positive aspects of the past nine months.

I seriously damaged my left knee when a perp tried to run me down. They recommended surgery, but I opted for a slower but more natural recovery. I wore a brace for eight weeks, then orthopedic neoprene support for a further six before starting physiotherapy sessions three times a week. Now, my knee isn't one hundred percent, but it's improving. What's more important to me is that I can run again, as long as it isn't too fast or too far. I'm getting there.

Another positive step I took was to offer the Sheriff my resignation.

When I was suffering the worst pain I have ever experienced, I stupidly accepted painkillers from a local drug pusher. I foolishly thought he was being kind. He wasn't. He was setting me up for blackmail. I was to be what he called his *inside blue-bitch,* feeding him information. When I explained this to the Sheriff, he waved away my concern. Instead, he told me to focus on my recovery and return to work as soon as possible. I was genuinely grateful for that.

Turning off the faucet and stepping out of the shower, I dry myself, study my face in the mirror, and ask myself if I'm sure I'm ready to return to work.

I don't know what I expect to hear, but I'm still disappointed when I don't get an answer. It certainly isn't a resounding - yes!

Regardless, twenty minutes later, the running gear is on. My badge and Glock are clipped at my side - I've learned once before always to keep them available. A lesson I do not need to learn twice. One last look around the apartment, and I'm off.

Early mornings in February are cool in Florida, so I have an extra lightweight jacket on top of my running gear. Today, I select a middle-length route and quickly settle into a simple rhythm, pounding the empty streets and heading towards the beach. Before my recent difficulties, my brain would switch off as I ran, but not now. Today, I'm thinking about Bossy-boots and how he or she would already be a reality by now. I only recently admitted that I had secretly assumed it was a girl. I was forever told what to do by this tiny monster inside me. It had to be female.

By now, she would be six weeks old. I don't know if I would have been breastfeeding or not. Would I have her in a routine or feed on demand? Would my bottle of Corona have made way for bottles of prepared milk in the fridge? Would my apartment smell of baby? Would I smell of baby? Would my breasts leak at work? Would I even be at work? I feel like shouting aloud at myself to shut the fuck up and concentrate on running. But I don't.

Forty minutes later, I rock up at EJ's eatery. I do warm-down exercises, then enter and slide into my usual booth. My first coffee of the day arrives before I even open the menu. I order waffles and syrup and sit back to think ahead. Will the office be different? My direct boss, Dan Weissman, has regularly checked in with me, so I know he hasn't changed.

I also know he will understand the challenges I will face.

What about everyone else? What will they think about me killing a two-year-old? Will they say? If they do, will they say what they really think or be polite? How will I know? Fuck. I accept that I will have to face all this, but I'm not looking forward to it.

I demolish the stack of waffles, finish my coffee top-up, put it all on my tab, and head in. The office is only ten minutes away. I walk instead of running. Somehow, the closer I am, the less enthusiastic I become. The thought of my colleagues not being straight with me is causing my stomach to churn.

I see my vacant space as I cross through the carpark behind the Sheriff's office block. The area where I used to park my trusty steed. My clapped-out Chevy. Sadly, that's one thing I've had to sacrifice in the past nine months. I got nine hundred bucks for it, which helped me clear my previous tab at EJ's and hold a few hundred in reserve. I'm not flush, but I am getting by.

Inside, I take a second shower in the locker room and change into my jeans and a simple black round-neck T-shirt. Clip on my badge and Glock, then head upstairs.

The Detectives' Bureau is a large open-plan office with around thirty cubicles. Usually, even at seven-thirty in the morning, the place is buzzing. We start early and finish early. Well, start early anyway. When we're on a case, the clock doesn't have a say when we knock off.

Today, the place is empty. No sign of life. I head towards my cubicle when suddenly there is a roar, and people spring up from their cubicles, cheering my name and chanting. 'Sammy! Sammy! Sammy!' They're all smiling and laughing. Then they gather around, clapping me on the back, and offer support. This floors me and isn't what I'm expecting.

The last to greet me is Dan Weissman, with a massive grin on his face. 'You didn't think you would slink back in with no one noticing, did you?'

I can't speak. I'm tongue-tied.

Without saying another word to me, he turns to the gathered detectives and asks. 'Who here has been responsible for a fatal shooting?'

A third of the room raises their hands. I'm astonished. I had no idea.

'I'm having Sammy head into the small conference room, and I want each of you to talk with her one-on-one. I want you to tell your story and tell her how you have learned to deal with it. I know how boring you guys can be, so I'll supply regular coffee to keep her awake. I'll go first.'

Dan picked up two coffees and led me into the small conference room.

After that, the morning is a blur. People kept coming in and telling their stories. How bad they felt taking a life, even though they had no choice. How they dealt with the guilt. At one point, both the Sheriff and the Under-Sheriff also came in.

If you ask me now who did what, I wouldn't have a clue. I have learned that I'm not alone, which counts for a lot. And they are all genuinely glad I'm back. Any doubts I've had are washed away.

2

After lunch, I log on at my desk, expecting five-trillion emails. Instead, there is only a handful, and they're all current. I stand above the cubicle wall and shout across to Dan. 'Has someone stolen my emails? My account's empty?'

Dan's voice drifts back. 'Don't complain. It's the only break you're going to get. I think we've just got a new case.'

Instantly forgetting my missing emails, I walk the few steps to his cubicle and sit. 'Tell me more.'

'No time. It looks like we've lost one of our own. Let's go.'

On the way, Dan explains that they've just found a detective from the Narcotics Division dead in his apartment. He hadn't turned up for work the previous day, and two of his colleagues checked out his place on their way to work this morning. Getting no answer, they badged the super and gained entry. Found the body and called it in twenty minutes ago.

The apartment is in Jasmine Circle, a better area than mine. But, there again, almost all places would be. It's in a small circle of blocks around an open grassed area between Goodlette-Frank and Rte 41, only a ten-minute walk from work. So we're there in less than that.

Two patrol cars and an unmarked are already outside when we arrive. Patrol officers have already secured the scene, and one records those who enter. Looking at the list, I can see that

Arnie Collins, the Medical Examiner, is already onsite with a team of three from Forensics. The two detectives who found the body stand to one side, smoking and looking pretty shaken up. We head their way.

Dan asks if they are okay, then they tell us what happened. They had convinced the super to let them in and found Mark Jason in bed. His eyes were closed, and they assumed he was asleep. However, when they went to raise him, there was a small stain of dried blood on the duvet, and his body was cold and stiff. So they touched nothing further, called it in, and stepped outside to wait.

We slip on plastic booties and gloves and enter the apartment with nothing more to learn from them. I'm right; it is much nicer than my place. More windows, so much lighter, and it looks recently decorated. The furnishings are comfortable rather than flashy, but I see enough to wonder if detectives in Narcs are being paid more than in homicide. One of the forensic team is taking pictures of anything and everything while a second is dusting for prints.

We leave them to it and enter the bedroom where Arnie is examining Mark Jason. He nods his acknowledgment as we enter but continues his work in silence.

He has folded the duvet to the bottom of the bed to reveal that Jason is still half-dressed, wearing loose gray jogging bottoms with a string tie around the waist and trainers. He's lying on his back, eyes closed, with a small pool of congealed blood underneath his upper torso. Arnie is muttering to himself as he examines a small puncture wound in the chest, the source of the blood.

Looking around the room. Nothing seems out of place. No signs of a struggle. It looks like he had simply gone to bed two nights ago.

* * *

Arnie speaks first. 'Brilliant, this one.'
'What do you mean, Arnie?' asks Dan.
'Small narrow blade. Slipped between the second and third rib. Severed the aortic arch, but with a very small entry wound.'
'Meaning?' I ask.
At that moment, Arnie truly notices me for the first time and welcomes me back before answering my question.
'A severed aorta usually means a lot of blood, which is also true in this case, but it's mostly internal bleeding. Just as lethal, but not nearly as messy.'
'Professional job?' I ask.
'Could be. Or a medically qualified person? Maybe I can tell more when I start the autopsy.'
'Today, Arnie?'
'Definitely, Dan. I'll clear everything aside and get started by mid-afternoon. You attending?'
'I'll let you know.'

At that point, Arnie closes his bag of tricks and heads out. Two of his assistants move in to remove the body, and we follow Arnie outside.
'What do you think, Sammy?'
'What do you mean, Dan? It's a homicide for sure.'
'No, Sammy. What I mean is, are you ready?'
'Me?'
Dan nods. What can I say? No, I'm sorry, Dan. I don't feel up to it yet. I'm still suffering from self-recrimination and guilt. I might never be ready.
What I actually say is, sure. I'll take it.

On the way back into the office, Dan reassures me he'll be available 24/7 if I need help and that if the case becomes complicated, he'll allocate more people to work with me. He also promises to deal with internal communications if I keep him up to speed. He's speaking code for keeping the Sheriff and Under-Sheriff off my back. This is a subtle reminder that when we lose one of our own, everyone wants to know everything - all the time. Dan's offer will let me focus on solving the case without worrying about office politics and the Press.

I'm glad Dan didn't force more people on me at this early stage of an investigation. I much prefer doing the basic groundwork myself. I trust myself with details. I'm not so good with others.

When we arrive at the office, I sit in my cubicle, organizing my thoughts. The first thing is obvious. I need to open a case book. Although we're all encouraged to develop electronic case books, most of us still like the old paper version. I find a large folder and write Mark Jason's name on it.

Next, I call Arnie, and he promises to give me a shout when he's about to start the autopsy. He confirms his best guess as mid-afternoon.

I will need to interview the two Narc detectives who found the body formally. Then speak to other colleagues to find out if he was working on anything that might have gotten him killed.
After deciding that, I head to HR.
I'll need to review Jason's Personnel file to get next of kin, family members, and other personal details. Then break the news.

Bureaucrats piss me off. HR, Finance, Admin, and Unions are all the same. Fucking hopeless. The man is dead. Still, I can't gain access to his file without the Sheriff's permission. But, even given that, I still can't remove it from HR. Yet, they're happy for me to take pictures of everything with my cell. Go figure!

Back in the office, I send all the details to my email account and print everything off for the case book. His next of kin is a sister living up in Punta Gorda. His parents are dead, and he has gone through two divorces. I reckon that would knock a hole in his finances, yet he still had a better apartment than me. I'm now convinced they pay Narcs more.

One divorce was a year ago, the other five years before. Both exes lived here in Collier County. Other than that, there is no one else. After checking the time, I know I can get up to Punta Gorda and back before Arnie starts the autopsy. It's about an hour north. First, I call to make sure she's at home. It's an awkward call. I don't want to tell her on the phone, but I can't avoid her being worried.

As soon as I hang up, I head for the duty sergeant. I need a pool car. Unfortunately, none are available, so I end up in a patrol car with a driver I've met before. He's what I would describe as one of the good guys. Around fifty and heading for retirement, he's usually a training officer for newbies. On this particular day, his newbie is off sick.

Like everyone else, he knows about my shooting history and is happy to share a few of his own experiences with me. The more I hear, the more I feel I can manage my guilt. I don't talk with him about terminating Bossy-boots. That's one for me to deal with on my own.

We take I75 to save around ten minutes because there's an exit ramp at Jones Loop Road, and the address we're looking for is just off that. So we turn into Tuscany Isles Drive and continue until we stop outside forty-five. It's what I call a two-in-one. Single-storey, divided down the middle. Two driveways, side-by-side, with double garages. She has a bland silver Toyota parked in her driveway.

Jason's sister's name is Susan Entwhistle. According to the file, she's a nurse, which immediately puts her on my suspect list. But I have to assume she'll be a grieving relative as far as this visit will go.

She's already standing at her front door when I climb out of the Patrol SUV. Walking towards her, I can see her nervously twisting her hands. Her face looks strained. She's already expecting bad news, and I'm not going to disappoint...

I follow her inside before saying anything, and we sit opposite each other. When I tell her what has happened, the news clearly shocks her. I guess, in a situation like this, you may expect the worst, but when you're told someone has murdered your brother, that's a whole different level of surprise. Shot in the line of duty or killed in a vehicle collision. She would get that. But stabbed to death in his bed. That's a hard pill to swallow.

The surprise on her face is evident. This woman didn't kill her brother. No one can pretend like this. It's just not possible. The color drains from her face entirely as the tears flow freely. She's trying to say something, but can't get it out, so I offer to make her a coffee. She nods. I head for the kitchen, glad to get out of there.

Five minutes later, I'm back with two steaming mugs. I place one in front of her. She doesn't acknowledge it. She's staring into space. She's in shock. I move over to sit beside her, take one of her hands in mine and gently rub with what I hope is a reassuring touch. I'm not good at this sort of thing, but I give it my best shot. She seems to respond. She turns, looks me in the eye, and thanks me for the coffee.

I move back opposite and start asking my questions. She falters a little at first, but she relents and starts answering when I give her the old line about me needing to ask if we're to catch whoever is responsible.

Honestly, I learn nothing useful. She only saw her brother three or four times a year. He was a loner. Their parents died in a car crash over ten years before, so there were only two of them. They weren't close. She knew nothing about his friends or his work. She knew he was a detective but didn't even know he worked in Narcotics. This all left me wondering what they talked about when they were together.

When I say I learned nothing useful, that's not true. When I asked about Jason's previous marriages and exes, Susan was less than forthcoming. This left me wondering, so I added the two exes to my interview list.

After leaving Susan, I have time to think on the return journey. Who would want to kill Jason? Was it work-related, or had it something to do with his personal life? At that moment in time, I'm fifty-fifty. I don't know, but I will find out.

3

We stop and grab sandwiches on the way back to the office, and I'm glad we have. There's unlikely to be any time later. There's a message already waiting for me. Arnie is ready to start the autopsy on Mark Jason. The message was timed thirty minutes before.

I head downstairs immediately and arrive after Arnie has made the Y-incision, sprung the rib cage open, and is up to his elbows, removing organs to measure, weigh and take samples from.

I can't think of the body on the autopsy table as Mark Jason. I can't think of what I see as human at all. The flesh on both sides of the body is folded open, and all I can see are two mounds of yellowish fatty blubber. I know we all have fat and need it, but when you see it like this, it's gross. It makes me want to go veggie.

'Dan not coming?'

'Fraid you're stuck with me, Arnie. My case. My autopsy.'

'Well, you've already missed the exciting part. The heart's over there,' Arnie tells me, indicating a stainless steel bowl - one of many.

'What did you find, Arnie?'

'Even more sophisticated than I thought at the crime scene. Whoever did this maximized the damage to the aorta while minimizing external bleeding. As a result, the aorta was ninety percent cleanly severed, leading to massive internal bleeding. I would say he died within thirty seconds at most. If the knife remained in the wound for as little as a minute after doing the damage, the heart would have no blood left to pump.'

'Hence, minimum blood at the scene.'

'The blade used was most likely a stiletto, with a narrow cross-section and acuminated tip which would reduce friction upon entry, allowing the blade to penetrate deeply with relatively little pressure being applied.'

'Acuminated?'

'Just means tapered to a needlepoint.'

'But if it was such a fine blade, how did it manage to almost sever the major artery? Isn't it a couple of centimeters across?'

'Excellent, Sammy. Yes, it looks as if the killer first inserted the blade, then moved it back and forward pendulum style, cutting in both directions.'

'But without enlarging the wound in the outer wall of the chest?'

'Exactly.'

'But there were no signs of struggle, Arnie. So, why would someone lay there and allow this to happen?'

'Did you notice the beer bottles in the lounge?'

'Yes.'

'I suspect they will contain traces of sedative or paralytic. The toxicology results will determine that.'

'Anything else of note, Arnie?'

'No. It seems Detective Jason was an otherwise healthy individual. From his physique, I would say he probably worked out regularly, but I didn't see much equipment in his apartment, so you could try looking for a local gym. Besides that, I don't expect to find anything else to help.

'Can you call me if you turn anything else up?'

'Sure, and I'll write up the preliminary before the end of play today. So you'll have it first thing tomorrow.'

Back upstairs, I check in with Dan and update him on my visit to Jason's sister and what I've learned from the post-mortem. He's busy with his caseload, so I leave him in peace and head to pick up a Folgers from the coffee area before returning to my desk.

My next stop is to visit the head of Narcotics, Jerry Stillman, but first, I want to do a little online research. I want to find out more about Mark Jason's previous wives.

As a detective, online sources are incredibly useful. But as a private citizen, I'm not so enthusiastic. One of these days, I will check myself out online, but I'm not in any hurry. It would only take seconds to find out I had shot and killed a two-year-old.

I avoided press articles back when it happened and have no wish to see them now.

Jason's most recent ex, from just over a year ago, is Emily. She's thirty-five and a stewardess until the Covid pandemic. Since then, there's no word of what job she may have now, if any. A fine-looking woman. I can't tell her height from the picture, but for looks, she was what most guys would call an eight out of ten. It doesn't tell me if she has a brain, though.

I copy her address, print off her details, and set out to look for the second ex.

Minutes later, I find her. Lynda Goldway. I guess she reverted to her single name, or else she married again real quick. A little older at forty, but another stunner. A few wrinkles spoil the overall effect, but she would have been a real catch twenty years ago. We're talking nine out of ten. Mark obviously liked attractive women. There again, most guys do, so no surprise there. She's working at Walgreens on Pine Ridge.

Given Arnie's comments about drugs in the beer bottles, I mentally add her to my suspect list. Less than half a day in, and already two suspects. I'm never sure if that's a good thing or not. The greater the number of suspects, the more work I have to do. I get why some detectives tune into one suspect. Unfortunately, so does the District Attorney, and he is unforgiving if we try to railroad one particular suspect.

***

With that thought, my mind switches to thinking about Bossy-boots. Our District Attorney here in Naples would have been her father. Cliff Bodie. Would have been, or should have been? Talk about railroading. I didn't even let him have a say.

I add Lynda Goldway to my follow-up list. Next, it's time to talk with Jerry, who heads up the Narcs division. I've worked a few cases with Jerry over my few years here and like him. He's a straight shooter with a sense of humor. He also genuinely cares about people, and I love him for that.

When I arrive at his office, he stands and hugs me. Not a casual *it's-the-right-thing-to-do* type hug. Nor is it the politically correct light hug with virtually no physical contact, like an air kiss. Instead, this is an *honest-to-goodness* hug.

We spent a few minutes with him checking that I'm okay and sharing his views of my shooting nine months before. Once that's out of the way, I ask him what he can tell me about his detective, Mark Jason.

In summary, Jason's a highly-rated detective. Has been in Narcotics for twelve of his twenty years of service. He was on patrol before that. He had several commendations. A popular figure with all the guys in the department.

Given that last information, I realize something I haven't noticed before. Sounds silly. But there are no female detectives in his squad. None. There again, there are only two of us down in homicide, so we aren't a lot better off. When I think about that, I realize that the Women's Liberation Front would have more to complain about than Black Lives Matter. At least a third of both departments are black or other ethnic minorities, myself included. But still, only two women. A female Native American would count as two wins for the department. I wonder for a moment if that has had anything to do with my rapid rise to detective second grade, as probably quite a few of my male colleagues suspect.

Jerry pokes me in the arm, snapping me back into the conversation.

'You still with me, Tiger?' he asks.

'Yeah, sure. So, are you aware of anyone in the squad who may have a grudge?'

'Nope. None.'

'How about the cases he was working on? Anything jumping out there?'

'First thing I did when I heard the news. Got the group together and brainstormed all his cases for the past few years. We have a list, but being honest, Sammy. I don't think the killer's on there. These guys are all into drugs, and half of them are users. Whoever did this to Mark was a professional or knew what they were doing. It won't be one of these Candy-flippers or pill-pushers.'

'Yeah, that makes sense to me.'

'I'll shake their trees to see what might fall out, but I'm not expecting much.'

'How about his best friends, Jerry? Do you know who they are?'

'Sure. He was close with a couple of my guys, but I think he was particularly tight with two guys at the gym he used to work out with. *Addicted-to-fitness* up on Airport-Pulling by the airport. You can speak to my guys right now if you like. They're both here. They'll tell you who his friends at the gym were.'

We talk a little more about Mark's cases before Jerry introduces me to the two detectives who were closest to Mark Jason and leaves me with them. They have nothing particular to add other than to agree that they didn't think the cases he had been working on had anything to do with his death. But they give me the two names at the gym, and I add them to my growing list of people to talk with.

Back downstairs in my cubicle, I access Mister Google again and find out what I can about these two gym buddies of Mark's.

Tyrone and Xavier. The first is a twenty-five-year-old African American from the Bronx. A middle-weight boxer with a fair percentage of wins. Must be decent. Single. Must have made some cash as he lives in another upmarket apartment downtown. Then Xavier. Puerto Rican. Two years older than Tyrone and an accountant with a small local firm. Again, he is single and lists his interests as kickboxing and karate. I wouldn't want to meet either of them on a dark night. Both also list their membership of *Addicted-to-fitness*.

Although both guys are interested in physical pursuits, I couldn't see either of them having the skill or patience to position a stiletto accurately and then use it to sever the aorta. They would be much more likely to beat someone to death. This isn't their scene, but I still need to talk with them.

I print everything I've found and add it to the case file.

4

I check the time and reckon that if Tyrone and Xavier are regular gym bunnies, they'll probably be there more often than not. So a random visit might just be successful. Fortunately, this time, when I ask about a pool car, there's one available, so I sign it out after promising to bring it back in the same good condition.

I have a terrible history with pool cars.

Ten minutes later, I pull up in the car park in front of *'Addicted-to-fitness.'* The building itself is hardly inspirational. Single-story white with a green shallow-sloping roof and matching green shades over multiple floor-to-ceiling tinted glass windows. The logo over the door has a stick figure acting as if he has hornets up his ass, but I guess they mean him to be exercising. I badge the receptionist and ask to see whoever's in charge. It turns out that he's stepped out for thirty minutes, but I can talk with the security guard if I like.

Well, that's a conversation doomed to disaster from the get-go.

When I meet the guy, there's instant mutual recognition. This is a guy I had reported for sleeping on the job up at the Seminole Brothel the previous year. He lost his job because of me.

Needless to say, he is less than helpful. I'll have to come back another time.

* * *

As I push out the front door, I recognize the guy approaching me from the car park as Tyrone, the African-American boxer. As he steps up onto the sidewalk, I show him my badge and ask if I can ask him a few questions.

When you've done this a few thousand times, you begin to recognize the various responses you get. Some are bewildered as this has never happened to them before. Others are matter-of-fact, as if a random person has asked to talk with them, and the badge makes no difference. Then are those who assume they have done something wrong - the group I always feel sorry for. And finally, the group that Tyrone's in - thinking fast about how best to avoid me.

He has no chance. Once I get on a roll, no one can avoid me. Besides, I'm standing directly between him and the entrance to *Addicted-to-fitness*. So he has nowhere to go.

I reckon there's no way the security guard will allow me to go back inside and sit in reception, so I ask Tyrone if he would mind sitting in the car while we talk. He hesitates, still thinking, but not fast enough.

I start heading for the car. Defeated, he follows.

I reach the car first, climb in and watch him walk towards me. I say walk, but he's an ambler. He has that casual sway that African-Americans sometimes have. He isn't the build I'm expecting for a middle-weight boxer. He's taller and skinnier, with not much fat. I suppose the height is an advantage; I don't know, I'm not a boxer. But I wouldn't like to fight a guy this height, so I suppose his opponents would think the same. He opens the door, ducks his head, and climbs in to join me, leaving the door open.

I follow Questioning 101 and don't give away anything until I find out what he already knows. So, I start by asking him to confirm he knows Mark Jason. He does, so I ask him how long he has known him.

'Bout ten years. We met here at the gym. He's more of a fitness freak than I am. Has been since day one.'

'And do you also know Xavier Rivera?'

'Sure. Mark, Xav, and me are all members here. We hang out together. Sink a few beers. Watch a game. That sort of thing.'
'When did you last see Mark Jason?'
'Day before yesterday. He was here after work, around six-thirty.'
'You talked with him?'
'A little. He was focused, man. When he gets like that, he's too intense, so I just let him be.'
'Did he leave alone, or were you with him?'
'He left round eight. Said he was tired. Wanted to catch some Zees.'
'Did you see anything unusual about his behavior? You say he was intense. Was that normal?'
'Yeah. He could get like that sometimes. I thought it was the job. He was working through stuff.'
'You mean being a detective?'
'Yeah. You must know what it's like. He told us about all kinds of shit he had to deal with. I don't envy you guys.'
'So, are you expecting to see him tonight?'
'Yeah. He rarely misses a night.'
'Well, I have some bad news for you, Tyrone.'

When you have to tell someone this kind of news, there's no easy way. What I can do, is spare him the details. So I tell him Jason is dead, and we're looking at it as a homicide. He seems genuinely shocked and close to tears, which surprises me. I have all these preconceptions in my head about people. But they're more often wrong than right. My mind's thinking male, boxer, tough. What I get is a male, boxer, willing to cry for a lost friend.

I do my best to console him before restarting with the questions.

'Are you aware of anyone who might have held a grudge against your friend?'

Tyrone gives me a negative shake of the head, not trusting himself to speak.

'Did he have problems with anyone here at the club?'

Another negative shake.

'Can you tell me anything about what may have happened to him?'

'No.'

The guy is seriously upset, and I realize I'll get nothing else out of him right then. So, I rustle up my standard condolence phrase, hand him my card, and ask him to have Xavier Rivera call me as soon as possible. Then, tell him I would probably talk with him again in a few days.

He climbs out of the car and ambles back towards the gym with heavier footfall and lowered shoulders. I reckon I can strike him from my suspect list.

I sit quietly for a moment, thinking about what to do next. I'll leave talking with the two exes until I can arrange appointments with them. I guess my preconceptions are at play again. An ex would be female, emotional, and may still have feelings for Mark, so I shouldn't spring the news on them. But, boy, am I wrong?

Instead, I decide that as it's nearly knocking-off time, I would swing by Mark Jason's on the way home and have a second look around. During the first visit, the place was swarming with Forensics, and I didn't realize it would be my case. But, this time, it is *my* crime scene, and I want to study it at leisure with no one else around.

When I arrive, I check in with the patrol car sitting out front. The officer's glad to have someone to talk to. I get that. Been there. I didn't mind spending a little time with him. Nothing has happened since the body had been removed and forensics finished up. I explain I want a second look around, and he asks if I want some company. I thank him but say I'd rather do it on my own. He opens the front door and returns to the patrol car.

Only six-thirty, but it's already getting pretty dark outside, so I flick on the lights and stand back to get an overall impression of the place. It's a man's home, for sure. Something I hadn't noticed earlier in the day. There are no women's touches anywhere. Curtains, cushions, and photographs in a variety of frames. The only pictures on the walls are sport related. Apparently, Jason is a Hockey fan with a poster for the Blades at Hertz Arena from the previous year, taking pride in place above the faux fireplace. The Blades rock. I'm a huge fan.

The furnishings are functional rather than comfortable. He has a pair of two-seater sofas, a coffee table that has seen better days, a sixty-five-inch screen mounted on the wall, and a training bike set up so he could undoubtedly watch sport while he exercised. This agrees with what Arnie Collins said about not noticing weights or other training gear in the apartment. Some books are lying around, mostly fiction. I flick through a few, but nothing grabs my attention. Most of the magazines I see are sports-related. No surprise there. It seems following sport was almost as important as keeping fit for him. The magazines cover rifle shooting, angling, para-gliding, and surfing. And that's just the first few I look at.

I move into the kitchen area. Tidy and clean, which surprises my inner sense of preconceptions again. I'm expecting classic single guy, messy, piles of unwashed dishes, dirty sink. I get none of that.

The fridge contents are even more surprising. Jason liked his food and ate pretty healthily. There are a few beers that make me feel normal. But there are stacks of vegetables and yogurts, cheeses, and a steak that presumably he intended to cook that evening. The freezer compartment is also well stocked - not with the ready-made meals I expect, but mainly meat, veg, and fruit.

What a shame all this stuff is going to waste when my fridge and freezer are nearly empty, which is their natural state. I half-think of confiscating everything for evidence, but stealing from the dead doesn't sit right with me.

Moving through to the bedroom, I notice a scent as soon as I enter. I say scent, but it's more of a smell with some scent mixed in. If I'd been blindfolded, I would still have known this was a man's bedroom. But there's also a definite lingering scent, and that's undoubtedly female.

No surprise. The guy was single. Worked out. Reasonably attractive, why not have a woman or two visit?

What I'm wondering is how long a woman's scent would linger. I've been in the room too long and can no longer detect it.

Would she have been here the previous night? If so, was she involved in Jason's death? Or maybe she visited a few nights before? Something I might discuss with Arnie Collins, the medical examiner. He would have an opinion, at least.

I start opening drawers and looking in the wardrobe but come up with nothing to indicate a woman's presence.

One thing I do find is his cell phone in the bedside unit drawer. I slip that into a plastic bag and write the time and location before putting it in my pocket.

One last look around, and I'm confident I have everything I can get from the place.

I stop for another few minutes to talk with the officer outside, and when I finally draw away from the curb, he's re-locking the front door. The late shift would take over at eight, so he doesn't have much longer to wait. I head straight home, feeling I've achieved virtually nothing.

I get this in every case. We all do. The highs and lows. Sometimes you're following leads left, right, and center. Other times, you feel stuck and have no idea what to do next. When you're stuck - that's when working a homicide is the toughest. You think you're letting the victim down, and that's how I feel at the end of day one. I'm letting Mark Jason down.

5

Alexa kicks in at six, playing my choice for the day. Nickelback and *'This Afternoon.'* When Chad Kroeger kicks into the lines *'Beer bottles layin' on the kitchen floor if we take 'em back, we can buy some more,'* it reminds me I'm out of Corona. So whatever else I do this day, I have to get more Corona.

Thanks to having the pool car with me, no morning run. So I shower, shake my hair, and hand-dry it. Choose my outfit for the day - like I have a vast choice. I pull a bright-yellow V-neck T over my head. Pull up yesterday's jeans. Clip on the badge and Glock, then raid the fridge, feeling jealous when I recall Jason's from the previous evening. Mine is empty. I head out the door, hungry. First stop, EJ's.

Forty-five minutes later, topped up with over-easy eggs, bacon, and a side of sausage, I arrive at my cubicle. Now, with me only being back twenty-four hours, the empty desk is still an unfamiliar sight. Usually, case files would be everywhere, mixed with research summaries and messages left for me overnight. Today, nada. This should please me, but it has the opposite effect. It reminds me I've been out for nine months, and that reminds me why. Suddenly, my mood takes a nose-dive. I feel no one needs me.

Shrugging my shoulders and accepting this erroneous conclusion, I head for the coffee area and prepare a new pot of Folgers.

While I'm there, Dan arrives and checks in with me. When I

say checks in, I mean he places his coffee order before heading for his cubicle.

Ten minutes later, after leaving Dan's mug with him and giving him the lowdown on Jason's gym buddies, I sit down and log on. I'm hoping for something interesting in my inbox, but there's nothing besides a summary of events during the night shift.

Then I remember I have Jason's cell in my pocket and walk it down to forensics. They'll dust for prints and produce a cell phone record of all incoming and outgoing calls for me, then pass it over into the evidence locker for safekeeping.

Back in my cubicle, after I update the case book, it's still too early to call Jason's exes, so I do the only thing I can think of. I open Mister Google, look at knives with long thin blades, and eventually tune into the stiletto. Apparently, it was first invented in the fifteenth century when they intended to stab between the gaps in chain-mail armor. The blades vary in cross-section - triangular, square, diamond-shaped, or round, and became popular with assassins. Italian immigrants brought the stiletto to New Orleans initially. Pasta and stilettos - quite a contribution.

The modern switchblade version originated in the fifties. Easy to conceal. Spring loaded so quick to open and potentially lethal.

I look where I might buy such a knife in Naples but quickly find that eBay is the most likely place. I might as well requisition transaction information from them. You never know. I might get lucky. I've been down this route before and found eBay willing to help. That instance had related to a fraud I was investigating. Homicide would trump that, so I'm hopeful.

I spend the next hour thinking exactly what I want to know as I'll only get one chance at this, then, convinced an open question may be the best way to go, I end up asking for all the information they have on anyone purchasing a stiletto with a Collier County address. Then add either buying or winning a bid for a stiletto. When the form I'm completing asks for a timeframe, my first thought is to say the past few months, as I figure Jason's death was personal. Someone is perhaps seeking revenge, and more than likely, that was for something relatively recent. Then I realize that I might rule out possibilities by making that assumption, so I request all history.

Next up, I call Jason's most recent ex - Emily Jason. She answers almost immediately and agrees to meet me in an hour. She's curious, but I avoid talking about her ex, knowing I need to break the news in person. I'm not entirely insensitive.

The following call is almost identical. Lynda Goldway answers after just a few rings, and when I ask to meet, she agrees, but it must be before her shift at Walgreens starts at two o'clock. We agree I would be at her place around noon. My morning is set. I'm raring to go. Something needs to break in this case, and I'm hoping the exes can point me in the right direction.

Emily lives out at Rattlesnake in the Huntington Woods suburb. Her house could have been her late husband's. It's almost identical. Single-storey, two-in-one with two driveways beside one another. In this case, she lives to the right of the building, not the left, as Jason does.

A red Honda Civic is in the drive. I park across the back of it, and as I do, I notice someone peering through the blinds next door. In a generous moment, I consider this might be some community watch, but I doubt it. More likely a nosy neighbor.

Emily is already waiting for me when I reach the front door. She's clearly apprehensive but welcomes me in and offers me a drink. Never known to refuse, I ask for a coffee and look around the lounge as I wait. No pictures of her ex. No sports posters on the wall. No weights or training bike. Curtains on every window and lots of cushions. This woman is everything that her ex was not.

When she returns, I thank her for my coffee, and we sit at opposite ends of a three-seater. I dive straight in.

'Emily, I'm sorry, but they found your ex-husband dead yesterday morning, and we are treating his death as suspicious.'

Now, here go my faulty preconceptions again. What am I expecting? Shock? Tears? Hysterics? I don't know. But I can tell you, I'm not expecting acceptance and relief.

Seeing the reaction, I have to ask.

'You don't seem upset, Emily?'

'Me! Upset because that bastard has finally got what he deserves. I'm only surprised it's taken so long.'

'So, your split with your ex wasn't too amicable then?'

'Fuck no. Excuse the French. Everything started fine. He was sweet and caring before we married. But after that, he became physical. Sex was a nightmare. The bastard hurt me repeatedly. I only escaped because I bought a nanny cam and recorded him, then threatened to go to the police. Being that he was already a detective, I wasn't sure that would worry him, but it did. Probably didn't want his reputation harmed, or he was protecting his pension. I don't know. But after that, when I thought things would get nasty, the opposite was true. He was decent with the separation agreement. We shared everything fairly evenly. He even helped me find this place.'

'When did you last see him?'

'Not since I moved in here just over a year ago.'

'Have you stayed in touch at all?'

'No. No calls or texts. Nothing. And being honest, that's fine for me. I'm trying to put it all behind me and get on with life.'

'Do you have any idea who might have killed him?'

Before answering, she bites her lower lip and hesitates. She's trying to decide whether to tell me something. I need to help her.

'Look, Emily. There is someone out there capable of murder.

This is not just about who killed Mark. If they can kill once, they can kill again. Whatever you know or think you know. Please tell me.'

'You should talk with his two cronies. They hang out together all the time. Christ, they spent more time with him than I did.'

'You mean Tyler and Xavier?'

'Yes, that's them.'

'Why should I talk with them?'

'They're just the same as him.'

'They're abusive?'

At that, tears appear in her eyes, and she wipes them away, nodding.

'Did he bring them home sometimes?'

Tears are flowing faster than she can wipe. I don't need to ask anymore. I have the unique insight on Mark Jason I've been looking for. Not to mention his two cohorts.

After that, I don't press for further details. Instead, we talk a little about what being married to a detective was like for her in a more general sense, and I guess that was more for me than anything else. When Bossy-boots was still around, one of the options I had been forced to consider was whether I would like to be married. I hadn't concluded then, and I guess I'm still curious.

When I have everything I'm going to get, I thank her again for the coffee, especially for sharing her information with me, and leave her watching me from the doorstep as I head back to the car. The next-door neighbor has another peek between her blinds, and I give her a friendly wave.

Back in the car, I check the time. I need to head straight to meet with Jason's other ex - Lynda Goldway. Where Emily lives to the South of Naples, Lynda is to the North. It will take twenty minutes straight up Santa Barbara Boulevard. I should just about make it if the traffic is kind.

Bang on midday, I enter the Island Walk gated community off

Vanderbilt Beach, east of I75. I've visited a friend here previously, two years before. It's like a small town with a post office, cafe, bank, and gas station. There's also a clubhouse with an impressive fitness center and half a dozen tennis courts. They carefully constructed the complex around waterways. Lots and lots of waterways, such that virtually every home had a waterfront view. I'm interested to find Jason's ex living here. Presumably, her name change implies she has remarried and remarried well by the look of this place. You don't live here on a detective's salary.

If I'm being critical, she has picked the wrong road to live on. It doesn't directly connect to the central complex. You can see it over the water but not get to it. I would find it frustrating to have to walk around the outside of the estate.

I follow that perimeter road until I reach Hawkesbury Way, then turn in and look for her house. The houses are nice, don't get me wrong. But they're nothing special. Well, yes, I would swap in a flash. But for five hundred grand, I would expect a little more. I should never face such a choice. Dream on.

Like many houses in Florida, the exterior walls are a pale primrose, and the roof is shallow with pale red tiles. The house has the mandatory two-car garage and an archway over the front door. There must be thousands of these across the State. Comfortable, but boring. I suppose if you're retired, that might work for you. But Lynda works at Walmart Pharmacy, so what does that tell me?

I ring the chimes on the front door and wait only a minute before hearing footsteps approaching. When the door opens, I feel like a rag-doll compared to the woman in front of me. She looks younger than the picture I had seen of her online. Either her wrinkles have disappeared after her divorce, or I need to know which face cream she's using. Her skin is clear and smooth, her eyes shine, and her auburn hair has highlights and hangs down to shoulder length in loose waves.

She smiles, and I swear my day improves right there and then. She waves me in and directs me to the outdoor area out the back, where we can sit by the pool. Kids' inflatables and toys are around the place, but no sign of kids. She follows my gaze and tells me the toys belong to her husband's kids. But they're at school.

She has already prepared a jug of iced lemonade, and without asking, she pours one for me, and we sit under the shade of an enormous umbrella before she finally asks me how she can help.

I tell her about her ex, but I'm better prepared for the response this time. The only difference is that Lynda is much more forthcoming about her ex's two friends being involved. Not only was she shared around, but sometimes they would bring a girl home with them, forcing her to watch and then join in.

After these sessions, they always left her bruised, but they were careful about where. Her face was out-of-bounds, but sometimes she had to wear high-necked roll-tops for a week or two to cover the bruises on her neck.

When I ask her how she got out of the marriage, she hesitates but ultimately decides to tell me. I can almost sense the relief. Something she's bottled up for over five years.

'My brother came home from Afghanistan. He was a marine. A tough guy's, tough guy. He nearly blew his stack when I told him what was going on. I could barely stop him from finding Mark and killing him and his two friends. He was all for shooting them down like rag-heads. That's how he described them.'

'But you stopped him?'

'Let's say I avoided him killing them. He waited until one night when Mark had his two friends over for a session. He used a key I had given him to let himself and a few ex-marine buddies into the house.'

'So, they sorted Mark out?'

'You bet. I wasn't the one with the bruises the next day and wasn't sorry about it. Not for a second.'

'So, your divorce was straightforward?'

'No problem. After that, he was decent enough, although not what I would call generous. But I didn't care. I just wanted out.'

'Have you seen him since?'

'Not once. And never wanted to.'

'Have you any idea who might have wanted to kill him?'

'Not my brother, if that's what you're thinking. He got himself married a couple of years back and lives up in Kennebunkport, Maine. He knows I've remarried and am safe and happy. He hasn't been back down here since.'

'Anyone else?'

'How about his most recent wife? I don't remember her name.'

'Emily.'

'Sure. That rings a bell. I doubt she would have fared any better than me.'

'Did you try to warn her before she married him?'

'Nope. I might feel bad about that, but I wasn't going anywhere near the slime bag ever again.'

'Well, she got out a lot quicker than you did. So you needn't worry about her anymore.'

'Good.'

'Anyone else you can think of?'

'Probably a whole trail of one-night-stands that will struggle to stand after their one night with the three of them. I doubt he and his friends have given up their sessions. I dread to think how many others have gone through what I did.'

'You feel guilty you didn't report them back in the day?'

'Sure, I feel guilty. But I needed to get out. That was all I cared about.'

We talk a little more about her current life, and she has moved on. When they met, her husband already had two kids, so they're raising them together. She has no plans for any additions. She likes her job as a pharmacist, although she hates the daily struggle to explain to people why essential prescriptions are so expensive. Ultimately, she thinks that might eventually cause her to give up her job. But it hasn't so far. Maybe one day.

When we finish, I thank her and leave. The iced lemonade

had been great, but the new perspective she had given me on my victim was better still. According to two independent people, Mark Jason is a serial abuser. He and his buddies together. And that opens up a whole new avenue of investigation. I'm buzzed. At last, the case is beginning to go somewhere. How little do I know?

6

Back in the office, fate is smiling kindly at me. There's a message for me from Mark Jason's other friend - Xavier Rivera, leaving me a cell number. I call, and he answers immediately. Given my recent new insight into how these three guys have behaved, I decide on a more formal approach.

'Hi, Xav here.'
'Is that Xavier Rivera?'
'Sure, who's this?'
'Detective Sammy Greyfox. Thank you for calling.'
'Oh, yeah. Sure. Is this about Mark, man?'
I avoid his question.
'I would like you to come into the Sheriff's office and talk with us as soon as possible.'
He will worry about why I was happy to speak to his friend at the gym, yet I want to see him in person.
He doesn't give up so easily, though.
'Can't you just tell me what you want to discuss?'
'I think that's better discussed here, Mister Rivera.'
'Can't we like meet at the club or something?'
'No, Mister Rivera. It needs to be here. How about first thing tomorrow morning, say nine?'
'I suppose.'
'Is that a yes, Mister Rivera?'
'Yeah, sure. It's a yes. See you at nine.'
The line goes dead.

* * *

My plan had been in three parts. First, sound more threatening - done. Second, get him onto my turf to make him uncomfortable - done. Finally, give him an entire night to worry about it. I'm pleased with myself. I can almost imagine him scurrying off to find Tyrone.

I'm just beginning to plan my approach when one of the forensic technicians stops by to tell me they've finished the review of Mark Jason's apartment. Unfortunately, they only have a couple of things they think might be of specific interest to me.

The prints from four of the beer bottles. Three sets match the victim, but the fourth set is unknown. They've already run them through the AFIS system without finding a match.

The second thing is a single long red hair, believed most likely from a woman. When I ask why a woman, he explains that although hair is the same between both genders, men usually wear their hair shorter, and if they use styling products, they have a matte finish. Women often wear their hair longer and use softening products that show off their shine. This was long shiny red hair. This hair has come from a woman.

I thank the technician and can already see the significance of that last discovery. I've already noted the absence of the female touch from Jason's home: no female partner and no signs of even casual stay-over company. No extra toothbrush or makeup accidentally left behind. Nothing. So this long shiny red hair is screaming at me. What I don't know for sure is when it was left there. My gut is saying we've just found a hair from the killer. But I need more.

The beer bottle prints are also interesting. I decide to take the theory forming in my head downstairs and talk with Arnie Collins.

I find him hunched over the autopsy table, happy as ever. I know as homicide detectives, we get used to bodies and learn to cope, but opening them up and rifling around inside, takes it to a whole different level for me. I don't know how he stays so cheerful.

I asked him once, and he said that because the dead couldn't speak for themselves, it was his job to do that for them. That he was pleased and honored to do that. Hence, he would either have cheerful music playing in the background or as today. He would be happily humming to himself. I guess whatever turns you on.

I stand behind the observation screen and wait until I catch his eye. When I do, he stops work immediately and strips off his gloves and gown before coming around to talk.

'Sammy. You got to me first. I intended to call as soon as I finished with my client. Anyway, now you're here. I have some interesting news for you on the death of Detective Jason. Let me get my notes.'

We cross the room to his admin area, where there is no evidence of the paperless office. Not in Arnie's world, anyway. Regardless, he always knows where everything is and goes straight to the file he wants. Then, opening it, he reads aloud.

'Whoever supplied the beers laced them with over-the-counter medications. Zaleplon which causes drowsiness. Often used when treating sleep disorders. Eszopiclone which is also a sedative-hypnotic, and Zolpidem as a muscle relaxant.'

'Interesting, Arnie. But why the chemistry lesson?'

'I'm reading the results of your detective's blood toxicology tests. With these three drugs, there was enough in his system to paralyze an elephant. Also, sufficient to kill him.'

'So someone paralyzed him first, then stabbed him. Is that what you're saying?'

'Looks that way. But honestly, the stabbing was superfluous. Left long enough, his heart and lungs would have stopped working. As soon as he had those three beers, he was already dead. He just didn't know it yet.'

'What about the other bottles?'

'They were the same. Whoever did this laced all six bottles

and avoided drinking them.'

'Wouldn't he have noticed the taste?'

'That's what I thought, especially with such a high dosage. The only conclusion I came to was that someone must have distracted him.'

'You examined the fingerprints on the bottles?'

'I did. Three bottles had his prints on them, which would explain his condition. And there were a clear set of prints on one other bottle.'

'Do you know if the additional prints are male or female?'

'Funny you should ask that. I wondered about that myself. If you care to come with me, I'll show you rather than tell you.'

We cross to a work area between his desk and the autopsy room. He stops at a high-resolution microscope, bends over, and starts twiddling knobs. When satisfied, he stands back and instructs me to look.

I bend over and do as asked, wondering what he wants me to see.

'The print on the left is your victim's. The one on the right is from the fourth beer bottle. I have altered them to be the same overall size, but can you notice anything different between them?'

I look from one to the other and have to admit my ignorance. The patterns are different, but that is as it should be. I'm looking at prints from two different people. I'm missing something. Arnie explains.

'Look at the distance between the epidermal ridges on the left first. Then look at the same spacing on the print on the right.'

I do as he suggests. I look at the one I know to be Jason's first, then over to the one on the right. Then back and forth a few times to be sure.

'There's more detail in the one on the right?'

'Correct, Sammy. Now it's not one hundred percent proof, but women generally have a higher epidermal density in their fingertips than men. Hence they have a greater sense of touch.'

'So, the other beer drinker was a woman?' I suggest, pleased that he's inadvertently supporting my theory of a woman being present in Jason's apartment. But this time, it would be on the night he was killed.

'At this point, possibly,' he replied, bursting my bubble as quickly as I'd allowed it to blow up. 'But to be sure, I had to run a second test, so I checked for amino acid levels.'

'Amino acid? Why?'

'Certain Amino acid levels are twice as high in women's sweat as in men.'

'So? Was the other beer drinker a woman?'

'Yes, Sammy. I think your victim was paralyzed and stabbed to death by a woman. Moreover, thanks to the long red hair we found, I'm fairly confident she was a Caucasian woman. Advances in genetics are allowing us to identify gender and ethnicity these days. However, the tests are still expensive. I've gone as far as I can without a further budget allocation, but hopefully, I've given you enough?'

'Thanks, Arnie. This fits with another question I came down to ask you. How long do you think a woman's perfume will linger in a bedroom?'

'You mean Jason's?'

'Yes.'

'Well spotted, Sammy. It was something I had noticed myself. It was very noticeable when I first arrived, and that would be approximately thirty-six hours after death.'

'So, it could still be there a day later?'

'Probably, as long as the apartment had not been further disturbed.'

Given my earlier musings about how anyone can be happy opening up bodies, I virtually skip out of there and back upstairs. The case is taking shape already, and I'm still only a day and a half in. Now I need to consider how best to approach Xavier Rivera in the morning. Perhaps something done best at my retreat. I pack up and head home.

My retreat is the Rusty Nail. A serious drinking bar less than ten minutes from my place. More specifically, it's the stool at the end of the bar in the Rusty Nail, with a Corona in front of me. This is where I truly relax. No one bothers me here. I can think. And on this particular night, I've plenty to think about. I don't realize then how helpful the eBay security team is about to be.

7

Alexa gets me up and running fast this morning with another of my favorites. *'Boulevard of broken dreams'* by Green Day. In the shower, I'm hair-flipping and throwing my arms in the air as I sing, *'My shadow's the only one that walks beside me. My shallow heart's the only thing that's beating. Sometimes I wish someone out there will find me. Til' then I walk alone.'*
At least Green Day gets me. I feel understood. Great song.

I've already dried off and dressed when Christine Aguilera tells me *'What a girl wants.'* She tells me, *'If I love something, let it go. If it comes back, it's mine for keeps'*. Well, that didn't work out too well with Bossy-boots father.
I let him go, and that's as far as we got.
So much for lyrical advice.
The fridge is still empty, and I still need Corona. I need to shop. I put the thought on my to-do list - where it will be doomed. Still, I have to try. I leave for the office wondering how long they will let me use the pool car. They expect most detectives to have their own vehicle, but I'm not *most* detectives. If I ever repay my education loans, I may afford a second-hand cycle. Until then, I scrounge what I can get.

In the office, I update Dan, then head for my cubicle, Folgers in hand. No messages again. I feel like a complete newbie. I log on and read the previous night's report. Nothing exciting there. Then I see it. A message from eBay security. There's an attachment, which I quickly pull up. There have only been six stiletto knives bought in Naples since they started maintaining records, and they've sent me all the transaction details. I look the six orders through and initially discount four of them as men purchased them, and I'm becoming convinced that Jason's killer is a woman.

I justify this further by remembering Arnie's answer when I asked him if Jason wouldn't have noticed the taste of the drugs in his beer, and he said he must have been distracted. Who better to distract him than a beautiful woman with long red hair?

I will keep the four men's names on my B-list in case the woman angle doesn't work out. I have to prioritize somehow, and this seems the right way for now.

So that has narrowed my potential killer list down to two. I'm undecided about which looks the more promising. One woman purchased the first ten years before, and someone else the other around nine months ago. I study the detail of each transaction and look the knives up on the website to find the technical information. The two knives are similar in basic design. Both are the *'flick'* variety and easy to conceal, with stylized handles but different blades. I lift the phone. I need to speak with Arnie.

Two minutes later, I have my potential killer. The blade that killed Mark Jason had a diamond cross-section. Only one of these is on the eBay list, and one of the women purchased it ten years before. The name on the order is Pamela Wilson, with an address down in Belle Meade, south of the city. I type her name into the DMV system and find her driving license confirming the current address.

She's thirty-eight and has red hair. In her picture, it's shorter than the hair found at the crime scene, but the picture is several years old. Women change their hair. This is the one. I can feel it. I want to rush out the door, but Xavier Rivera is due in ten minutes. I print her DMV picture and put it in a blank folder. This is coming with me.

Rivera is fashionably late, and by the time he turns up, I'm pissed and struggling to hide it. At the same time, he's cool, calm, and collected. The talk with his buddy and a night to think about everything has calmed him down rather than worried him. That is about to change. I start gently enough.

'Thanks for coming in this morning, Mister Rivera. I appreciate your cooperation.'

'Yeah, sure. No problem.'

'As I'm sure you know by now, we're investigating the death of your friend Mark Jason two nights ago. I want to ask you what you might know that could help the investigation?'

'Nothing I can think of. Mark was a cool guy. We hung out. Drank some beers. Worked out at the club. Watched sport. Not much more to tell.'

'Where did you drink your beers? A sports bar somewhere?'

I'm fishing. But fishing with a purpose.

'Here and there, you know?'

'No, I don't, Mister Rivera. That's why I'm asking. I'm sure there must be a regular bar you guys would hang out at. I only want to know which one?'

He looks cornered. He doesn't know what I already know and doesn't want to give anything away, yet he doesn't want to appear to avoid the question either. I have him where I want him.

'The bar, Mister Rivera?'

'Well, if you must have a name, I would go for the All American Sports Bar on Ninth Avenue between Fifth and Sixth.'

'Busy place, is it?'

'Yeah, pretty crowded usually.'

'Decent food?'

'Burgers, steaks, that kind of thing.'

'Nice waitresses?'

'Sure, if you're into them so young.'
'You prefer them a little older?'
'Straight shooter. No youngsters for me.'
Time to fish again.
'So, you were there with Mark the night someone killed him?'
'What? Me?'
'Yes, you, Mark, and Tyrone. Just sinking a few friendlies.'
My bait is innocence, and he buys it.
'Well, only a couple.'
'What time did you finish up?'
'Tyrone and me, we left around ten.'
'And your friend, Mark. When did he leave?'
'I don't know. He was still there when we left.'

I open the folder and place the photograph of Pamela Wilson in front of him. 'So you didn't leave with this woman then?'

He's flustered. He recognizes her but doesn't know what to say. I prompt him.

'I can ask at the bar if I need to.'
'Sure, I recognize her. But not from that night.'
'Which night then, Mister Rivera? Which night did you three leave with this woman?'

He doesn't even see the trap. Just walks right in.
'It was a few nights before.'
'And you had a few drinks with her, then left together? That right?'
'Sure. Tyrone and me were heading home, and Mark was going to see her safely to her place.'

He's recovered a little. I push again.
'But that's not what happened, is it, Mister Rivera?'

I can see the sweat forming in his armpits. He's in trouble and should ask for an attorney, but I'm not charging him with anything. We're just talking. I'll take the heat for this afterward if I have to.

'How do you mean?'

More fishing.

'Well, you all went back to Mark's place for a little party, didn't you?'

'Who told you that?'

'Mister Rivera. I'm a detective. Finding things out is what I do, and I'm good at my job.'

I prompt him again, then give him the old silent treatment.

It takes him a few minutes to phrase his denial so that at least *he* thinks it sounds plausible. I can almost see his brain working.

'We might have, I don't really remember.'

'We're talking four, five, maybe six nights ago, Mister Rivera. And you can't remember?'

I make my incredulity ring around the room. He gets it.

'Look, I'm not a hundred percent sure. You *get* that, right?'

'So, you're what ninety percent sure? Does that sound about right?'

He doesn't answer.

'So, how did your little three-on-one soiree go, Mister Rivera? Did you enjoy yourself?'

By now, the sweat patch has spread right down to his waistband. He's noticeably paler, and his hands are twitching.

'Look, Tyrone and me went home. There wasn't no party. Not that I recall. She was fine when we left.'

Now I have to decide what he's telling me. By saying she was fine when he left, was he claiming that nothing had happened while he was there or acknowledging that maybe something happened after that? It could be either, but having listened to Mark's two ex-wives, I suspect I know which one it was. More fishing is required.

'I thought you were ninety percent sure you went back to Mark's place with her? So, do you mean that she was fine when Tyrone and yourself left Mark's place?

'Yeah, that's what I meant. Sure.'

'So you were there the entire time with Mark, Xavier, and Miss Wilson?'

'Yeah, but nothing happened. We were having a few drinks and some fun.'

'So, nothing violent happened?'

'No, of course not. Nothing like that?'

'So, let me see if I've got your facts straight, Mister Rivera. This attractive young single lady accompanies three men, who have been drinking, to one of their homes. Shares a beer or two, then leaves. That about right?'

The penny finally drops, but I know I've got as far as possible. And we have recorded everything. So when he asks for an attorney, I thank him for coming in and show him out. I reckon I can go after him and his boxer buddy later. But, for now, I have a killer to catch, and it isn't one of these guys. I'm already sure of that.

8

Back upstairs in my cubicle, I update my notes and add them to the case book. I also add the forensic report from Jason's apartment and a summary of my position relative to my number one suspect.

I then go looking for Dan to discuss the next steps with him. He's out of the office, so I call and leave a message for him, then speak to the duty sergeant and arrange two patrol cars and four officers to accompany me. We're heading out to Pamela Wilson's place. This woman has already killed one detective. I've no intention of letting her make it two.

The address eBay has given me is about fifteen miles south down Rte 41. She lives in one of these vast housing complexes, which grow like weeds in Florida. Nice enough, but another house in the middle of the hundreds just like it. Hers is the only house in the row with a blue-tiled roof. It makes it stand out. Everywhere looks deserted. Early afternoon. People at work, kids at school. Grandparents napping in the backyard. No-one around. I send two officers around the back as I approach the front with the others. I knock, but there's no sound from inside. I knock louder and shout that we're from the Sheriff's office. Still no answer. I tell the officers to check the windows and see what they can see inside. It only takes thirty seconds for one of them to call me over and ask me to take a look.

There's blood on the floor by the entrance to the lounge. A

significant amount of blood.

I send an officer back to the patrol SUV to bring a ram. Two practice swings, and we're in.

A woman I recognize immediately as Pamela Wilson is lying a few yards from the front door. Dead, but I check anyway. No pulse. No breathing. Definitely dead. I tell the officers to secure the perimeter while I call it in and ask for the medical examiner, forensics, and other half-dozen officers for door-to-door.

I'm tempted to glove up and look around inside, but we've already interfered with the crime scene even by breaking the door down and me checking for signs of life. No point in making things worse.

I tell one of the officers to take control of access in and out of the crime scene, and he heads off to collect a clipboard.

A long thirty minutes later, the forensics team arrives. I recognize one of them. The one who had given me the print and hair information from Mark Jason's place. He nods his recognition in return.

They take time at their vehicle to pull on their one-piece forensic suits, pull up the hoods and add gloves before finally entering the house.

I now have eight officers on the scene, so organize the door-to-door before following forensics into the house, booted and gloved.

Standing just inside the door, I watch as they briefly examine the body before methodically photographing and measuring everything in sight, laying markers wherever they find something of interest.

One of Arnie's assistants arrives next. They have a duty roster for situations like this, and I guess they have pulled him from something he was doing with his family. He has a disgruntled air hanging over him and a snappiness I haven't seen before.

I wait patiently as he examines the body. He knows I'll have questions; I don't need to say. He'll get to me when he's ready. See, I can be patient and considerate.

When that moment finally arrives, he confirms my assumption he didn't want to be here when he starts his update without a preamble.

'Dead between ten and twelve hours. A single knife thrust into the femoral artery,' he explains while bagging what looks like a medium-sized kitchen knife soaked in blood.

'Looks like the assailant deliberately left the knife in the wound, then the victim removed it sometime later. I'll confirm the cause of death later, but for now, I would say she bled to death. We'll be able to say more when we get her on the table.'

'Why do you say the killer left the knife in?'

'Blood spatter patterns. If you cut the femoral, there will be immediate spray, which would cover the assailant.'

'So, if you leave the knife in….'

'You get minimal spatter and can walk away.'

'Why do you think the woman took the knife out on her own?'

'Instinct. Something enters your body, and you want it out.'

'She killed herself?'

'Essentially. Mind you, if the knife weren't there in the first place….'

Leaving him to finish his work, I check with one of the forensic technicians if they're finished with the lounge and kitchen before I start to look around the house. See what I can find out about Pamela Wilson.

There isn't much to the place. The entrance hall, two bedrooms, a lounge, a kitchen, and a rear porch with a bare backyard. I find a bowl of cat food in the kitchen, but no sign of a cat. The contents of the fridge look normal. The freezer is stocked mainly with fruit and veg. No signs of meat anywhere. Probably a vegetarian. There's a calendar on the fridge door. It looks like she attends regular yoga and dance classes. Apart from that, no names jump off the page. No boyfriends or girlfriends, come to think of it. Just yoga and dance. I note the clubs she attends and move on to the lounge.

Comfortably furnished. It reminds me of Mark Jason's place but with more of a feminine touch. Not a lot, though. Cushions, and a few paintings on the wall. No curtains. She's also a magazine reader with piles everywhere. I glance at a few. Women's Fitness, Woman's World, People, Women's Health, Cosmopolitan. Nothing about men. Maybe she's gay? Perhaps she simply likes women's magazines?

Then I see another thing is missing - family. Not a single framed photograph. Not even parents. So a loner with a troubled background? Unhappy childhood?

When I'm convinced the lounge has nothing else to offer, I see the technician coming out of the main bedroom and confirm it's okay for me to enter.

He gives me an unusual grin and tells me I'm in for a treat.

I push the door open and start looking around, still unsure what he was grinning about.

Nice sized room. But then, it needs to be. There's a super-king-sized bed against the far wall, with bedside tables and lamps to either side. I run a finger along one table and leave a score in the dust that has formed there. It doesn't seem like she's been there for quite some time.

I open a drawer on one of the bedside units and find a strange contraption made from wood with hinges. I lift it out and am examining it more closely, trying to figure it out when a technician asks if he can start in the other bedroom. When he sees what I'm holding, he explains it's an adjustable cell phone stand. It allows you to position and direct your cell any way you want. For example, people use it for hands-free video calls. I put it back in the drawer and carry on looking.

The headboard is a fancy wrought-iron piece. Not comfortable to lean against when you're reading. Just not practical. On the wall facing the bed, there's a shelf mounted at almost my shoulder height. Just about three feet long. It's empty, apart from a matching layer of dust.

Fitted wardrobes with floor-to-ceiling mirrored fronts run along the left-hand wall. I start at the first and look inside. Skirts, tops, and a few dresses. Nothing fancy. She wasn't a clothes person. The second is much the same, although there are a couple of long evening dresses. The woman would probably have looked good in either of these.

When I try the third, I begin to get the technician's grin. The clothes inside are very different, although she would also probably have looked good in these.

An outfit that reminds me of a school uniform - white shirt, plaid tartan short skirt, and, would you believe, a tie? Then, uniforms - police, air-hostess, nurse, and something that resembles a hangman's outfit from an old movie, complete with a black hood.

Then there's my favorite - a black faux-leather figure-hugging one-piece jump-suit. I can only imagine trying to squeeze into this thing and look sexy. It wouldn't happen. I would look like a stuffed sausage.

I move on.

To one side, there's a set of drawers. I open the top one and lift a few pairs of flimsy knickers. Different colors. Lacy. Crotchless. I'm now thinking I may have underestimated Miss Wilson.

The second drawer is even more interesting. The contents would be best described as paraphernalia. Dildos of various shapes and sizes, some of which make me cringe.

A pink anal solid-glass bulb. Blue leather floggers. A PVC hood with no slots for the eyes. Various gags, one of which sported bright red lips open in a letter 'O' attached to a leather strap. Something I could only describe as a finger rake with sharp nails. And, inevitably, handcuffs. Now I'm positive I had

Miss Wilson all wrong.

I check the final wardrobe only to find more sexy outfits. It looks like she could cover most men's fantasies with this lot.

I carefully leave everything as I find it for cataloging and collecting later and move on to the second bedroom.

The technician's finished, and I'm free to look around. It's not as large as the first, but still a decent size. Measured against my own, it's enormous. The room is more effeminate than the rest of the house. A queen bed with a patterned duvet. Curtains that pick out a couple of the primary duvet colors hang on either side of the window. I check the bedside cabinet. There are a few over-the-counter regular medications, a couple of magazines, hairpins, an underarm deodorant, and a Coco Mademoiselle Perfume spray, the cost of which would feed me for a week.

I remove the glass topper and take a sniff.

I can't be sure, but I think it's the same as I detected in Jason's apartment.

I lift the magazines and find three small transparent bags with white powder inside. I guess cocaine, but forensics will tell me the answer to that. I shout the technician back in and ask him to bag these up while I continue to look around.

There's a dressing table in the far corner, but it seems like Miss Wilson didn't believe in makeup. There's hair spray and several face creams, and that's about it. A woman of simple needs - at least in her personal life. Maybe any other needs she had were being fulfilled in her professional life?

On the way out, Arnie's assistant is giving instructions on Miss Wilson's removal. I sidestep out the front door and head for my pool car. Just walking towards it reminds me of my transport problem. I already know a bank loan is out of the question, and the limits on my credit cards won't cover what I need. So, maybe I have to consider a cycle seriously. But then, I imagine turning up last at a crime scene and everyone laughing. So no, I definitely need a car of some description.

I decide to stop by my friendly garage on the way home and discuss the options. He had kept my previous car alive way longer than I thought possible. But, eventually, the cost of further repair wasn't worth it, and it had to go.

First, I have to fill in the incident report for Pamela Wilson's death and start a second case book. When there are multiple homicides in a case, the District Attorney's office insists we keep separate case books. That way, at least, we give each victim the same respect and attention.

Then I'll worry about a car.

9

The conversation at the garage goes better than I expect. Jonny, who owns the place, says that his daughter has an old banger but can't afford the insurance anymore as she's attending college. It's a Honda Civic, one-point-six liter, two-door in metallic blue. But, hey, at four hundred bucks, it could have been puke colored, and I would still bite his hand off.

I'll have to ask my parents for the money. They'll have no problem with that, but I will. It's always the same. I run out of cash. They bale me out. I'm thirty-six, for God's sake. I carry my education around my neck like a fucking anchor. I'll see them tomorrow.

Having missed my morning run, I quickly change into my running gear and add a lightweight wind-cheater. After the sun goes down, it gets chilly in February. I'll be glad for the extra warmth. It also helps cover my shield and Glock. Since I started wearing them when I run, I always feel very self-conscious.

I leave the apartment, head west towards the gulf, and then turn north. Going this way, I can run for as long as I like. Tonight I'm planning on around ten miles, so five up and five back. It doesn't happen.

I'm only a couple of blocks north when I notice a woman shouting at someone I assume to be her teenage daughter. Wrong again.

As I get closer, I see they're tussling over a purse with long straps.

The teenager wins the battle, turns, and starts running in my direction, but when she sees me, she turns again and runs away. The woman is screaming after her from the car park and shouting that the girl has stolen her purse.

Even though my knee isn't a hundred percent yet, I'm still a damn fine runner, so I set off after the youngster. She must have heard me coming as she ups her pace. I not only keep up but start rapidly closing the gap. Then, looking over her shoulder, she sees the problem and makes what turns out to be a foolish decision. She suddenly hooks a right into an alley. A dead-end alley. There's a ten-foot-high meshed fence directly in front of her. She stops and turns. I stop ten paces away and lift my wind-cheater to flash my badge.

I expect her to be around seventeen or eighteen, but she isn't. More like fourteen or less. Skinny. No breasts are showing yet. Long hair could do with a wash. Intelligent eyes.

I watch her think. She's weighing up the possibilities. As I see it, she only has two options. Turn and try to get far enough up the fence before I catch her or give herself up. I'm wrong. She has three.

She pulls a kitchen knife from the back of her trousers and points it in my direction.

I play her at her own game, pull my Glock and point it right at her.

We stand like that for an eternity. She has no idea what to do. I don't want to shoot her, but I've learned not to mess around with someone pointing a knife at you, regardless of how old she may be. One of us will break, and it won't be me.

She seems to come to the same conclusion and drops the knife. I walk slowly towards her, lowering my Glock. She throws the purse in my face and tries to dash past me when I'm almost there. I duck and, in the same movement, hook her arm and spin her around. Before she knows what's happening,

I have both hands behind her back and tie-wrapped.

I turn her around and examine her more closely. Fourteen may be on the high side. Without the knife, she'd morphed into a tearful adolescent. Probably more like twelve. An age she would later confirm.

I frisk her quickly in case she has any more surprises for me. She doesn't. She has nothing at all. No cash, no cell, nothing. Just empty pockets. I bend down, pick up her knife, stuff it down the back of my running pants, and then reach for the woman's purse. It's faux leather. Nothing expensive. But it isn't the girl's to have. She hasn't had time to open it, so I assume the contents will still be intact. It's time to learn more about her, so I start with the straightforward stuff.

'What's your name?'

She mumbles her response, making me repeat the question.

'Name?'

'Trace.'

'Trace what?'

'Just Trace. I don't have no other name.'

'Everyone has a second name, Trace.'

'Not me.'

'Okay, Trace. Where do you live?'

'Around.'

'Vague, Trace. Care to be more specific?'

'Just around.'

'You live with your parents?'

'Ain't got none.'

She enjoys brief sentences. I get that. This is going to be hard work.

'How about we return this purse to its owner, then decide what we will do with you?'

She shrugs her bony shoulders. 'Suit yourself.'

She has a young teenager's attitude, for sure. But, deciding I would not get any more right then, I do as I've suggested and march her back down the few blocks we had run until we get to the car park. The woman is still there, waiting. Hopefully, I guess.

I whisper in Trace's ear. 'You're going to apologize. Say you're sorry and hope she doesn't want me to write you up. You hear me?'

The girl grunts.

When we arrive in front of the woman, I hand her the purse and explain that I didn't think the girl had been inside. The woman didn't believe me as she immediately opens it and starts checking the contents.

Seemingly happy, she stares at the girl.

'I think the girl has something to say to you,' I say, nudging the girl with my hip.

'Sorry.'

Not the most heartfelt apology I'm hoping for, but at least it's an attempt, and the woman seems to accept it.

'Don't you go trying that again, young girl.'

Without another word, she turns and heads towards one of the apartment blocks next to the car park. Leaving me thinking a simple thanks might have been nice. Fuck her.

She's dumped her problem on my shoulders and just walked away. Now I have to decide what to do with the girl. I look at her.

'You eaten today?'

We walk silently to the next block west, where I know there's an all-night diner. Just before we enter, I remove the tie, free her wrists and tell her not to try anything stupid.

Inside, we take a booth, and I hand her one of the plastic encapsulated menus.

'Order whatever you want,' I tell her, realizing I've hardly eaten all day either. I'm hungry. She's ravenous.

I drink coffee with several top-ups. She does the same with the 7Up. When the food comes, there's barely enough room on the tabletop. Between us, we demolish everything. Before we entered, I wasn't sure I was doing the right thing. Now I am. I don't think she's seen food for quite some time.

After the waitress clears our table, we have one more top-up of our drinks and stare at each other, neither of us knowing where the conversation is going. Again, she breaks first.

'What's going to happen to me?'

I sit back, studying her. That makes me look clever, but the truth is, I have no idea what is about to come out of my mouth. This stuff isn't exactly covered in 101 basic training.

I think I'll prove I *am* clever and turn the tables.

If you don't know what to say, ask someone else.

'What do *you* think should happen?'

'You arrest me, and I go back into the system.'

She provides me with my first two clues. She's already been in the system, and right now, she isn't. I've got a runaway on my hands. There's only one responsible route for me now. I take her in and enter her into the juvie justice system, where she'll probably initially go into a juvie offender public facility. After that, she may or may not enter a 24/7 residential shelter or a reform school. If it's the latter, at least she can continue her education.

'What happened to your parents?'

'Never had no dad. Mom was a gang-banger till she died. Never cared for me.'

'Drugs?'

'Sex, drugs, and rock n'roll, she used to say. Never heard her listen to music in my life.'

'You ran away?'

'Wouldn't you? Laying in bed at night listening to different guys banging your mum. Her screaming about how much she was enjoying it. Then, you come out in the morning, and some guy's still wandering around. Wants to touch you up.'

'How long have you been on your own?'

'I'm not on my own.'

'Who are you with?'

'There's a group of us. We look out for each other.'

'This group. Where do you sleep?'

'We got a place. It's crappy, but it's our home.'

'Where is it?'

I look at her for an answer, but she isn't giving her friends up. All I've found out is interesting, but it hasn't helped me decide what to do with her. I'm only too well aware of horror stories in the juvie system. It's way short of perfect, and I'm not convinced she would be any better off. I ask her if she's had enough to eat, then walk her out and tell her to follow me.

Another two blocks inland, there's a 24/7 that sells just about anything and everything a person could want. The shelves have shelves in this place, and they pack every square inch high. I nudge her ahead of me and step inside.

It only takes thirty seconds to pick out what I want. Apparently, throwaway cells are so popular here. They store them right at the check-out, where they generally sell sweets for kids. It makes me wonder about the clientele they're expecting. I buy a throwaway, open it, and ensure it powers up. Program in a number I know by heart. I should. It's my own. Then hand it to the girl.

'You need me. You call, got it?'

She stares first at the cell in her hand, then at my face as if checking that I'm serious.

'You letting me go?'

'You got a better idea?'

'No, but you're a cop?'

'Off duty.'

'Still...'

'If you got a better idea, I'd be glad to hear it.'

I swear she's about to well up, so I turn and walk away. She shouts after me.

'Can I have my knife?'

I keep walking, unsure about what I've just done.

10

First thing I do in the morning. I sweet-talk the duty sergeant into letting me keep the pool car one more day. Two homicides. People to see. Lots of travel required.

Afterward, I head upstairs and stop at the Juvie desk. I know a sergeant there well and want to discuss what I've done with Trace the night before. Carol is one of the good guys, but she works in a heavily regulated area.

My luck is good. Not only is she in and available, she's heading for a coffee. I don't need to be asked. So, of course, I join her.

Unlike our coffee-making area, Juvie has a room with comfortable seats. It used to be the smoking room. Not now. I never smoked, but I enjoy comfortable seats.

When we have our coffees, I take her through the events of the previous evening, up to and including Trace asking me for her knife back. Then sit back to see what Carol is going to say. I can see the reprimand in her expression before she says squat. I'm prepared for that. What I want is what comes next.

I'm spot on. She rips a new one for me. Then sits back and asks how much I know about the girl's previous involvement in the system. I tell her the truth - virtually nothing. Next, she asks if I can look through some photographs and pick her out. I say I'll give it my best shot.

She disappears for a few minutes, leaving me wondering what will happen if I identify the girl.

I don't reach any conclusion before she comes back carrying two heavy binders.

She opens the first.

Each book has six pictures per page and around a hundred pages.

With lightning speed, I ask if twelve-hundred kids have really fallen out of the system in Collier County alone.

She gives me one of those *don't be stupid* looks over the top of her glasses. I start turning pages.

Twelve hundred sounds like a lot, but it doesn't take long when you're looking at double pages, twelve at a time.

Trace is in the second book, halfway through. Her full name is Tracy Elaine Shaw. According to the file, she's now twelve. Much of the information about her family is as she had told me. The only new info is that her mother had eventually committed suicide, or at least OD'd, leaving Trace in the care of an uncle. Unfortunately, that only lasted a few days before she disappeared, and she ended up in the system for dealing drugs a month later.

After that, she has a string of minor offenses - shoplifting, more purse theft, and breaking into cars. She's been in and out of the detention and care system ever since. That's the past three years.

She's down as having absconded from a residential care home.

I've previously seen some of these and can't blame her.

Carol tells me that given the girl's track record, I'm lucky I hadn't given her the knife back. That could have had severe consequences. I get that. As for helpful advice, Carol came up light. Whatever might happen with Trace, it's clear I'm on my own and will have to figure it out on the fly. Maybe she'll never call. I doubt it. She has a homicide detective on speed dial. Who wouldn't want to use that?

Up in my cubicle, there's a note from the medical examiner telling me the autopsy on Pamela Wilson would start around ten. I have time to get some help with some further investigation I want to do. I wander around the department looking for someone who isn't busy and settle on Matty White. He's halfway through a tasty donut when I knock on his cubicle wall and invite myself in.

Caught with a mouthful, he wipes at his mouth with a paper towel and swallows too quickly. Spluttering, he gulps some coffee and sits back, at least pretending to be back in control. I avoid smiling. Only just.

He accepts his mission with good grace. Most guys never acknowledge my second-grade status unless I ask them if they would do something for me. I ask him to go to the *All American Sports Bar* and get their security footage for the seven nights before Mark Jason's homicide. I want to find out if Pamela Wilson was there and if she hooked up with the three musketeers - Mark, Xavier, and Tyrone. If she did, was this a one-off or a regular thing? Also, which night or nights was she there that week? I tell him all the details he will need are in the case book for Mark Jason in my office.

Leaving him seemingly happy to oblige, I head downstairs for the autopsy.

It doesn't matter how many of these you see or smell. You never truly get used to it. But, since the Covid-19 epidemic, things have improved in that we can no longer be in the same area as the medical examiner. Instead, we're in a viewing room, separated by perspex sheeting with audio connections so we can talk back and forth.

Again, I've missed the Y-incision, and Pamela Wilson's innards are already splayed out for all to see.

I tap on the screen to let Arnie know I've arrived, and he grunts his recognition. Although simply a grunt, it conveys his displeasure. He doesn't like people being late for his shows. Something again about respect for the dead: anyway, he's focused. That's fine with me.

I watch as he carefully removes each major organ one at a time and hands them to his assistant for processing. His maxim is *if you're late, you wait.*

Eventually, when finished, he turns to address me directly.

'Glad you could find the time to join us, Detective.'

He likes to play this game where he only addresses me by my title as if I'm a naughty schoolgirl.

But in this case, I *was* late. So, I suck it up.

'I've got a few things that may interest you today,' he continues. 'Even after a preliminary look, I would say this woman was a regular Cocaine user. I have already noted some left-ventricular hypertrophy and pulmonary edema.

I have yet to complete the craniotomy, but I can almost guarantee cerebrovascular damage. The toxicology tests will confirm, but I would say she has been a long-term frequent flyer.'

I mention his conclusion fits my finding of the white powder baggies in her bedside cabinet. He nods.

'What about the stabbing?'

'Simple enough. Whoever did this targeted the femoral artery with precision. Severed it in one quick stab.'

'Your assistant suggested that the assailant left the knife in the wound, and the victim herself removed it. Can you confirm that?'

'No. The blood spatter is the only way you can determine that.'

'Anything else you think might be helpful, Arnie?'

'Maybe,' he answers. He likes to be mysterious sometimes. To make me drag it out of him. I play along.

'Maybe, what?'

'Maybe I have something. Maybe even a *couple* of other useful things, in fact.'

'Can I ask what?'

'Bruising.'

'Where?'

'Many places, including vaginal and anal. But mostly on her arms and legs and around the base of her neck. I would say this lady had some rough treatment recently.'

'How recently do you think?'

'Looking at the bruising dis-coloration, I would say most

likely within the past few days, or certainly in the past week.'

Given her profession, I'm not surprised. There again, Mark Jason's two exes had painted the story of how he and his two friends treated them. I could see it either way. Arnie shakes me out of my thoughts.

'Do you know the most common ways to kill someone outright with a single blade stab?'

I have to admit it's not something I've ever considered. This seems to please him. I settle down and prepare for a bit of a lecture.

'Number one - straight through the eye, penetration of the frontal cortex.'

'That would do it, for sure,' I agree.

'Number two - direct punching motion through the side of the skull. The Temple. Again, penetrating the brain.'

'This is gruesome, Arnie. What's next?'

'Three - severing the carotid with a swipe across the neck. Not as fast, but just as effective.'

I'm ready to ask if there are more when he continues.

'Four, a direct puncture wound into the heart or preferably the Aortic arch as in the death of Detective Jason. And finally, the fifth would be the one we have in front of us. Severing the femoral artery. This is like the carotid in that it's not instantaneous but equally effective if you have a little time to spare.'

'Fascinating, Arnie. I suppose there's a reason for enlightening me in this way?'

My sarcasm always results in the same stare. But it never stops me. Take pleasure in life when you can - that's my motto.

After a strained moment, he explains.

'Do you understand the crucial difference between the first four and the last?'

I'm not expecting a test, have no idea what he's talking about, and tell him so.

'The first four accounts for over ninety-five percent of knife deaths and are above waist height. The last accounts for five percent and is not.'

'I get that, Arnie. But why are you pointing it out to me?'

'If there are four more equally efficient or better ways to kill your victim with a knife above waist height, why would you pick the lowest?'

I think about that for a moment. It seems he's onto something, but I'm unsure what.

'The accuracy of the single blow tells you that whoever did this knew what they were doing. And had planned it. So my question for you, Detective, is why did they pick the least likely point of attack?'

'I see what you mean. Most people would raise their hand to stab, so the impact site would usually be above waist height.'

'Exactly why the first four are the more common deaths from stabbing. So I ask you, detective. Why didn't your killer go for one of them?'

'Thanks, Arnie. That gives me something to think about.'

'One other thing, Detective. I examined the cervix just before you arrived and think your victim may have had a baby. If she did, I would say it would be many years ago.'

'Not like you to give me possibles, Arnie.'

'What can I say, Detective? The thing is, when a young woman delivers a baby, the cervix is more flexible and capable of more or less returning to its original state after delivery. So, given what I have found here. If Pamela Wilson had a child, she is most likely to have been in her early teens at the time.'

11

When I return from Pamela Wilson's autopsy, I think about everything Arnie told me.

I still have missing information. The toxicology report to confirm the plastic baggie content as Cocaine, and forensics to confirm the blood-splatter theory that the killer left the knife in the wound. I'm also now wondering if there is a younger 'Pamela' out there somewhere to start my list of suspects. There's certainly no indication of that around her home.

Thinking about possible suspects, another thing I need to follow up on is Pamela's professional engagements. Was her death connected to Mark Jason and his buddies or something else entirely? Someone who had not taken kindly to the professional treatment she had meted out? I have no idea.

What's becoming clear is that Pamela Wilson is responsible for the death of Detective Jason. A final comparison with the fingerprints found on the beer bottle in Jason's apartment will confirm her presence. Combined with the Coco Mademoiselle perfume and the red hair comparison should at least raise her to the top of the suspect list. The only problem is that the door-to-door has uncovered nothing. No one had seen or heard anything unusual on the night someone killed Jason. So, all I can be sure of is that Pamela Wilson had been in his apartment recently and given the fingerprints on the beer bottle, probably the night he died. But still not necessarily that she had killed him. I need more. I can establish opportunity and motive, but ideally, I need to find the stiletto.

At that point, my phone rings, interrupting my thoughts. It's one of the technicians from forensics. I can tell he's excited.
　'What have you got?' I ask.
　'There was a safe at the victim's home.'
　'Pamela Wilson's?'
　'Yes. It was a floor safe in a pantry cupboard in the kitchen.'
　'What was in it?'
　'We don't know yet. There's a safe expert out there now as we talk.'
　'Okay. Thanks for letting me know.'
　'I'll call you later. Let you know what we find inside.'
　'Great. Thanks.'

Now that's interesting. How many regular people do I know that have a safe in their home? Not many. I don't know any at all. But, again, that's too small a sample size to draw any conclusions. I don't know many regular people. Most of the people I know are cops. Please show me a cop who has a safe in his home! I decide to take a poll.

In the next ten minutes, I give the question to half a dozen guys in the department. Not one of them knows anyone with a home safe. So, what little secret is Pamela Wilson keeping in there? I'll have to wait to find out.

Meanwhile, when I get back to my desk, I realize autopsies make me hungry. But one thing I have to do first. File for a subpoena to gain access to Pamela Wilson's bank details. I do that through our in-house system online, and it only takes a few moments. After that, I try to concentrate on updating my two case books, but when I'm hungry, I can do only one thing. Find food.

I'm at EJ's thirty minutes later with a massive fried all-day breakfast. Finally, with food making its way into my body, my mind is prepared to cooperate.

First, I have to decide if there's a link between the two cases. The way I proceed will depend on that. I think back to the descriptions Mark Jason's ex-wives had given me of how Mark and his friends assaulted them. If for no other reason than getting justice for these two women, I would like to nail Xavier and Tyrone. I'm depending on Pamela Wilson turning up on the security videos from the *All-American Sports Bar*. At least I have a plan for them.

Now that Pamela Wilson is top of my suspect hit list for Jason's homicide, I need to think through the other possibilities and make sure I'm not zeroing in too quickly. My list of alternative suspects includes his two ex-wives, but having spoken to them, I'm almost ready to cross them off the list. I have to check their alibis as a last detail. That's something I can have someone else take care of. I'm sure neither of these women is a killer.

Then there are his two dumb-assed friends. I can see them falling out and getting physical. Fighting. But I couldn't see either of them climbing over him and pushing a stiletto through his aorta, so I'm convinced I can take them off the list. But, again, I'll have someone check their alibis.

That leaves me with either someone I haven't yet thought of or Pamela Wilson taking her revenge. I stop mid-sausage-bite and use my cell to call the forensics lab. The same guy who called me an hour ago answers. I ask about the hair and print comparisons, and he promises to get back to me ASAP.

Satisfied I've made progress, I get back to eating.

So, if I assume Pamela Wilson killed Mark. Who do I have on the list for killing Pamela Wilson? Mark's two buddies, for sure. They would know her and know what had really happened at Mark's apartment. They are top of the list. Revenge is the motive. Then I grind to a halt. I realize they're not *just* at the top of the list. They *are* the list.

I need more suspects.

That makes me wonder about her Dominatrix career and whether I'm looking for a dissatisfied customer. I'm also curious to find out the contents of her home safe. Maybe I'll find another possible suspect there.

Pamela Wilson's home was comfortable, but it didn't leave me feeling she was loaded. Everything was utilitarian, not expensive. It looks like her professional life gave her a particular lifestyle, which was fine, and I didn't sense ambition or drive to become super-rich. So, what could she possibly own that would require a safe? Maybe she inherited it? I should look into her family for that. I also need to follow up on the door-to-door I left the patrol guys doing. Maybe someone saw the killer come and go. It's happened before.

By the time I've emptied my plate, I feel I've done some helpful thinking. It's time to return to the office.

As I approach the Sheriff's building, my cell rings. It's my newfound friend in forensics.

'You got to come to see this, detective.'

A few minutes later, I'm doing just that. He has the contents of the safe laid out in a neat row in front of him: ten cell phones, each in a plastic evidence bag.

'What's this?'

'That's what was inside. Ten cells, nothing else.'

'Do they work?'

'Some do, some don't. They're not new. Some of them are over ten years old, I would say.'

I recognize a couple as older models of the Apple iPhone and another couple as Samsungs. Other than that, I'm at a loss.

'Can you charge them up and find out what's on them?'

'Should be able to with most of them. The newer ones might be a problem, though?'

'The newer ones? Shouldn't the older ones be the problems?'

'No. Charging them will be easy once we dig up the right cables for the older models. But getting in through the security will be much harder with the newer phones.'

'Why's that?'

'Apple, mainly. The FBI has been after them for years to build in a back door through their security screening so that they can get into terrorist cells. But they've refused point blank. They've even defended their position against a U.S. Magistrate's order to allow FBI access to an iPhone used by one of the perpetrators in the San Bernardino mass shooting. They plan to take it to a District Court and all the way to the Supreme Court if necessary. They won't budge anytime soon.'

'But we can get into the older models?'

'Sure can. We use a couple of external firms that do that. It usually takes a few days, but we can get into at least six or seven of these.'

'Ok. Let's do it. And as quickly as you can. These cells will probably tell us who killed the victim.'

The next hour I spend tracking down relatives of Pamela Wilson. She'd never married. Her mother is dead, but her father still lives here in Naples. She also has a sister up in Tampa. I call the father, and we agreed I would go directly there.

It takes me around thirty minutes to turn into the Everglades golf complex to the East of I75. This one complex has two or three courses, and I guess Pamela's father is a golfer. With his wife dead and living on his own, why not?

I pass the swanky clubhouse on my left. They're also into tennis. I can see five outdoor courts and three mini-courts for juniors or seniors for pickleball. The club is a sizeable single-story affair with a glass front and an octagonal restaurant to the side, overlooking a decent-sized swimming pool. You would probably never leave the complex if you could afford to live here.

Having seen the glory of the clubhouse, I have to say the basic construction of Mr. Wilson's home surprises me. Functional is the best way I can describe it. He has a golf buggy in the garage, several sets of clubs, and an old Dodge in the driveway. What more does he need?

I pull up and head for the garage. He's cleaning some clubs at a workbench in the back. I show him my badge and confirm that I was the one who had called. I ask if we can talk inside, and he leads me into the house through a door at the rear of the garage and offers me coffee. Much as I would have liked one, for once, I refuse, wanting to get on with the discussion.

I suggest maybe we can sit.

I then tell him what has happened to his daughter.

As he absorbs the news, I try to figure out his response and come up with - stoic. No extreme meltdown. No tears. Just a sad acceptance.

I offer to get him something. A glass of water, a coffee, anything at all. He declines.

So, I ask if he could tell me a little about his daughter. He doesn't go where I'm expecting. In this situation, most people tell you about the deceased's childhood and how they were when they were little. You know. Fond childhood memories. But not Mr. Wilson. He sticks with the present.

'I told her this would happen.'

'Told her what would happen, Mr. Wilson?'

'That someone wouldn't like what she was doing. That someone would harm her.'

'What was your daughter doing that you thought would get her harmed?'

He looks reluctant to say more. I nudge him along.

'I've been through the contents of her home, Mr. Wilson. I think you can talk freely without giving away too many secrets.'

'She was seeing people. Men.'

'By seeing, you mean having sexual relations. Is that right?'

He nods.

'So you knew she was doing this?'

'Yes. I tried to get her to stop. But she wouldn't, until recently.'

'How recently?'

'Oh, I think it was around two or three years ago. Strange that she should get killed over it now, though.'

'You think someone killed her because of that?'

'Why else? She was just a woman trying to get by. Never could hold down a regular job. Damned drugs. Couldn't get off them.'

'Do you know why she stopped seeing men?'

'She never told me. Just said she'd had enough.'

'Do you know how she managed for money? Did she ask you for help?'

'No. Just the opposite. She often brought me a week's shopping to stock up my freezer. She never asked for anything from me. She was good that way.'

'Was there any man in particular in your daughter's life?'

'No. They wouldn't have put up with her doing what she was doing, would they?'

'How about since she stopped? Say, in the past couple of years?'

'Not that I know of. She never seemed interested in men. I know that sounds stupid. But maybe she saw the darker side and didn't like it. I don't know.'

'You have another daughter?'

'Sure. Shirley. She lives with her family up in Tampa. I don't see her so often anymore. They're always busy.'

'Was she close to Pamela?'

'No, never was. She's five years younger. Different Mums. She never got along much. She would only ever see Pamela when she came here to see me. I would make a point of having them both together.'

'Was there animosity between them?'

'No. Nothing like that. They just weren't interested in each other. Sad, really. But I stopped trying to make it better a long time ago.'

'Will you tell Shirley what has happened to her sister?'

'Sure. I'll take care of that. Do you know when I can collect the body?'

'I don't know, but someone from the Medical Examiner's

office will be in touch over the next few days.'

We talk more after that, but he has little else to tell me. Although he knew that his daughter was seeing men, he never mentioned the specifics of the service she provided. So, I decide not to, just in case he doesn't know that level of detail. No point.

Back in the car, I look at the time and decide that as I'm driving up to talk with my parents, I should probably head off. I'm on top of everything I should be for the moment. I can afford a few hours with my folks.

My parents live north of Fort Myers, about an hour's drive from Naples. So I call ahead and make a reservation for Mama's home cooking. She's pleased to hear my voice, and that cheers me up as it always does. I dread the day I lose Mama and Papa. I feel so strongly connected to them both and worry that I might drift away when they go.

Tonight, I intend to enjoy the cooking and finish with an extra helping of dessert. Humble pie. I will ask Papa for a loan of four hundred bucks to buy my car. He'll have no hesitation in offering. Probably tell me it shouldn't be a loan but a gift. I'll insist it will just be a loan, and he'll back down, then agree. Both of us know I have no way of paying it back. But that's family for you, and I love them both very much.

12

Life at my parents' house has a reassuringly familiar pattern. Mama rises early and starts baking or cooking. Every day, rain or shine, Mama would be in the kitchen by six. I swear she feeds our entire tribe. There's probably an unbroken line of people in and out of the kitchen before I even open my eyes. I've just never seen them.

Papa rises, eats breakfast, and heads to the Medical Examiner's office in Fort Myers. He works as a porter and general helper there. They're always busy, so when he can, he works overtime. After work, he comes home, and they eat together. Mama always waits for him. Then, they clear up together and sit in the evening, discussing their days, remembering the past, and sharing their hopes and dreams for the future.

When I appear, I break the pattern as Mama assumes I never eat and insists on feeding me. She will eat with me in the evening. Papa will eat alone.

But then the three of us quickly ease into each other's company.

I talk to them about my work - not the gory stuff. Then they tell me how our broader family members are doing. That's when they suddenly ask me if I could help a cousin on my Mama's side. Joey Still Water.

They're worried he's mixing with *bad people* down in Naples. My neck of the woods. Listening to them, it's only a matter of time before he gets into trouble. If I can only have a word with him.

I remember Joey from when I was growing up. So if he's mixing with some bad people, he's in the perfect company as far as I'm concerned. An act as predictable as night following day. But I can't say that. So I agree.

That's when my mama admits she's already told her sister I will help and that she, in turn, has already mentioned it to Joey.

I don't mind this. It's how our family works. We help each other. There's no way I would refuse. I am curious about how Joey responded, but Mama tells me her sister said he seemed grateful, maybe even desperate.

After that, we talk some more before I head home, using the journey to get my head back into the deaths of Mark Jason and Pamela Wilson.

That had all been the previous evening, and when I wake up this morning, my mind has unconsciously shifted from my two homicides to thinking about my cousin.

Joey lives just a few blocks from me, although I'm unsure exactly where. According to Mama, her sister doesn't even have his address.

I live here because it's all I can afford. He lives here with his 'bad people' friends, and I very much doubt his friends will appreciate him having a visit from a detective. So I have to figure out where best to meet him.

I needn't have bothered.

I'm tooled up and ready to go. I tell Alexa to stop playing, head for the door, and open it to find Joey slumped unconscious against the wall opposite.

I check him over for obvious injuries, but he seems fine. I speak his name, and he responds slowly. He's on something, but I don't know what. Dilated pupils, skin discolored, hair dry, and lank. He looks half the weight I remember him being. I repeat his name.

It's like he hears me speaking from far, far away. He looks

around, trying to figure out where I am, then his eyes lock onto mine. Or at least try. Tears form and run down his cheeks. He whispers my name.

'Sammy, I'm in trouble.'

No shit.

I help him up to his feet. Half carry him into my apartment and dump him on my beanbag. I reckon he's dehydrated, so I start with a glass of water.

'Drink.'

To my surprise, he does, greedily. So now I know he's in trouble. I don't yet know which kind. If it's drugs, I can probably find him rehab through the department. But with Joey, things are never straightforward.

'Have you eaten recently?'

He shakes his head. I have little in the place, but I toast a couple of bagels and make him some scrambled eggs. I've never seen anyone eat so fast. He shovels it down. By now, I'm desperate for coffee, but that won't be best for him, so I pour us both tall glasses of water and sit opposite him at my small breakfast bar.

'Talk to me, Joey. What's up?'

I recognize the look in his eye - fear.

Big Joey, who used to bully everyone at school, is scared. When I say everyone, I don't include myself. I never took his crap. I guess he respected me for that. I never asked.

'I got mixed up in some bad stuff, Sammy.'

'No kidding?' I reply, trying desperately not to let my sarcasm be too obvious. He wouldn't have noticed, anyway.

'They killed a guy. He couldn't pay for his China White. So they fuckin' killed him. Slit his throat. Just like that.'

'Slow down, Joey. Who are *they*? And who did they kill?'

'They're new around here. The guy who leads them isn't, but the rest have come from Miami.'

I groan. I know where he is going.

'They call themselves the Savage City Gangsters.'

'Chico Vegas.'

'Yeah, that's the guy. He's a whole different level of mean,

Sammy.'

'Tell me about it. Who did they kill?'

'Just some poor fucker who couldn't pay for his China White.'

'Did Vegas do the killing?'

'No. One of his side-kicks. This one's not nasty. He's a fuckin' psycho. I don't know why Vegas keeps him around. He causes trouble.'

'Where's the body?'

'They put it in the car crusher. Inside an old Chevy.'

My heart skips a beat.

'What color?'

'How do you mean what color?'

'What color was the old Chevy?'

'Green, I think. It was covered in dust.'

At least it wasn't my old car. For a moment, I worried that I might have sold it only for it to end up in the scrap yard with a dead body squashed inside. Not a fate for a homicide detective's trusty steed. They'd probably given whoever scrapped this Chevy fifty bucks for providing a coffin. Not something the owner would have been told.

'Can you ID the killer?'

'Sure, but I won't. Do you think I'm stupid?'

'Look, Joey. You're the one who's come to me for help. So if I'm going to help, it needs to be on my terms?'

He looks at me blankly, like I'm speaking ancient Sumerian or something. I try again.

'To give you what you need, I need you to ID the killer. If you do this, I'll arrange for you to stay at a rehab clinic somewhere outside the area. Then, when you're clean, I'll ask the help of our families to find you somewhere else to live and get you a job. After that, you're on your own.'

As I watch, he goes into think mode. Not something that he often does, so this impresses me. I'm impressed even more when he agrees. Now I'm just plain shocked.

I leave him thinking while I quickly call Jerry in Narcs. I clue him in on my thoughts, and he agrees that if Joey gives up the killer, the department will spring for the rehab clinic. After that, it was up to me to fulfill the rest of the commitment.

I tell him I'll bring Joey in right then, and he says he'll look out his files on the Savage City Gangsters. So we'll meet at his place.

Thirty minutes later, Joey is sitting in a small conference room in the Narcotics division, reviewing the files and looking for the killer. Jerry and I are outside discussing how best to follow up.

It's an interesting situation. The SCG was number one on Jerry's hit list as the area's principal supplier of illegal drugs. But the killing of an innocent guy is homicide, and that makes it something my department would usually handle. Typically, homicide would trump drugs, but this is a unique situation, so I agree to talk it over with my boss and see if we can agree on how best to handle it. I promise I'll get back to him and leave Joey in his care, going downstairs to look for Dan Weissman.

Easy to find. He's in his cubicle. I grab the free chair and sit myself down.

He's just finishing a call. When he hangs up, he knows me well enough to know I have something for him. I spill the beans. No hesitation on his part. One thing I like about him. He's decisive and doesn't care about organizational boundaries. He agrees to Narcs taking the lead in this case, as long as Homicide is represented at the take-down. I say I'll make sure of that, knowing that it will be me and hoping that Dan hasn't figured that out.

I thank Dan, then update him on the apparent dead-end I'm at with finding Jason's killer. We agree that although the evidence against Pamela Wilson looks promising, it's still inconclusive, and we still need to find the stiletto.

I commit to organizing a second search of the areas around both Mark Jason's and Pamela Wilson's apartments and the apartments themselves and all the contents.

When I leave to call back upstairs, I'm pleased. Narcs taking the lead with my cousin's offer to ID a killer was the decision I wanted. I've enough on my plate with two homicides to solve.

When I tell Jerry, he says that Joey has identified Chico's man as Joaquin Montoya, nicknamed *The Joker,* with a certain amount of irony. He also said that if we want to find the body, we need to hurry before it ships out, so he's already started the application for a warrant and expects to have it through sometime mid-afternoon. He plans to hit the scrap yard before closing, probably around four-thirty. I say, to count me in. We raided this place a year ago when we removed the previous drug suppliers. And here we are, same old same old. In that last raid, the gang leader had been *Lucky Luke,* and Chico Vegas had tricked me into taking him down, so he could replace him at the top of the tree. I'd been used but couldn't do anything about it. I didn't like that, and I still hold a grudge.

I hope we can finally wrap up Chico and lock him away this time.

We need to keep Joey around until he can make the identification in person, so Jerry says he'll have one of his guys take him to a hotel for the night and sit on him. One less thing for me to worry about.

13

I'm back in my office and feel the need for one of my to-do lists. I am only a few days back at work and need a to-do list. How quickly things change. I guess that's one reason I stay in homicide. You never know what will happen, and a lot is going on.

A message on my desk from my forensic friend tells me there's a match between the red hair found at Mark Jason's place and on Pamela Wilson down in the morgue. So, along with the prints on the beer bottles, I now know she was there, almost definitely on the night of his homicide.

I still need to find out what they found on the security footage from the *All-American Sports Bar*.

I put that first on my list.

1. Security footage - check for Pamela Wilson, Mark, Xavier, and Tyrone. Were they all together, or was Pamela with Mark as the others suggested? Did they leave together or separately?
2. A new thought - check traffic cams and see who traveled where when they left the sports bar.
3. Figure out how to confront Xavier and Tyrone. Were they involved in the assault or death of Pamela Wilson?
4. Find out more about Pamela Wilson. Who else might want her dead?
5. The cells in Pamela's safe. Why were they there? What is

on them that made her keep them in a safe?
6. Was Pamela a victim or a murderer, or both?
7. Organize new searches looking for the stiletto.
8. Support Jerry in the take-down.
9. Check for results from the door-to-door at Pamela's place.

The only other thing that comes to mind is to collect my new car. Given that my day will only get busier, I decide I can hand the keys for the pool car in at the duty desk and walk to the garage. Pay with the cash Papa has given me. The cash I stubbornly define as a loan, even when I'm only talking to myself. Then bring it back here in time for a briefing session with Jerry and the Narcs team.

All goes well until I get to the garage. It's locked up. I take out my cell and call. I hear the phone ring inside the small building. No-one answers. I try looking through the grime-covered window but can't see a thing. Fuck. I have to walk back to the office. I'm not amused.

Instead of going directly to my cubicle, I stop to discuss the searches at Jason's and Pamela Wilson's with the duty sergeant. He will arrange both for later in the day. Happy with that, I stop at forensics on the way back to my office.

I find the technician dusting the phones for prints. Something I hadn't even thought of. I ask him how he's getting on. It turns out he's on the last cell. Of the ten, he has five with clear prints, which he's already running through AFIS, but the others have only partials or nothing. Still, five's better than nothing.

Given the same reasons I've used to rule Jason's two gym buddies out for his stabbing, the same logic applies to Pamela Wilson. If they were to take revenge on her, they would have beaten her to death. So, the chances are that the owner of one of these phones killed Pamela Wilson.

* * *

The only slight caveat is what Arnie told me about her having had a child a long time ago. Other than that, I've found no family or friends. I've had one of the other detectives visit with her dance and yoga classes, but she is known at both as very much a loner.

While waiting for AFIS, the technician walks me through a chart he's made up. But, first, he has listed the cells.

Apple iPhone 4
   Apple iPhone 5S
   Apple iPhone 6S
   Galaxy S8
   Samsung Galaxy S2
   Samsung Galaxy Note 5
   Google Nexus 5
   T-Mobile G2
   Sony Xperia Z3
   LG Nexus 4

'These are not new cells,' he tells me. 'The most recent is probably the Galaxy S8 which is probably only two or three years old.'

'The others are all older?'

'Yes, probably. Rather than bore you with the details, I've taken a shot at putting them into the most likely years, bearing in mind that some people keep a cell for many years. All I can go by until we unlock them are the years they were either introduced or most popular.'

He produces the following list.

2010
   Apple iPhone 4
   T-Mobile G2 Android
2011
   Samsung Galaxy S2 Android
2012

LG Nexus 4 Android
2013
Apple iPhone 5S
Google Nexus 5 Android
2014
Sony Xperia Z3 Android
2015
Samsung Galaxy Note 5 Android
2016
Apple iPhone 6S
2017
Galaxy S8

'Another way of looking at them is which operating system they use. This is important when trying to hack through the security. For example, we have three Apple iPhones. The first two should be possible, but the 6S may not be.'

'The rest are all Androids; because they're old, they should also be straightforward. The most recent, the Galaxy S8, we'll have to see. I can't predict that one.'

'So, you're saying that your external consultants should be able to gain access to eight or nine out of ten cells?'

'Yes, and possibly the last one or two as well. It may take a little longer, though.'

'What about the prints?'

'The three with clear prints are the three iPhones, which I guess has to do with the material they use to manufacture the case.'

As he answers, he walks back to a printer against the rear wall and returns with the AFIS results print-out.

'Bad break, detective. It doesn't look like these three are in the system.'

'What about the partials?'

'I'm running them now, but you will probably get a list of possibles for each. Still, you may find something that makes sense in your case. I'll email everything through to you as soon as I get it.'

I thank him and head back upstairs.

I still have some time to do some checking before Jerry's briefing.

Thinking about the ages of the cells, whatever Pamela Wilson was doing, she was collecting a cell per year, more or less. But, it also has stopped in the past three years, and I wonder why?

I've based my working theory on the use she has been making of the main bedroom in her home. Was she somehow able to use her client's cells to record their performance, then keep them? Surely they wouldn't allow that? But if she could somehow do that, was she then blackmailing them?

The timing also fits with the layer of dust everywhere in her professional bedroom and her father telling me she retired some two or three years ago. I've already concluded that she hasn't been in business for quite some time. That tied in with the ages of the cells. Maybe, she retired, and the blackmail income had become her retirement pension?

I need to add checking into Pamela Wilson's bank records to my to-do list.

14

I start research on Pamela Wilson. First, is she who she's supposed to be? I hadn't thought to ask her father for a photograph of his daughter, so I start by checking her birth certificate, school records, then college yearbooks. I can see the likeness in her photographs as far back as kindergarten. And the yearbooks confirm it for me. She is definitely Pamela Wilson.

Checking through employment records shows that she has moved around a lot. Her first job was at Walmart, then in an insurance company, an eye clinic, Costco, and finally as a bank teller at Bank of America.

As I add to the list, I note that virtually every job she had was in administration or finance. I suppose once you start down that road, you build experience, so new prospective employers would want you for that.

Her employment seems to stop around five years ago. After that, there's nothing. At least nothing in public records.

Criminal history confirms both Arnie Collins' supposition and what her father told me. She's been a user of Cocaine since her teens. There're two reports of her as a user between fifteen and eighteen, but no charges were filed. I guess we were cutting her some slack. From there on, she had several convictions and was in and out of rehab. Nothing major, though, and never a dealer. Just a user. This probably ties in with why she seems to move employment so regularly. Not a happy life.

* * *

Just being thorough, I check for marriage or divorce papers, but there are none. It wouldn't be the first time someone had hidden a marriage from their parents. But not in this case.

I log into the DMV system again and check her driving convictions, but apparently, she's an excellent driver with no offenses.

Her passport is current, and her Social Security and tax payments are up to date. Then I look into her property. She's the sole owner, with no loan outstanding. Paid her utility bills by regular banker's orders.

It's when I start examining her bank records things become interesting. There are all the regular outgoings you would expect, and I don't pay them much attention. What I focus on is one regular monthly income. This last few months, for ten thousand dollars, deposited directly from an offshore account in her own name.

I immediately request details for the previous ten years and print everything out. After collecting them from the printer and having armed myself with a fresh Folgers, I move into the conference room and spread the records out on the table.

I start checking the history of the incoming deposits. They started ten years before at five hundred dollars per month and increased every now and again up to the ten-thousand level about three years ago. Since then, they have remained constant at that level. I grab a pad and pencil and start mapping them out, year by year. The income increases nine times over the ten-year period. Sometimes once a year, sometimes twice. This is Pamela Wilson's retirement plan in action. I reckon I've found how she has managed to own her home, pay her utilities and taxes and provide her father with regular groceries.

At this point, I almost run back to my cubicle to print out the cell phone history that forensics have laid out for me.

* * *

Looking at the year of introduction for each model, I found a pattern year-by-year over eight years. 2..1..2..1..1..1..1..1.

When I look at the pattern of increases in Pamela's income from her offshore account, it isn't identical, but It's close enough for me. Every time she adds a cell to her safe, her income from this offshore account goes up. So in the first year, her income starts at five hundred and increases to a thousand before the year's end. And if I'm right, these two contributors had recently purchased new models of cell phones. As I say, it isn't an identical pattern match, but the general picture is that as newer cells become available, her income rises.

Then I notice that there are only nine increases and yet, ten cell phones. That puzzles me until I notice that her income doesn't increase when the last cell phone was available - the most recent.

I'm now convinced she was using recordings on these cell phones to blackmail her clients, apart from the final client, who is the owner of the newest Galaxy S8 for some reason. Now, I really want to know what's on them. I'll figure the Galaxy S8 discrepancy out later.

Before I can give this any more thought, Jerry calls down from Narcs and tells me the briefing's about to start, so I head upstairs, aware that senior management will see my involvement in this as unnecessary. But from a family perspective, it most definitely is. Besides, I feel I'm making steady progress with both homicides and still feel in control.

We aren't going in great numbers as we did the last time we raided this scrap metal yard. That time, we were taking down a major drug deal. This time there will only be four of us and a patrol car. The aim is much simpler. To find an old green crushed Chevy and see if there's a body inside. We'll take a flatbed with us in anticipation.

Jerry shows us a picture of the owner, who apparently works there every day. He's the one to whom we will serve the search warrant. Then there's a picture of the guy Joey told us is the killer we're hoping to nail - Joaquin Montoya, or *The Joker* as we know him. Given the appearance of the guy, I have to award top marks to whoever came up with his nickname. This guy is about as far from a joke as possible. Nothing funny at all.

At upwards of two-fifty pounds and six foot six, he's a big guy. In the picture in front of us, he's wearing his straggly hair to shoulder length and sporting an equally scraggy beard, long and unkempt, mostly brown but with flecks of gray. He's decorated himself with tats on every available patch of skin, including his face.

According to the file Jerry produces, he's thirty-eight, single, and the gang's fixer. No known pastimes or interests - just fixing. He has served time twice, but not for anything major. Not yet. There's no current address for him since he moved up from Miami a year ago. So we're really hoping to catch him on-site.

Jerry also shows a picture of my nemesis, Chico Vegas, but explains that it's unlikely he'll be there. I guess he's not really into scrap metal.

Half an hour later, we roll through the gates of the scrap yard and climb out of our vehicles. The owner walks towards us. I can only see two other people. One is controlling the crusher. Old car in, metal cube out. I bet he enjoys his work. The other is driving, I guess what you could call a pick-and-place mechanical hoist. He's collecting the crushed cubes and piling them neatly, presumably ready for collection and transport to some far-off place.

When I stop and look around, Jerry's already handing the warrant to the owner, who is looking it over. I decide to use the time to snoop around, so make for the office while the owner is occupied.

I've only reached the front door when I hear a noise and curse coming from round the rear somewhere. I draw my weapon, shout for an officer to follow, and run around the side of the building.

* * *

The Joker is trying to escape across an eight-foot high wire fence. He has jumped on top of half a dozen wooden pallets and put his foot through one of them. I imagine that was the reason for the cursing I heard. By the time I'm fully around the building and twenty paces from him, he has clambered up on a huge waste bin and is trying to swing his massive bulk over the fence.

I shout for him to stop, but know there's no way he will, so I holster my gun and sprint towards him, rapidly closing the gap.

He already has most of his body mass over the fence but has trapped one leg. The other trailed behind. When I'm almost there, I can see his problem is that his enormous belly is hanging down both sides of the fence.

I jump up on the same pallets, being careful to keep to the edges, but just as he gets his first leg over. It will only be a matter of seconds before the other will follow. I do the only thing I can think of and jump as high as possible, snagging his belt with both hands, then hold on.

With his momentum lost, he becomes stuck again. He pulls a knife from somewhere and starts jabbing it toward me through the links in the fence. I avoid the first few jabs but know I need to do something different before eventually he gets to me. I throw my weight backward, and as I swing back towards the chain-link fence, put my feet out to form an arch with my body. Not only can he no longer reach me, but I've increased my leverage, and his body is slowly reappearing over my side of the fence.

I think I'm doing fine until I look up and realize that all that's happening is I'm getting a magnificent view of the crack of his butt as his pants slowly slide down to his mid-thigh.

Fortunately, by this time, both of the patrol officers we brought with us have arrived and start helping pull him back over the fence.

All very well, but if we succeed, I stand a really good chance of being flattened.

Fortunately, the section of the fence he'd been climbing

collapses towards us, allowing me to jump clear and the two officers to secure and cuff our Joker. I almost laugh as his pants finally slide to the ground, but I was always taught never to laugh at a man's privates. I don't know. Something to do with a fragile male ego or something.

He's not a happy bunny.

I find the knife he had used and bag it for evidence. Even if we can't nail him for the body in the Chevy, we can get him for resisting arrest and assaulting a police officer. Although technically, we don't yet have any evidence to charge him with, so the resisting arrest probably won't stick.

As they bundle The Joker into the rear of one of the SUVs, I return to stand beside Jerry and watch the recovery operation take place. The owner says he recalls a car like the one we described but doesn't recall it being crushed. Once we explain when it happened, he then estimates where in the stack of cubes it should be, if it was there. He then directs the pick-and-place vehicle, which starts digging into the pile one at a time.

I tell Jerry I need to leave him to it, but would like an update later.

I don't want to squeeze in beside the Joker in the back of the patrol SUV, but two of Jerry's guys, who are also leaving, offer to take me back with them.

Half an hour later, I'm filling in the incident report form and drinking another Folgers. I stop by to update Dan, but again, he's out on the road somewhere, so I send him a text update and head home. It's been a busy day.

Only then do I realize I don't have a car? I try calling the garage again, but with the same result. I don't want to beg the duty sergeant for another pool car, so I called a cab. On the journey home, I'm not thinking about *The Joker*, dead bodies, or cell phones. I'm wondering why my garage is closed. I'll have to swing by again the following morning.

15

Six am, and Alexa awakens me to a Motown mix, starting with the old Smokey Robinson number, *Tracks of my tears*. Tired from the previous day's exertions, the melancholy guitar intro affects me. Then Smokey talking about how you can appear happy yet be so sad inside tears me up. It's months since my decision to terminate Bossy-boots, but the doubts still linger. There's no room in my life for single parenthood. I had to do what I did, but I can't help but hear her argue her case in some far recess of my mind.

Never one for dwelling too long, I get up and notice my left knee doesn't feel so good. As careful as I have been with my recovery, it still isn't one hundred percent. When I was chasing The Joker and jumped onto the stack of pallets, I knew my take-off wasn't right, but in the heat of the moment, what could I do?

I massage it gently, rub some anti-inflammatory gel into the joint, then knock back a couple of painkillers. That will have to do. No run for me today, so I shower, dress, and raid the fridge coming up empty. How often do I have to remind myself to get food on the way home at night? Angry with myself, I'll have to spring for another breakfast at EJ's. My tab must already be significant, and I haven't even been back a week.

I dress lightly but also wear my wind-cheater. It will still be cool outside.

As I'm almost ready to head out, I notice the bones my Papa had given me. They're supposed to warn you of what lies ahead. It's been a while since I last used them. When honest with myself, I've never believed what they are supposed to tell me anyway, but I've built up some guilt by not using them.

I'd sworn to my Papa that I would use them. So, I open the small box, remove the four bones, and cast them on the breakfast bar.

They tell me I'm going to see something new that day. Something useful.

I'm absolutely fine with that. At least it's upbeat. I repack them into their box and call a cab. It's still too early in the morning to head to the garage, so I tell the driver to make for EJ's instead.

This morning I settle for pancakes with syrup, two eggs over-easy on the side, and copious quantities of starter fluid - coffee. I'm bouncing off the walls when I hit the office.

The duty sergeant informs me they'd searched both locations I'd requested the previous afternoon and hadn't found the stiletto. I'm not too disappointed, as I thought it was an outside prospect anyway. However, it still leaves me with the problem of proving Pamela Wilson was responsible for Jason's death. Without the weapon, the case is still circumstantial.

In my cubicle, there's a note from the detective I'd asked to check out the security cams at the *All-American Sports Bar*. He wants me to swing by and see what he's discovered. But, unfortunately, he won't be in yet. So I add it to my to-do list for the day.

There's also a note from forensics asking me to call. They seem to work 24/7, so I dial their extension, and sure enough, the guy I want to speak with picks up.

'Good morning, Detective.'

He sounds as wired as I am. I wonder if it takes him as much coffee as me to end up in this state. I wish him good morning and listen as he explains his evaluation of the blood spatter checks at Pamela Wilson's home. It seems Arnie Collins was right. The attacker did leave the knife in the wound. It was Pamela herself who removed it some short time afterward. This confirms what I'm already thinking, that this was an attempt by the killer to avoid being soaked in the inevitable spray from the severed femoral artery.

I thank him and add this detail to my notes about the killer.

But I still have quite a few unanswered questions.

1. Why stab Pamela in the femoral artery when ninety-five percent of stabbings happen above waist height? Am I looking for a dwarf from a circus? Fuck, am I even allowed to think that these days?
2. Why was there no trace of the killer found at the crime scene if they were after the contents of the safe? Nada.
3. Check for door-to-door results
4. Smart enough to leave the knife in the wound implies forethought. So this was no random killing.

I don't have much to go on. Still, having refreshed my memory, I look through the online reports from the previous twenty-four hours and find the one I'm looking for.

During the door-to-door, one officer spoke with a neighbor walking her dog the night Pamela was killed. She reported seeing an unusual car parked a few doors from the apartment. She paid little attention to it then but noticed a disabled badge prominently displayed on the dash.

Other than that, no one else had seen anything unusual.

Even though the car with the disabled sticker was a couple of driveways away, the killer may have parked there deliberately to put us off the trail. Although, I'm sure what to make of Pamela having a disabled visitor. I make a note to call her father and ask if he knows of anyone it might have been.

I recheck the report and confirm that the neighbor was taking her dog for a walk that evening *after dark*, not late at night. Dusk is around six-thirty, dark by the tail end of seven.

Given Pamela's apparent lack of family or friends, it seems

highly unlikely she had a disabled visitor that evening. But you never know. I'll have someone speak to registered local charities in the area, see if anyone there knows my victim, and check with her father.

I look at the time and decide it's late enough to call Pamela's father. He's a golfer. Probably already on the tenth hole. He isn't. He answers right away. I ask him. But he knows nothing about a friend with a disability, nor is he aware of his daughter being involved with any local charity. I thank him and apologize for disturbing him, then end the call.

I add the possible disabled visitor to the unanswered questions list in my head. I'll also ask someone to check other houses in the area for likely visitors that night who may have a disabled sticker on their vehicle.

As I'm sitting mulling things over, the detective who wanted me to review the sports bar security info passes by and invites me for a coffee in the small conference room. He's already set up and ready for me. I happily accept and follow him there.

He has seven discs. One for each night leading up to and including the night someone killed Mark Jason. They're date-stamped. First, he slips the disc for the night of Mark's death in and fast-forwards to a time he has already noted, and I sit back and watch the events of that evening.

All three men are there, starting around eight-thirty and finishing by ten. Nothing particular happens. They're just buddies sinking a few, then going home.

I'm disappointed. I'm hoping for an argument or a fight or something. I get nada.

Next, he loads a disc from two nights previous and fast forwards until I can see the three of them again. Creatures of habit, they're in the same corner. They're there for a while, and then a woman joins them. I recognize her immediately. It's Pamela Wilson. It seems like Mark's the initiator of the initial conversation. He chats with her at the bar for a while, then buys her a drink and encourages her to return to where his friends sit. They stay there for just over two hours, each man buying her drinks.

At around ten-thirty, Xavier and Tyrone get up, make excuses, and leave Mark and Pamela. It looks like he offers her another drink, but she refuses. Next thing, they go together. They are not precisely arm-in-arm, but they're getting cozy.

Damn. This supports what Xavier and Tyrone said happened. More disappointment.

But the show isn't over.

Another disc goes in. This is from the car park outside the sports bar. The first thing I see is Xavier and Tyrone leave and walk out of the camera shot. Then Mark and Pamela some ten minutes later. As I watch, Mark's car drives across in front of the camera, leaves the car park, and hangs a left. He could be heading anywhere, but I think his place is the most likely possibility.

I'm about to speak when I'm told to pay attention to the screen.

Thirty seconds later, another two cars follow the same way, one after another, both hanging a left.

I'm puzzled until I'm told that Xavier Rivera and Tyrone Ross are the registered owners of the two cars.

Now I'm much more excited, but there's more in store. I'm told to keep watching as yet another disc is loaded. This time, it's footage from a traffic cam near the entrance to the small enclave Mark Jason lived in. I watch as a procession of three cars turn in, one after another. It's clear they're all going to Mark's place.

My colleague has impressed me so far, but his next revelation is the coup-de-grâce. He quickly opens up Google Maps and starts pointing things out to me. I get his point. This is a fine piece of essential detective work. I congratulate and thank him and exit the conference room with newfound confidence.

It's now looking like I can deliver justice for what Jason and his buddies did to Pamela Wilson - before solving either homicide. If I can finally prove that Pamela Wilson did kill our detective, this new evidence may help me identify the motive.

Of course, if I were the Sheriff, I would tell me to solve the murder of one of our own first. If only life were so easy.

16

I'm back in my cubicle when my cell rings, and I answer it to find cousin Joey wanting to know if I've forgotten about him. It's one of those white-lie moments. So, I reassure him that he's still very much in my mind and ask him where he is. It turns out he's back in the building, upstairs in Narcs, so I tell him I'll be right up.

When I see him, his expression is sullen. I'd forgotten he would be desperate for a fix by now, not to mention worried about his death-defying intention to finger *The Joker* as a killer.

Before I talk with him, I stop by Jerry's cubicle and ask for an update on the cube-shaped green Chevy. It's now in the basement with forensics trying to figure out how to unwrap it. They have affirmed there is a body inside, and a DNA sample is already being analyzed. If the dead guy is in the system, we'll know soon enough. They say it may be two or three days before they can extract the body or whatever's left of it. I can't imagine a more gruesome task and don't envy them at all.

I enter the conference room and try to sound upbeat to Joey. It doesn't work. My presence seems to make him feel worse.

'I need a fix, Sammy. I really do.'

'I know, Joey. But we've come a long way since we spoke the other morning. We've found the body and caught the person you say is responsible. All we need to do is have you formally ID him, and we can get you out of here and off to a rehab clinic. You can get something there to help with your DTs.'

'But I need something now. I don't think I can face him feeling like this.'

'Of course, you can. You'll be able to see him, but he won't be able to see you. You ID him, and before you know it, you'll be heading up to Tampa.'

'Tampa?'

'That's where Jerry has found a great rehab clinic for you. It's far enough away that you'll be safe there.'

He doesn't say anymore after that. Instead, he draws deeper within himself.

Sure, I can get no further with him, I leave him like that, but instead of going back downstairs, I head out of the building. I want to see my garage and see if my new car is available.

Someone has rolled the rusty steel door up when I get there, but the interior is still dark. At least there's someone there this time, and I can find out what's happening.

I catch a brief hint of some movement in the office off to the side, so I head on in. I would have seen the padlock lying on the ground outside if I'd been more observant.

I shout for the owner, but instead of a reply, everything is eerily silent. I'm just reaching for the office door when it bursts open, catching me full in the face and knocking me back on my butt on the hard concrete floor. I get a glimpse of someone flashing past. After that, all I remember is jeans and dirty white trainers.

I sit up and gently feel my nose. Not broken, but there's a lot of blood. I look around and see some rolls of the blue absorbent towels they use for cleaning oil. I climb to my feet, cross shakily to the bench where they are, and tear off a few.

As I use them to staunch the blood flow, I can feel an egg-sized lump growing on one side of my forehead. I'm going to look a real mess.

Throwing the blood-soaked towels in a bin, I take a new one and check the bleeding. It's already more or less stopped.

Nevertheless, I hold the towel in place and head into the office again.

The owner is in a chair, slumped over his desk. I check for a pulse, but there's nothing. From the look of him, he's been dead for at least a day. No wonder he hasn't answered my calls. I can't see any immediate sign of foul play, but I can see the cash drawer hanging open and empty. I suppose that's what I've interrupted. Whoever took the cash is long gone.

I call this all in and sit on a spare chair to wait.

A patrol car and the paramedics arrive at more or less the same time. I give a brief statement to one of the officers, then allow a paramedic to clean up my face. She also gives me a couple of painkillers. The lump on my head is hurting, but I've had worse. She recommends I have an X-ray, but I can tell from her tone that she doesn't expect me to listen. I won't disappoint. It's time to get back to the office.

I check in with the duty sergeant and acknowledge I look a sight. He already knows about the incident and asks if the youngster who hit me is still in primary school. I give him the finger and ask for an incident report form, which I dutifully sit and fill in.

Twenty minutes later, I'm in my cubicle, turning my mind back to how best to approach nailing Xavier and Tyrone, when Dan stops by and asks how I've been injured. He wants to know how I am. He's concerned, which is nice, although I hate people fussing over me.

I'll never know how quickly news travels around the place. When I ask how he found out, it appears they received my call as an officer needing assistance. I hadn't meant it to sound like that.

So, as my direct supervisor, one of the officers on the scene had given him a verbal report, and the duty sergeant had also spoken to him. All this as I was climbing the stairs. Can a girl have no privacy?

When he asks how I am, I still feel a little shaken. To make me feel better, he offers a sit-in lunch at a local Italian at his expense. I accept.

We're just finishing lunch when I take a call on my cell. It's Forensics. They have some preliminary information on the cell phones from Pamela Wilson's safe. I promise I'll be there within thirty.

When I stand to leave, I feel light-headed and, rather than fall, sit back down again. Dan has witnessed this and has no hesitation in ordering me to get checked out for a concussion. Normal me would laugh it off, but I'm not feeling normal right then. So he tells me to stay where I am while he picks up his car. He'll be back in ten.

I sit like a pathetic obedient puppy, sipping water, feeling like shit. My head throbbing, my nose hurting, and now my butt is joining in. I must have bruised it when I fell. With my face being the more obvious injury, I haven't even noticed, but now I certainly do. I don't know if you can get a concussion in the butt? I should have it checked out.

Dan drops me off at the emergency area of the NCH hospital. He offers to stay, but I don't want him to know I'm having someone check out my butt, so I thank him for the ride and insist he gets back to the office. Before I climb out of his car, I ask if he will call Forensics and tell them I'll be around first thing in the morning to discuss the cell phones.

Inside the NCH emergency area, I'm half expecting the doctor to be the same one who helped me when I injured my knee the year before, but of course, it isn't.

They must have more than one. Clever me.

This doctor is a walking, talking advert for Black Lives Matter. It turns out he's originally Nigerian. Softly spoken and heavily accented. I struggle to understand much of what he's saying. Regardless, he checks me out thoroughly. I have what he describes as a mild concussion. He confirms that my nose is not broken, although it has swollen to a Pinocchio size - only in all directions. But I have a hairline fracture of something he called my coccyx.

Apparently, this is a small collection of bones at the bottom of the spine, a residual of us having tails, and now of little practical use. He tells me nothing needs to be done with it. It will self-heal within a few weeks, but I might find sitting uncomfortable.

He then asks if I need a painkiller prescription, but I refuse. Sometimes I can be so dumb. And I think men are macho!

By the time I leave, I feel a like big Mack has run over me. I'm stiff when I try to walk.

I call a cab from reception and go straight home.

After climbing six flights of stairs, my butt hurts something awful, so in my apartment, I strip off and stand under a shower, aiming the water jet at my nether parts. Twenty minutes later, I suddenly remember I intended to shop on the way home. Instead, the fridge is as empty as a field of corn after a plague of locusts passes through.

I call for a pizza.

Italian twice in one day.

As I wait, I stand naked in front of the full-length mirror. What the hell am I doing to my figure?

Turning sideways, the conclusion was nothing too bad. Thirty-six and still trim. A body most twenty-five-year-olds would die for. Well, that's what I tell myself, anyway.

I pull on a pair of joggers and a loose-fitting T and sit down on my beanbag in front of the tv to wait. At last, something comfortable to sit on.

It's difficult to judge time when you're waiting for something, and you don't have a watch. I'm sure I have been waiting an hour when there's a knock at the door, and my pizza finally arrives. I recognize the delivery guy. I should. I see him several times a week. He hands me my pizza. Compliments me on my sweats with a smile. I give him fifteen bucks and tell him to keep the change for the compliment. He laughs and disappears back down the corridor.

I'm on slice three when my cell rings. I answer, and it's Jerry in Narcs.

'He's gone.'

'What? Slow down, Jerry. Who's gone?'

'Your cousin, Joey. He's done a runner.'

'Fuck. Weren't you monitoring him?'

'Yeah, but we're not a babysitting service. He went to the washroom and never came back.'

'Did he ID *The Joker*?'

'No. That's what we were about to do when he split.'

'How long can you hold *The Joker*?'

'About another eighteen hours. We need to find Joey. Do you know where he might go?'

'No idea, Jerry. But I know he was desperate for a fix.'

It's at that exact moment we both have the same horrible thought. I voice it first.

'He's returned to whoever his dealer is with the Savage City Gangsters.'

'If he's gone there, and they've found out we were holding him to ID *The Joker*, he's dead, Sammy.'

Jerry promises me that his entire team will be on the streets as soon as we finish the call. I tell him I'll see what I can learn from my contacts.

So much for resting my butt.

17

I dress as quickly as I can, but I have to sit to do it when pulling up my jeans. With a sharp pain in my butt, raising my leg is as painful as when a dentist pulls a tooth.

A quick look in the mirror frightens the life out of me. But my hair is okay, so I'm good to go.

I clip on my badge and Glock, cover them with the windcheater, and head out to look for my nemesis. I'm going to gamble with not only Joey's life but my own.

I've never been to the Hunter's Chase before. A grotty, man's drinking place, with titties on show and blow-job booths in the rear. The department knows it well as a drug-pushers paradise, but regardless of how often they raid it or even close it down, it always seems to spring back up again. I'm looking for my nemesis, Chico Vegas. If anyone knows who is supplying Joey, it will be him.

I push open the front door and feel like I've entered a saloon in the old-style cowboy movies. It's like someone has switched off the sound, and everyone in the room has turned to look at me.

It seems they see nothing interesting, as after a few seconds, the sound switches back on again, and everyone starts to ignore me. I'm more comfortable with being ignored anyway.

The decor in the place isn't as bad as I thought it might be. They've painted it within the past ten or fifteen years and use picture frames to more or less disguise the damp stains. But, as different as the pictures are, their essential topic is the same - naked or near-naked women. Quite a collection, and it adds a certain something to the ambiance of the place. Something that makes my skin crawl and me feel unclean.

The place is busy. Gone ten, why wouldn't it be? Some women are plying dubious skills, but ninety percent of the clients are male. Two pool tables are in the rear corner, and a dartboard that looks never used hangs on the wall to my left. There's no light bulb in the overhead spotlight. Maybe it's for blind dart players. Who knows?

Customers occupy all the seats at both the tables and booths, but there are a few spaces at the bar, so I make for one of those.

Two guys are tending, but they're both at the far end, so I have to wait. A big guy to my right asks to buy me a drink. I decline. He asks again. I decline a second time. Finally, he puts his hand on my shoulder. Mistake. Within five seconds, he's bent over the bar, his arm up his back, breathing real heavy.

'What the fuck, lady!'

'I'm no lady, ass-hole. And you touch me again, and I'll give you something to remember it by. Now, fuck off to the other end of the bar and take your drink with you.'

I release him and stand back. He glares at me, weighing his chances, rubbing his wrist, and flexing his arm before finally taking his glass and disappearing with a snort. Just as well. I had surprise on my side the first time. I'm not sure how the second round would go.

As I settle back onto my bar stool, a barman asks if I want a drink on the house. I decline the offer but say I'll take a Corona.

When he returns with a beer mat and a cold Corona, I ask if Chico is in.

He studies me, trying to decide my threat level, before asking who is asking. I give him my name and say I'm a friend of Chico's. He would want to know I was here. The barman takes a cell from his pocket and calls a preset number. There's a conversation I can't quite make out before he ends the call, replaces his cell in his pocket, and tells me to wait where I am.

As I wait, I can't help but notice that the space around me at the bar is growing in size as people slowly move away. But of course, they needn't have bothered. When Chico appears twenty minutes later, the barman has already cleared out one of the back booths and steers both of us in that direction before placing a fresh cold Corona and some kind of scotch on the rocks in front of us and returning to the bar.

Chico looks at the drinks, nudges the Corona in my direction, then lifts his glass and toasts my health. I do likewise, even going as far as clinking my bottle against his glass.

We sit silently for a few moments, each weighing up the other and trying to figure out what relationship we have. It's easy for me. He's an ass-hole, and I'll bring him down hard and heavy if I get a chance. On the other hand, he's probably figuring out what I want from him and what he can get in a trade. He breaks the silence first.

'Good to see you again, Detective.'

'Can't say the same, Chico.'

'Hope you're not still holding a grudge from our past little misunderstanding, man?'

'You mean when you tried to blackmail me? That little misunderstanding?'

'Nah, I wouldn't call it that. More like we were to be helping each other out.'

'Whatever.'

'Looks like you wantin' something now, though, Detective? Am I right?'

This is the point at which I have to swallow hard. The last thing in the world I want is to be due this guy anything, but I also need to find Joey. But, sometimes, you have no choice. You have to do what you have to do.

'I need to find someone. He's family. Cousin goes by the

name Joey. He hangs with one of your dealers. I don't know which one.'

'Skinny dude. Long scraggly hair.'

'Sounds about right.'

Chico sits back and gives me the *'what's in it for me?'* look.

I tell him I'll not be in his debt, but I will remember if he helps me when I need it most. Subtle, but a definite distinction. If I'm in his debt, he can call it in. But if I only remember him helping, I'm more in control of any next step. Or that's what I try to convince myself, anyway.

He nods his agreement, takes out his cell, and calls. After about two minutes, he turns to me and asks if I know a place they called the Project on the East Side. A series of burned-out apartments due for demolition over a year ago but allowed to stay in place through the pandemic as a shelter for people without homes. The local government would face the cost of putting them in empty hotels if they weren't there.

I tell him I do. He tells me I'll find Joey there, but he isn't in good shape.

As I stand to leave, he throws me his parting shot with a sickening grin.

'Nice doing business with you again, detective.'

I can't get out of the place fast enough.

Outside, I call a cab, then Jerry to tell him what I've found out. It doesn't matter how brave you are; you don't go into the Project without serious backup.

Thirty minutes later, I'm standing outside the Project with Jerry and his team. It's pitch dark both outside and inside. The street lamps never survive more than twenty-four hours around here. I don't know whether the County is responsible or Florida Light and Power, but either way, they have long since given up worrying about them.

The Project building shows no signs of life, which couldn't be further from the truth. I've only been here once before, looking for a suspect, and it's one of the scariest and most depressing places I've ever been in.

Formerly a block of some forty apartments, a ground-floor fire had spread quickly through all levels thanks to some shortcuts in the cladding material used in the original construction. As a result, civil lawsuits are ongoing years after the event.

We agree to work in pairs. There are six of us, so we take a level each. Jerry and I take the first floor, the others the two floors above.

The first thing I notice is the smell of urine and feces, with weed a distant third, followed by the awareness you get when you can't see anyone - but you know they're there.

Jerry and I switch on our cell torches to shine light where no one would ever want to look. The sight of these people is both sickening and sad in equal measure. Disowned by the wealthy Naples residents and seen as problems by the County and trouble by the Sheriff's office.

Some have sleeping bags, but most just lay where they've fallen. A few huddle together for warmth.

The floor is littered with drug debris. Broken pipes, tin foil, needles and small spoons, straws, aerosol cans, and even tubes of glue with the life squeezed out of them.

Cold and dampness hang in the air.

We move, staying close together, checking each soul one by one. Most are men, but there are some women. Then Jerry finds a girl who could be no older than ten. She's stiff under a blanket, her corpse riddled with maggots and beetles. It takes all my willpower not to throw up, not just at the sight but at the knowledge that girls as young as this are dying alone and unloved in our very midst.

Jerry covers her back up. We can call it in and deal with her later. The corridor is clear, so we start checking individual rooms.

We're in the third when Jerry's cell rings. One of his team has found Joey on the second floor. We double-time it and see all four of the others already gathered around Joey, sitting on the floor, leaning against the wall. His skin is flushed, and he has vomit down the front of his T-shirt. He's also icy cold. I take off my wind-cheater and drape it over him. He's in and out of consciousness. We debate calling for the paramedics but end up agreeing it will be quicker to carry him down to the cars and get him straight to the emergency department at NCH.

Two guys lift him in a chairlift easily and head for the stairs. I follow. Jerry calls in the death of the young girl we found downstairs and offers to wait behind with one of his team. What a crappy night for everyone.

18

I stay at the hospital with Joey till three in the early morning. The doctor eventually declaring him past the worst, but far from out of the woods. I accept that as being better than I expect and take a cab home. It's only on the journey I remember I still didn't know what happened to my friendly garage owner.

Alexa wakes me up with that question in my mind. The song she plays is an old Huey Lewis number everyone knows. *Workin' for a livin'*.

Given that my new ride is doubtful, and I can only afford the four hundred my papa loaned me, it seems very appropriate. Jonny at the garage had offered me the Honda Civic for four hundred. I now don't know where that offer stands. I need to find out. These cabs are costing me the earth. It feels more like I'm *Scratchin' for a livin'*.

I check with NCH, but there's no change in Joey's condition. My tailbone is still aching, and my face is a mess, so this morning, I don't hold back on the painkillers, downing four instead of two. I can hear my knee thanking me in the back of my mind. I sure as hell know my butt is. Given all these aches and pains, my busted knee seems like a lifetime ago.

At the office, I head straight to Arnie Collins' area.

I need to find out what happened to Jonny, my friendly garage owner.

As luck would have it, Arnie is at his desk reading some file or other.

He looks up as I enter.

'Good God, Sammy. Are you due on my table anytime soon?'

I try a smile but suspect it comes out as a grimace.

'I'm fine, Arnie. I appreciate your concern.'

He grins and asks if I'm about to spring another body on him.

'No, Arnie. Unless you count the dead girl we found at the Project earlier this morning.'

'Was that you?'

I nod, feeling guilty. Arnie and his two assistants must be the three busiest people in the building, and I have a habit of delivering more work than most - hence his earlier question.

'I want to ask you about another case, Arnie. White male, around sixty. Garage owner. Came in yesterday.'

'Ah, yes. I know who you mean. I didn't take care of the gentlemen. It was Carrie, I believe.'

'Does she have a cause of death yet?'

'What's your interest, detective? Not a case of yours, is it?'

White-lie time. If it isn't one of my cases, I'm not officially entitled to the autopsy report.

'Related to a case,' I lie smoothly.

He gives me one of these 'lie detector' looks that see right through you before nodding his acceptance.

'Heart attack, I believe. Natural causes. Would you like me to send the report?'

'Thanks, Arnie. That would be great.'

Then, keen to move the conversation on, I ask him about the girl we found at the Project.

'Poor young soul. I don't have an answer for you there. She's scheduled for this afternoon. Do you want the report for this one?'

'No, Arnie. She's not related to anything I'm working on. Please send it to Jerry. It's a drug-related incident.'

* * *

With that, I leave Arnie and climb the stairs to my office. When the doctor told me I had a fractured coccyx and I might find it uncomfortable to sit - I didn't know he actually meant damned painful. Then I remember refusing the painkillers and realizing how stupid I can be again.

When I reach my cubicle, I find out.

Dan hears my yelp and stands, looking across the partition, wondering what's wrong. I give him a lame smile and lower myself out of sight, trying to position most of my weight on one buttock. When I'm as comfortable as I can be, I log on, check the overnight reports, and read the Project report submitted by Jerry. Afterward, I scroll up to the most recent message and find my garage owner's autopsy report from Arnie Collins. Quickly looking it over - there's nothing suspicious. What I learn is the deceased's home address and cell number. I note them down and log out. Mission accomplished. I can deal with this later.

My most important task for the morning is to plan how to get after Mark Jason's two buddies, Xavier and Tyler. I know they'll bring attorneys, so I need to plan the confrontation carefully. I also hope to get one of them to rat out the other. I realize I'll need an assistant district attorney to sit with me for that. One prepared to offer a deal.

But before arranging that, I must put together photos from the sports bar security cam and the street cam outside Mark's address.

I need a detailed local street map and several photos of Pamela Wilson. One is from before her death, and the others are taken from both the crime scene and the autopsy.

It takes me until lunch to pull all I need together.

Recalling how Joey had recently accused me of forgetting about him and feeling guilty, I call NCH for a second time. No change. He's still unconscious, which the doctor says is not unusual with the quantity of drugs in his system.

My detective radar fires. 'Quantity?'

'Sure, detective. The toxicology report shows that he had enough cocaine in his system to kill him off. I can't explain how he's still alive?'

'How much are we talking?'

'A single dose for an addict varies between ten to a hundred milligrams, as you probably know. But a lethal dose varies from person to person. I gather this individual was a habitual long-term user, and they often develop a degree of tolerance. So a lethal dose would normally be around twelve-hundred milligrams, but it would probably have been higher in this case. Say as much as five thousand.'

'Five grams!'

'As I say, Detective. I'm surprised he's still with us.'

Hanging up, my mind is already back at my conversation with Chico at the Hunter's Chase. I was so desperate to find Joey; I didn't stop to think how quickly Chico had tracked him down. It's obvious now. He knew where Joey was all along. He was playing me. He was sending me to remove a corpse. Fuck!

Furious is the word. I was stupid going to him in the first place. But to then trust what he told me. Doubly stupid.

I'm still stewing some half hour later when Forensics call to ask if I got their message from the previous day that they have access to data on some of the cell phones. I tell them they're top of my to-do list. Another white lie. I've forgotten completely. I reckon I can make it a non-white-lie if I *actually make* them top of my list and hurry to see them.

When I arrive, they spread the cells in a line on the workbench in the lab. The technician walks me through what he knows about each.

'The consultants have accessed nine of the ten and are still working on the final one.'

'The Apple 6S?' I suggest, hoping to prove that I'd been listening on my last visit.

'No. It's the Galaxy S8. The most recent model. They have

now hacked into the 6S. They also tell me they're hopeful about the Galaxy S8. It's just that they thought I would want what they have rather than wait for the last one. They're running some code-breaking software on it, but because it has to try billions of combinations, it will take some time.'

I nod sagely, knowing nothing about such things.

'So, have you extracted everything from the nine we have?'

'Oh, yes. You're going to love this stuff,' he says, reaching for a stack of folders and opening the first to reveal a snap of a middle-aged man laying naked on Pamela Wilson's bed, with his hands cuffed to the wrought-iron headboard.

'These are selected frame-prints,' he tells me, spreading a dozen compromising photos in front of me. 'But they're extracts from a video. These are all the same,' he finishes, passing me the stack. 'I would say you've found yourself a blackmailer, Detective.'

I guess I'm expected this, but seeing these makes it real all of a sudden. Pamela Wilson was up to no good for sure. My theory about her regular income is much more likely now.

'What about the owners? Do we know who they are?'

'All in the individual files. The owners' names and a printout of their contact details. I'll send you all the video files. Apart from that, there's nothing more we can do for you right now. We'll call when we get the last set of results from the Galaxy S8.'

Once again, I head for the small conference room in the Homicide Department. I'm going to need the conference table again and a strong coffee. I'm no prude, but this sort of porn has never appealed to me. Why someone would want to be deliberately humiliated is beyond my understanding.

19

I spend the rest of the day sifting through the mounds of information from the cells and using a laptop to track down the owners. One of the department's few secretaries - I say few because there used to be lots of them, but not now - brought me a soft cushion. I'm genuinely grateful and tell her so. My butt is still sore, and the plastic chairs in the conference room are hard.

It's dark outside by the time I finish.

I tidy up and call a cab to take me home. This time I remember to have him drop me off at the local twenty-four-hour mini-mart, where I pick up some groceries and carry them back to my apartment.

It's after eight-thirty before I sit down to scrambled eggs on toasted bagels with a cold Corona. Alexa is playing some miscellaneous smooth jazz in the background. I need time to think. To sort out my priorities.

This all started with the death of Mark Jason. I'm almost sure that Pamela Wilson was responsible for that, but I still doubt that I can prove it beyond a reasonable doubt. Not that I approve, but she's already met with justice for that particular crime.

Then there's what I'm pretty sure has caused Jason's death - her motivation. She was sexually and physically assaulted by not just Jason but also his two gym buddies. So even though she's dead, it's still up to me to get justice for Pamela for that.

Then there's the question of who killed Pamela.
I'm not sure, but I don't like Xavier or Tyrone for that one. Nor do I like the two ex-wives, which leaves me with a list of nine names from the cell phones in her safe. If she were blackmailing them, then that would be the motive.
There may be a tenth to follow. I don't know yet.
According to her father, she has no ex or close friends, and she and her sister hardly ever talk. This woman seems to have been a real loner and a Dominatrix with a sense of responsibility to her father.
I don't know any details of her past other than she has been a steady user, with a long list of previous employers I'll need to contact.

I turn my mind to thinking about the list of cell owners. I'll need to look into these in some depth. The thing that's bothering me is that according to Pamela's financial records, she hung up her whip almost three years ago. She's had no new clients since then. That means all her clients have paid her regular sums for at least three years and up to ten. If they're all prepared to do that, why would one of them suddenly kill her? Why would he leave it so long? Why not strike when the blackmail starts?
I don't have an answer to that.

Stacking my dirty dish in the washer, I take a cool Corona from the fridge and remember my promise to Joey not to forget him. I call the hospital.

Two minutes later, the doctor who first treated Joey comes on the line.
'Detective, I was just about to call you.'
'Has he come round?'
'No, I'm sorry to have to tell you, Detective. He passed away peacefully about ten minutes ago. He never recovered

consciousness. I'm sorry for your loss. I know this was a family matter for you.'

'Thank you, doctor,' I reply, the words coming out automatically.

He says something else, but I don't hear what it is.

When the call ends, I'm in shock. I know Joey was in trouble, but I never once considered he might die. Not for a second.

I haven't moved when my cell rings sometime later, and I answer it to hear Jerry offer his condolences. He's the official contact for the hospital, and they called him immediately after speaking to me. He asks if I want him to come over, but I say no. That I would prefer to be alone. He says to give him a buzz if I need to talk. I say I will and end the call.

My mind's replaying all the good times when Joey and I were both kids. Going over the good stuff as it happens at a time like this. But that doesn't last.

I wonder if Chico Vegas knew Joey intended to finger *The Joker* in the killing at the scrap-metal yard and had him killed. If that's the case, he was just fucking with me by sending me to find him. Some kind of revenge for me having spoiled his plan to have me act as a blue-bitch for him last year.

The more I think about it, the more convinced I become. I now have Chico Vegas firmly in my sights. This is personal.

After that, it's another rough night trying to sleep and failing.

When I open my eyes, it's five-thirty, and Alexa isn't due to kick off until six. My butt hurts, my head is throbbing, my nose feels enormous, and worst of all, my knee is coming out in sympathy with what seems like every other part of my body. What a wreck. I need a shower.

Twenty minutes later, I've got as far as pulling underwear on when Alexa starts playing the same smooth jazz loop from the night before. I've forgotten to give her new instructions. I tell her to lower the volume and leave her playing as I force some muesli and plain yogurt down. I don't feel hungry but know I should eat. It's going to be another busy day.

My plan starts with borrowing a pool car and driving to see my Mama. Papa will be at work, but at least I can tell her personally before she finds out some other way. I'm not looking forward to that. I was supposed to be helping Joey, not getting him killed.

Realizing I need a pool car again reminds me I'm planning to talk to the garage owner's wife about the car he promised me.

I'll need to fit that in somewhere.

I finish dressing as fresh coffee brews in the background. I love the smell. As bad as I'm feeling, it lifts me - at least a little.

Two cups later, I'm downstairs, into a cab, and off to the office. First stop, duty sergeant. I'm hoping he'll be in a good mood. I'm lucky. He is. Ten minutes later, I have keys to a patrol SUV in my pocket and am upstairs looking to update Dan. He isn't in his office, and no one has seen him yet, so I call him. He's driving in when he answers. I tell him about Joey and where I'm going. He gives me his condolences and promises to cover for me in the office if anything urgent arises. And tells me that I should take care of my family.

I worry about breaking the news all the way up to my parent's house, but I needn't have. Mama has already heard through her sister and has already cried herself out. She gives me a big hug when I arrive. I tell her a little about trying to help Joey but skip many details. She doesn't need to know what a mess he had been in. I leave her thinking he had just taken some bad drugs. Something that happens all the time. I don't share my suspicion that he has been murdered. If that's true, I'll deal with it later.

I stay with her the rest of the morning, and we visit my

aunt. She seems more accepting than I expect. But I suspect she's more in the know than my mama. We all eat a light lunch together before I drive Mama home, then head South again. En route, I called Jerry and discuss my theory with him.

He agrees that Chico 'finding' Joey so quickly was at least highly suspicious and that he might have discovered that we had both Joey and The Joker simultaneously in the Sheriff's office. He could easily have put two and two together all on his own. Then, when he found out Joey had turned up again at the Precinct, desperate for a fix, it would have been easy to have given him to have a lethal dose.

I feel good that Jerry agrees with me but bad because I can't think of any way we can prove it. Chico will get away with murder, and there doesn't seem to be anything I can do about it.

Accepting that, I'll swing around and talk with my late garage owner's wife rather than return to the office. See if she knows anything about me being offered her daughter's Honda.

I take Castello Drive off Tamiami and think I've fallen into a dental wonderland. Island Coast Dentistry is on my right, then another Dental specialty center, a Dental group, and Towncare Dental, all within a block. Nowhere for knees, head bumps, or fractured butts. At least I'll know where to come if I ever have a toothache.

Jonny's Place is a small detached property on West Lake Boulevard. I pull up outside, aware of the attention my SUV is drawing from neighbors. Looking around, the houses are tightly packed but pretty well maintained. It must be trash collection morning as everyone has their multi-colored bins waiting. Some have extra black bin bags and piles of cardboard. It's messy, but it will all be gone by lunch.

Jonny's wife, Alice, opens the door. Her eyes go to the SUV first, then back to me. I introduce myself and tell her I've known her husband for a few years since moving into the area.

Then give her my standard condolence speech. She invites me in.

Having seen how Jonny kept his shop, his wife obviously rules the roost at home. The decor isn't to my taste, but it's clean, tidy, and smells fresh. Alice tells me she's just made some fresh coffee and asks if I would like some. I accept.

As she disappears into the kitchen, I look around. There are several pictures of Jonny, Alice, and a young girl I assume to be their daughter. The most recent looks like it was taken at a coming-out prom. She's an attractive young lady.

There's also a picture of the happy couple on their wedding day. It's an old black and white but has lost nothing for that. It's an excellent picture that caught the auspicious moment perfectly. Alice had been an attractive catch for Jonny when she was that age.

I'm just replacing the frame when Alice returns and confirms that it was taken on their wedding day in nineteen eighty.

I run the math and wonder why their daughter is only now attending college, but I don't hide the thought very well because Alice answers before I can ask.

'We tried for kids from the day we married. We both wanted a large family, but it wasn't to be. We tried everything until we ran out of cash. Jonny even took out a bank loan, but nothing took. It devastated us. Then, I lost my sister and her husband in a car crash. So we took their little one in and made her our own.'

'You adopted her?'

'Initially, we were only keeping her in care, but then, yes. We adopted her.'

'And now she's about to go to college?'

'You know about that?'

'Yes. Your husband told me. That's why I'm here, really.'

'You're not here about the robbery then?'

'No, Alice. I'm sorry. I'm not.'

'It was you that disturbed whoever killed him, isn't it? Is

that what happened to your face?'

I had forgotten how my face would look to someone else. But confirm both her questions, then explain how I know her daughter is starting college.

'Your husband had just offered to sell me her car.'

'The Honda?'

'Yes. I was to pick it up the day he died.'

'I see. And do you still want it?'

'If you don't mind. Yes, I would.'

'How much did he say he would sell it to you for?'

'Four hundred.'

'Four hundred,' she repeats. 'Why would he give it away?'

'I don't know, Alice. He helped me out several times in the past with my previous car. I guess he realized I was down on my luck.'

'But you're a detective?'

'Yes. But I'm still paying for two degrees and will be forever at the rate I'm going.'

She seems to take that on board. Perhaps realizing how expensive her daughter's further education will be. I hope that might do the trick. But just the opposite happens. I think the realization makes her worry about how to afford her daughter's college fees. She asks me to wait and disappears into the kitchen before returning with an old laptop.

Sitting back down, she powers up and waits for it to connect to the wifi. Then I watch her access Autotrader and type in some details.

'Six grand for the car in excellent condition. I guessed a hundred thousand miles,' she told me.

I choke. I know Jonny was generous with his offer, but I didn't understand how generous.

'Mmm,' is all that comes out of my mouth.

'I'm guessing that you're not so interested now?'

'I'm afraid not, Alice. Thanks for seeing me, though, and again, I'm very sorry about what happened to your husband,' I say, standing to leave. 'He was a nice guy.'

'Sorry about letting you down, Detective.'

'No problem.'

Then, just as she's showing me out the door, she throws me a lifeline.

'Tell you what. If you find the little shit who broke in and emptied the register while Jonny was lying dead right in front of him, I'll let you have it for four hundred.'

20

It's gone three before I get back into the office. Dan asks me how it had gone with my parents, but I'm not in the mood for conversation, so I tell him everything went fine and keep going to my cubicle.

The first thing I do is check through the incident reports until I find the one when my coccyx suffered, not to mention my face. There's *my* report, which I don't bother reading. But there's also a report from the first officer on the scene. Reading through that, I learn two things. They found the padlock intact. And the hasp it had been through, cleanly severed. Whoever had broken in had used bolt cutters on the softer material of the catch. He knew what he was doing. He'd done this before.

I need to find a detective. Someone who will want to suck ass with a second-grade detective. Someone who won't mind chasing down a kid with a pair of bolt cutters. I have the perfect choice in mind. Our newbie, George Jimisson, or Jimi as we call him. They promoted him from patrol while I was on my nine-month garden leave. So fresh, enthusiastic, and still trying to make his mark. Perfect.

As luck would have it, George is at his desk twiddling a pencil when I stick my head over his cubicle wall.

'You busy?' I ask, carefully keeping the sarcasm out of my voice. It isn't so long ago that I was the newbie, although given everything that I've been through since it feels like forever ago.

It's only three years and a two-year-old-shot-dead ago.

I explain what happened at Jonny's place and my theory that whoever had broken in has done it before. Perhaps many times before. That it's time a detective tracks him down and puts a stop to his career.

I can see George sit up like an eager puppy. This is too easy. I almost feel guilty. I won't mention I'll get a Honda for four hundred bucks if he catches the guy. Sometimes it's better to keep some things to yourself.

Back in the office, I have to decide whether to find out where following the leads from the cell phones will take me with solving Pamela's death or to bring in Xavier and Tyler for a grilling about her assault. Much as I would love another go at the drinking buddies, I have to stay focused on my homicide case first.

I decide Xavier and Tyler aren't going anywhere for the time being. Besides, if I leave them for a while, they may think I've dropped the ball and become complacent, so I opt for following up on the information in the cell phones from Pamela's safe.

Nine cells. Nine names. I have to find a way to prioritize. I go back to my previous thinking about why anyone would pay the ransom for anything up to ten years before suddenly deciding to kill their blackmailer. It makes little sense. So, I start with the most recent model I have information from - the iPhone 6S.

I recheck AFIS to make sure one more time, but there's no match in the system. The cell is owned by a Wade Dooley. I have an address for him in Marco Island, half an hour south. I don't particularly want to wander into any of these people's lives with the information I have until I have good reason to do so. They've already paid enough for what is merely a personal choice in how they like their sex.

I must admit that I'm still intrigued about the bondage and whipping thing, but it's more out of curiosity than sexual interest. There's that author who became one of the world's most published authors with her *Fifty Shades of Grey* and the follow-on books. I've never read them. They got crap reviews, but people bought them by the bucket load. Again, curiosity. A human trait around the world.

So, I start my investigation by looking into Wade's life.

Born in Cincinnati, Ohio, he attended school and studied finance at Pittsburg State. After that, he married a Florida girl and moved to Naples around twenty-five years ago.

He landed a job with Bank of America on Fifth, and as far as I can see, he is still with them.

He and his wife have three kids in high school or college. Another three reasons I won't be trampling through his personal life unless I'm sure I need to do so.

At one point, he took a career break for three years of military service with the Finance Corp. up in Fort Bragg, where he worked in Payroll. There was no break in his household records for that period, so I guess his family stayed here in Naples.

There's no Facebook page, but both of his daughters have them. I look through and conclude this looks like a happy family. I can't see this guy slitting Pamela's femoral. I put him to one side and select the second most recent model of cell - the Samsung Galaxy.

Owned by Chris Lover. Interesting surname, given the context of my search. I start the same as before but quickly stop short with surprise. Chris is a woman. Full name Christiana. It seems my prejudices have no bounds. I would never have thought of a woman going to a dominatrix, but yet, why not? Sex is sex. What's good for the goose and all that?

Chris was born in Paducah, Kentucky, where she grew up on a farm. Her school records show she was a modest performer but good athletically. She was awarded an athletic scholarship at Louisiana State and played in the Varsity hockey and basketball teams.

Her career started with Collier County public schools as

part-time boys coach. Having seen her DMV photo, I imagine her being popular with pre-adolescent boys.

After that, she held various jobs until working in Human Resources at Costco, where she's still employed. A sad end to an athlete's career. Still, it happens. Some folks I saw in the Precinct the other night could tell much worse stories.

She's married with one son at senior high. Her husband's a car salesman at Sterns on Airport Road. I wonder what he could get me for four hundred bucks?

Looking through what I've discovered, I can't see Chris as a femoral slasher. Although, there again, I wouldn't have expected her to be enjoying the services of a dominatrix, either.

I start on the third most recent model - the Sony Xperia. I had one of these for a while when it first came out. I thought it was cool at the time until I sat on it and snapped it in half.

Now I'm a Samsung girl and will never go back.

The proud owner of this cell is Denis Meaker. Fifty-five-year-old, single, successful entrepreneur. He was born in New Orleans, the son of a famous Jazz musician. He studied at Tulane Campus in uptown New Orleans and achieved a Degree and a Master's in Business Administration. After that, he graduated from the Indiana School of Optometry. This guy has more qualifications than I have.

After working in several eye clinics, he raised some private funding and opened a chain of eye clinics of his own, mainly in the Southern States. These were a major success, so much so that he made the front page of Business Week.

This guy isn't having any problem paying off his student loans. He's seriously wealthy.

The headquarters of his eye-clinic empire is here in Naples, in a residential district by the coast. I figure he lives in one of these super-expensive villas I've seen and works from home. With the money he undoubtedly has, he can afford to hire a dozen dominatrixes to whip him into a lather.

I can't see him being responsible for Pamela's death.

I doubt he'll miss it if he's paying some monthly

contribution to Pamela's retirement plan.

Three down and six to go. I need coffee, so head to the place we laughingly call the recreation area. Unfortunately, the coffee jug isn't just empty. It's cold. I know it's sexist, but men are hopeless at things like this. They would walk in, see the empty jug and decide they didn't want one anyway - rather than make a fresh brew. Too much trouble for them.
    If it's too much trouble for them, I can play that game too.
    I can look into the other cell phone owners in the morning.
    I look out the window.
    It's pitch dark, which means it's at least after seven, and I'm hungry.
    I can't think of anything exciting I have in the apartment, so a takeaway kebab is the way to go.
    I still have the patrol SUV, so I sneak past the duty sergeant on the way out. Kebab store, here I come.

Half an hour later, I set out two kebabs on a plate, pop the cap off a cold Corona, and determined to cheer myself up after my cousin's death, I settle down to watch an episode of MASH. This one is where Hawkeye is trying to repair the stove in their tent, which blows up in his face. He wears bandages over his eyes through the entire show after that but still gets one over on Frank, who is running a scam taking money from people betting on a baseball game back home, where he already knows the final score.
    These shows never grow old for me. I love the characters.
    I'm managing to laugh when my cell rings, and I have to pause.
    It's Jerry.
    'Hi, Sammy. Sorry to disturb you. A couple of things I thought you might want to know.'
    'Don't you ever go home, Jerry?'
    'Hey, you can talk. Anyway, the first thing is I had to release *The Joker*. So you should watch your back. Sammy, I don't think he liked you up his ass.'

'A feeling we share. What was the other thing?'

'We're clearing out the Project early tomorrow. I know it's not directly your bag, but I wonder if, seeing as how that's where Joey died, you would be interested in joining us?'

'Sure would, Jerry. When do we start?'

'We're meeting there just before sunrise, around six.'

'See you there.'

With my cousin firmly back in mind, MASH no longer has the same appeal.

I switch off and get ready for bed.

21

Alexa doesn't complain when I change the alarm time from six to five. Good girl. I let her choose a random selection to wake me up as a reward. That's a mistake.

Apparently, she learns my music preferences so that her playlist will become more tailored to me. She hasn't yet learned that I prefer quiet or happy music first - not Agalloch. The tune she chose starts loud and gets louder - much louder.

Into the Painted Grey.

I nearly hit the ceiling at the opening bars. I love the song, but not at five am. I shout over the noise to tell Alexa to shut up. It takes three goes. I only hope my neighbors enjoy Heavy Metal as much as me.

Everything is an effort from there on, but by five-forty, I'm clipping on the badge and Glock, ready for action.

Bang on six, I arrive at the agreed congregation point and look for Jerry. I find him in one of our remote-headquarter command vehicles. I'm impressed. It isn't easy to get one of these. There again, looking around, he has some size of an operation going.

There are at least a dozen patrol cars, numerous unmarked's, three fire tenders, and an endless line of ambulances. Others are milling around, which I guess would be from Social Services or Child Welfare. Only a few people from inside the Project will be walking out unassisted.

I get his attention, and he invites me into the climate-controlled environment. It's still chilly at this time of the morning, so I'm glad to get inside.

He explains the plan quickly. Sheriff's department enters the first floor, bringing people out if they're capable, flags them as needing assistance, or cuffs them if they cause trouble. The paramedics follow, and the fire service is there to deal with structural problems in the building because of the increased number of people inside. I'm right about there being folks from Child Services and Welfare. Given the body of the ten-year-old, we found on the previous visit, that's probably a good call.

A wing at NCH has been prepared in advance and staffed with people who understand how to best treat the various drug-related problems they'll face.

He has thought this through.

He's leading the first wave; I'm going with him.

Outside, the sun is just rising into the pale blue cloudless sky, and it's time. The forward party teams up in twos and enters the building, quickly spreading out along the main corridor, stopping at each person sprawled on the floor or wedged in a doorway.

It takes nearly two hours to clear the first floor. The count is thirty-eight homeless and helpless souls on their way to NCH and two dead bodies for the County morgue.

We repeat the whole thing on the second floor, with a further forty-five and three bodies.

On the third floor, Jerry and I are reaching for a huddled shape in the corner of one room when suddenly the floor gives way underneath Jerry, and he almost falls straight through but manages to wedge himself with his hands.

I shout out for help, but before anyone can arrive, a huddled figure in a nearby corner rises, grabs me around the waist, and squeezes tight. Caught unawares, I can hardly breathe. I can't kick, so I do the only thing I can think of and poke over my shoulder at his eyes.

I must have hit the target as my attacker yelps and lets me

go.

I gasp air into my lungs and turn to see *The Joker* rubbing one eye/

I go for my gun, but it's fallen out in the struggle, and I can see him eyeing it. It's slightly closer to him than me. We're both rooted to the spot, deciding what to do.

Unseen, Jerry reaches out and tugs at the leg of *The Joker's* pants. Not enough to trouble him, but enough to give me the time to get to my gun.

I dive and gather it up in one quick motion, allowing the momentum of my slide to take me away from *The Joker* so that by the time I turn and aim, he's six feet away, glowering at me.

Behind him, I see Jerry slip a little further through the floor and wonder where the hell everyone is. Surely they must have heard my shout.

The Joker steps in my direction; I hold out my Glock and issue a warning. I will shoot if I have to. I tell him to get down on his knees. He doesn't. He takes another slow step toward me. Taunting me.

I warn him a second time. He's now only four paces away. I should shoot. But I can't. All I can see is the surprised expression of the two-year-old girl I shot dead last year.

The Joker steps again and, before I can do anything, smacks the back of my hand with his giant paw, spinning my Glock off into a distant corner of the room.

I'm his. I can see it in his eyes.

He's just about to grab me when Jerry pulls his impressive bluff by shouting for *The Joker* to *stop where he is and raise his hands* - with as much authority as he can manage.

I see the indecision on *The Joker's* face for the first time.

Then he does what Jerry intended. He turns to see who is challenging him. As soon as he does, I bend, pick up a charred six-by-four lying at my feet, and hit him on the back of his head as hard as I can.

The wood snaps and flies out of my hand. *The Joker* turns

back my way and actually snarls. If it were under different circumstances, I would laugh. But this isn't funny. I shuffle back to the wall, pushing as far away from him as possible. He starts towards me, but without warning, he suffers the same fate as Jerry. The fire-weakened floorboards give way under his two-hundred-fifty pounds, and he disappears in a cloud of dust and splintered wood. The sound of his landing down below is sickening.

I maneuver around the new hole in the floor until I reach Jerry. Unfortunately, there's nothing I can do to help. He's tightly wedged between floorboards. But at least it doesn't look like there's any risk of him falling further. I'm just going for help when two deputies appear in the doorway. It seems like my shout hadn't been loud enough. No one heard me, but they heard *The Joker* falling through the floorboards.

We quickly agree that we need one of the fire-rescue teams to get Jerry out, so one of them disappears to get them while the two of us stay with Jerry.

It's surreal sitting beside half a man. I crouch as low as possible to make it feel less unnatural, but it's still weird. I ask him if he feels seriously injured in any way. He replies, saying there are probably a few cuts and bruises, but he doesn't think anything is seriously wrong. He can still wiggle his toes, although we are unable to see them. I have to take his word for that.

Anyway, I thank him for his quick thinking. By distracting *The Joker*, he saved my life, and I want him to know I'm grateful. If he had been able to move his shoulders, he would have shrugged my comments off, but he can't. So, he accepts my thanks graciously.

The deputy who has stayed with us gives an update on how the overall operation is going. Only two rooms are still left to clear, and deputies are already there. So it will all be over by the time they have Jerry out.

* * *

It actually takes the best part of an hour for the fire-rescue team to free Jerry, and his cuts and bruises are a little more severe than he had let on. They stretcher him into a waiting ambulance, then down to NCH.

I go down to the command center, where one of Jerry's guys seems to have taken control of the mopping-up process. He has a couple of joinery firms already on site, boarding the whole place up. They're bolting metal frames over every door and window on the ground level. No one will shelter in there anytime soon.

He tells me that a hundred-twenty-three people are down in NCH, and eleven dead bodies, including *The Joker,* who had not survived the fall, are heading for the city morgue.

If Arnie finds out, I'm involved in sending this lot to him. I worry he'll never speak to me again.

It's a job well done, and I'm pleased to have been a part of it. But it leaves me wondering what's likely to happen to the hundred-twenty-three people after they're released from NCH. They'll undoubtedly soon be back on the streets, but now, with nowhere to call home, and that worries me.

22

Later that morning, I'm in my favorite back booth in EJ's when Dan Weissman finds me. I've been pushing an all-day cooked breakfast around my plate for the past twenty minutes.

I'm just passing the time and not paying the food any attention.

He asks if he can join me for coffee.

He doesn't explain how he has tracked me down. Nor does he mess around getting to the point.

'You could have died, Sammy.'

I guess he's been to see Jerry at NCH and found out about my run-in with *The Joker*.

I laugh him off with some stupid joke about it all being in a day's work. But he isn't having it.

'Jerry told me what happened.'

'Yeah, it was a close call for him. Lucky he didn't fall straight through like *The Joker*.'

'I'm not talking about him, Sammy. I'm talking about you.'

This confuses me.

'When you had your gun pointed at him, you froze.'

All I could think about right then was the little girl's face. The surprise, the shock. She never had a chance. My bullet went straight through her. She didn't have time to be angry with me or to hate me for killing her. She just died in front of me.

It takes a nudge from Dan to bring me back.

'Sammy!'

I feel disoriented. Like I'm there with Dan, but I'm not really.

'Sammy!'

I shake my head and try to focus. What the hell's happening?

'Sammy, are you with me?'

'Eh, yeah. Sure, Dan. Just lost a moment there.'

'You need to go back to the shrink. You know that, don't you?'

'Whatever, Dan.'

'Sammy. This isn't a request. I'm serious. You could have gotten yourself killed today.'

I stare at him, tears forming in my eyes. Not for me. For the young girl, I shot almost a year ago. She haunts me and won't go away. Maybe she will never go away.

Dan's still talking.

'Today, Sammy. As soon as we leave here. I'll take you up there. I've already called ahead and made you an emergency appointment.'

The tears are now running freely down my cheeks. I don't care. Somehow, Bossy-boots is also in there. I don't understand how. But she is. I'm only dimly aware of Dan now. He's saying something, but I can't make him out. He's spinning round and round, and I can't figure out how he's doing that……

When I come round, I'm on the ground, laying face down with one leg curled up and my face to the side. Either I've been lucky in how I fell, or someone has positioned me in recovery where I can breathe and not swallow my tongue.

I hear someone groan. It's probably me.

I slowly sit up and lean on the padded seat of the booth, with Dan helping me. The first thing I notice is the ache in my butt. Then, after a moment or two, I feel the familiar headache and realize I've just been out cold.

Looking at Dan, I can see how genuinely worried he is. That makes me feel even worse.

I get back into the seat with further help from Dan, aware

everyone in EJ's is watching me. I cringe and try what I hope is a reassuring smile. Probably scare the customers away completely.

Dan passes me a glass of iced water, and I gulp greedily.

'How do you feel, Sammy?'

'Great, Dan. Sorry about that. I don't know what happened. Did I pass out?'

'Like a first-rate drama queen,' he smiles.

'Haven't done that before.'

'Do you feel you can make it to my car? It's right outside?'

'Sure.' I tell him with false bravado.

We make it. He helps me in, then goes to the driver's side and joins me inside.

'Do you remember where I said I'm taking you, Sammy?'

I do. I groan but realize I'm not on a solid footing to argue. Sometimes you have to go with the flow.

'This will be a treat for you. You're going to see someone you haven't seen before. She's fantastic and will help you. Luisa del Roy. Do you remember her?'

'Your on-off-almost girlfriend?'

'That's her, other than it's off. I could never get over her being my best friend's girlfriend before he was killed. It kept coming between us. But we're still friends, and she's agreed to see you.'

We sit quietly for the rest of the journey until Dan pulls up outside a two-story building in a small strip mall. We get out, and Dan leads the way upstairs to Del Roy's office on the second floor.

As we enter, there's the wonderful aroma of freshly brewed coffee, and the receptionist asks if I would like some. I accept. Dan introduces her as Maggie. She has an Irish accent and a cheerful manner about her. A good attribute for a psychiatrist's receptionist, I suppose.

Once I'm settled, Dan backs out, saying I should call when I'm ready, and he'll return for me.

I have no intention of calling, and I suspect he already knows that. But he offered, and I appreciate that.

I chat casually with Maggie until Luisa del Roy emerges from her office and welcomes me with a smile. We remember each other, although we only briefly met once before.

She invites me to take my coffee and go into her office with her.

Her office is more like a comfortable lounge, decorated in pastel colors, nice and light. She has the mandatory writing desk and high-backed swivel chair, but there are also two soft sofas with a coffee table for more informal discussions. She indicates that's where I should sit.

I had months of this stuff after the Critical Shooting Investigation last year. I'm not a big fan. But here I am, back at the starting post.

I think she's reading my mind.

'So, Sammy. I bet you would rather be almost anywhere other than here. Am I right?'

I nod my agreement.

'Tell me what you need my help with?'

I don't know where to start. I don't know if I *want* to start. I sure as hell don't know the answer to question number one.

Seeing my confusion, she tries again.

'Let's try a different question?'

Like I said, reading my mind.

'You've been through a tough year and think you're back to one hundred percent, but Dan doesn't. That sound about right?'

Another nod from me. I'm worried that if I started talking, I might never stop. I can feel the anxiety building up inside me, threatening to overcome me completely.

'You're probably reluctant to talk about everything that's happened. You might let the cat out of the bag.'

Now I'm convinced the woman is a witch.

'Now you probably think I'm some kind of mind-reader?

Am I right?'

Scary.

'Well, let me assure you I'm not. But I have something *you* don't. It's years of experience talking with people who have been through difficult periods. And you know what, Detective?'

I stare at her like a moron.

'Although the precise details of your difficulties will differ, the overall effect is the same. You're battling to deal with whatever has happened to you in the past while struggling to appear normal. So you're fighting on two fronts, and that's a losing strategy.'

'I'm not losing,' I tell her stubbornly.

'So, let me ask you again. Why has your boss brought you here?'

At that point, she might as well run up the victory flag and start the celebrations. I've lost, but I don't feel bad about it.

Our session lasts a bit longer than the scheduled hour. It's already four in the afternoon as I grab a cab and head back downtown. It would be over the top to say I've enjoyed the discussion, but it hasn't been as difficult as I expected.

She even had me laugh a few times, and it's only now that I realize how seldom I've done that in the past year. If I hadn't found the MASH reruns, I don't think I would have laughed at all. I feel like my life has no room for laughter and happiness. Like I don't deserve them. I've taken two lives, and now I've managed to get my cousin killed. So what is there to laugh about?

Just before the session wraps up, she says something to me that is both confusing and encouraging at the same time. She says she doesn't think there's much wrong with me and that another two or a maximum of three sessions will be enough. From how I've been feeling, I was expecting once a week for the rest of my life.

I agree to a date the following week for a second session.

* * *

As I pass the duty sergeant back in the office, he asks where his SUV is. I have to stop and think for a moment. Have I left it at the Project? I can't remember. I'm considering another little white lie when he laughs and holds up a set of keys.

'Dan told us you had trouble at EJ's and asked us to pick it up.'

Now, I do something else I don't ever remember doing before. At least, not since I was a little kid. I blush. Not a little flush. I'm talking beetroot red. All this achieves is to get a bigger laugh.

I virtually run up the stairs.

As I pass Dan's cubicle, I give him a thumbs up and keep going. I know that will be enough for him.

Back on my home turf, I already feel more like my old self.

I log on and check the daily incident reports. The most significant is the clearing of the Project. It makes for gripping reading. They've formed a team of volunteers to help identify all one-hundred-thirty-four people and research their backgrounds. The Sheriff has agreed to pay overtime for the work. For that, he's gone up, in my estimation. I'm hoping the County will support helping these people get re-established afterward.

I open the folder I've created with the details of the nine people who own the cells in Pamela Wilson's safe. I have already developed a background for three of them. There are still six to go. But I can't face it right there and then.

I close the folder and call a cab.

I'll take the folder with me and do the work at home.

23

I feel more alive after a shower. I pull on clean knickers and a Blades shirt with a large gator on the front. Knock back a few painkillers and make myself a cheese sandwich. Along with a bag of Ruffles and a Corona, I'm all set. I intend to eat, then research the remaining six names on Pamela Wilson's list, but I fall asleep on my beanbag.

I must have been exhausted because Alexa woke me up again with Agalloch. This time, I only vaguely heard the initial sounds before slowly dragging myself out of the deepest sleep I've had for a long time. I tell Alexa to play something more soothing as soon as I can, and she switches to classical piano. I don't know what the music is, but it's quieter, which is fine with me.

Standing, I feel like my body has been through a meat grinder. Stiff and achy all over. I try a few stretches but know that only one thing will help - another shower. Then, at least afterward, I will be sparkly clean … and sore all over.

I underestimate the effect of the second shower. I feel almost normal when I step out, apart from my sore butt.

After drying off, I apply the deodorant-for-men I use. Much stronger and lasts longer. Dress in a red cotton top and white chinos. Then refill the coffee pot and switch it on.

* * *

While the coffee is brewing, I put two bagels in the toaster, then a pillow on one of my breakfast bar stools, and sit. I open the folder I brought home with me the night before. There's that little niggling detective voice in the back of my mind again. I know I'm missing something. Something obvious.

I spread out the details of the three people I've already started building backgrounds for and look them over. Wade Dooley, Christiana Lover, and Denis Meaker. What is bothering me?

One man is married, but one is single, as is the woman. They're born all over the place. New Orleans, Kentucky, and Cincinnati. All are in their fifties, but I can't see how that similarity can help me. They work not only for different companies but different industries.

And that's when it hits me. Pamela Wilson had drifted from job to job across all kinds of companies. I look her file up and check. Insurance company, Sears, Costco, Walmart, I-4-U, and Bank of America. I know there are others, but this is as far as I've gone. I see what I'm looking for immediately.

Bank of America - Wade Dooley and Pamela
   Costco - Christiana Lover and Pamela
   I-4-U - Denis Meaker and Pamela.

She's been moving around and using her employment to target clients. But not only that. She's targeting highly placed individuals. For example, Wade Dooley was the bank's Senior Financial Investment Executive. Christiana Lover was the Human Resource director for Costco South East division, and Denis Meaker was the founder and principal shareholder of his eye-care company I-4-U.

I'm now positive that if I look through the careers of each of the other names, I'll find Pamela Wilson had worked in the same place.

I head for the coffeepot and pour my first cup of the day. My bagels are cold. I press the toaster a second time and return to the breakfast bar. I have one last check to make. I need to check the order of the cell phones against the order in which Pamela worked at the various establishments. I have all the information. I need to lay it out.

The order of the cell phones implies that the most recent target had been Wade Dooley, then Christiana before that, and Denis Meaker before that. I also remember that the most recent cell is the Galaxy S8, but I have to ignore that for now.

Looking back through Pamela's employment history, most recently, she was with Bank of America, working in administration in the investment branch. Dooley's responsibility. Before that, she was in Payroll in the Human Resources department of Costco, where Christiana Lover worked.

I'm on a roll now. Her previous job to that had been to work in administration at I-4-U. Denis Meaker's start-up company.

I get her game. She would take a new position. Seek an interested party. Target only high-wealth clients, then invite them to have fun. The only thing missing is that I don't know how she would find people interested in being dominated. Perhaps I can ask Luisa del Roy the next time I see her?

Another issue with my theory is I still can't figure out how she used their cells to take a video of the action, then managed to lock it in her safe without them stopping her.

I understand why someone who liked what she could do for them might want a video to remember the action. I learned about that when I visited Tommy Hawk at the legal brothel on the Seminole reservation last year. This video stuff is big business.

I also understand why they wouldn't want Pamela to take the video on her cell. Too risky. So if they wanted one, it would *have* to be on their own. One thing I'm getting about Pamela Wilson is that she was no amateur. She would have known this and probably offered to use their cells. That would have sounded reassuring.

But how did she keep them?

If I'm to figure this one out, I need to watch one of the videos again. I'll have to do it in a conference room, or if word gets out about what I'm doing, the whole department will gather around to *help* me.

I spread peanut butter on the bagels, pour a second coffee, and head for the beanbag to think, not about the case but me.

I start recalling my conversation with Luisa del Roy from the day before. The first memory that comes to mind is when she told me there probably wasn't much wrong. But just that one short phrase has me so jammed up. Something that rarely happens so easily. It implies the exact opposite of how I feel. Yet, she's a very experienced professional. And someone I already trust. So, I'm struggling to make sense of it.

I shot an innocent two-year-old, who died instantly. Sacrificed motherhood for my career. I ran away from a man I liked. I terminated an unborn child, having denied the father's involvement in the decision, and now I am responsible for getting my cousin killed. I feel guilty as hell about everything. How can there not be much wrong?

Then she explained how I'm fighting battles on two fronts at the same time. I get that. She's spot on there. I feel like the classic swan gliding smoothly across the lake, but with its feet working like crazy underneath the surface. But if I stop paddling like fuck, either I won't get anywhere, or more likely, I'll sink under the weight of the burden I carry.

Surely it's better to keep going?

Then I recall watching a series on Netflix about the Second World War and Adolf Hitler's mistakes. The worst by far was to attack on two fronts. Europe and Russia. He was fucked as soon as he headed East. It just took time, but that poor decision cost him the war.

To avoid losing, I need to figure out what to concentrate on.

Luisa said that the present was a war worth fighting. It was my actual present-day existence. The past was just that and no longer worth my time or effort. She's right, of course. I agree with her. But how can I do that when I always think about the past? When I see the young girl's face, if I pull my Glock? When Bossy-boots haunts my dreams? And now I can add how Joey accused me of forgetting him, and I know that's the truth.

Del Roy has said this is where she's going to help. She told me about a technique that would allow me to process these thoughts from my past and calm them down. Then, once I've dealt with them, I'll be more able to live in the present, not the past. I like the sound of that and am astonished to find I'm looking forward to the second session in a week.

24

For once, when I get to the office, I actually do what I intend to do. I grab a laptop and head into the small conference room to watch some of Pamela's dominatrix performances. I have nine to choose from, yet don't hesitate. I load up Christiana Lovers. I don't know if this is just curiosity to see a woman subjected to a dominatrix - something that has surprised me. Or whether there is some more profound, more personal interest. Regardless, when the video starts, Christiana is already wearing her minimalist black underwear. I don't know if she would always wear knickers like this, but looking at them makes my butt even more painful. They must be so uncomfortable.

I watch as Pamela, dressed in her black faux-leather outfit, performs her various tasks - apparently on demand. Within thirty seconds, I've already decided no one will ever do any of this to me. But Christiana - loves it. Well, I assume she loves it. Most of it looks painful to me. She keeps asking for more or for something to be harder.

The more I watch, the more ashamed I feel for them. Irrational, I know, but I feel embarrassed just watching this. Sorry that a woman would want this when there are thousands of women suffering physical and sexual abuse every day who don't want it and can't stop it. Pamela herself, for instance. Then I realize that what happened to Pamela with my fellow detective and his gym buddies happened recently, long after she retired from her dominatrix business.

As I half-watch, I disassociate, allowing my mind to think of other things I would have to do that day. I begin to pay full attention again when Christiana is naked and Pamela is cuffing her to the bed rails.

After that, it's more of the same, and again I lose interest. But I do notice that when the video stops, Christiana is still cuffed to the bed.

I play the Wade Dooley recording but fast-forward through to near the end. But, again, he also remains cuffed when the recording stops.

So, now I have at least partially answered how Pamela manages to get their cells locked into her safe. She puts them in and locks them away before releasing her clients.

But, if I were one of them, I would be livid when she finally set me free. I can't see them just happily walking off into the night.

So there's only one possible conclusion I can come to. She had an accomplice. At the end of each session, she called someone who would protect her as the client dressed and left. A man. A big muscular man would be my guess. I need to find him.

I have everything I need from the videos for now, so close the laptop and return to my cubicle. The next step is to get hold of Pamela's cell phone records. She would have had to call this man, so there should be a record. I send a request to her provider, hoping that she wasn't a huge cell phone user.

Most providers are quick to respond; she was with T-Mobile, so I'm pretty confident I'll have the information back the following day.

* * *

I notice a couple of message slips only after I've done that. One is from my Mama, the other from one of Jerry's guys. Both want me to call.

I call Mama first. She wants to let me know the greater family is having a ceremony for the passing of Joey's spirit that night at seven. I tell her I'll be there. I owe him that, at least. There goes that guilt again.

Next, I call Mike Gibson, Jerry's right-hand man in Narcotics. He tells me he's attending some of the project's postmortems and thinks my stopping by might be worthwhile. He doesn't say why. Intrigued, I tell him I'll be right there.

Down in the morgue, there are three of Jerry's guys watching what's happening, and I think that a little strange. I mean, sad as this whole thing is, why the sudden interest in the deaths of these poor people?

Mike thanks me for coming down and suggests we go to Arnie Collins' office. I shrug, unsure why I'm there, but follow him anyway. On the way, he gives me an update on Jerry. The splintered floorboards have made a mess of his thighs and stomach, but most of the wounds are superficial. They're expecting him back in a few days. Until then, he has been asked to run the show.

When we reach Arnie's office, I'm surprised to find him there. I'd thought he would be up to his elbows with all the bodies we had discovered, but here he is.

He has his stern look on, so my guilt fires up, and I start frantically thinking about what I might have done that would earn his wrath. Besides my involvement in sending him more dead bodies, I can't think of anything. I'm in the clear.

* * *

'Thanks for coming, Sammy.'

Shit. Not detective. This is personal. I'm not ready for that.

'I guess what I'm about to tell you will also affect your cousin, Joey Still Water.'

Now he has my undivided attention.

'We've not finished the work on all the victims from the Project, but we can draw some preliminary conclusions, and I want you to hear them from me rather than by reading a report.'

He clears his throat. Whatever's bothering him is already bothering me, too. I'm tense.

'Each of the victims had extremely high levels of drugs in their systems.'

So far, so good. No surprise there.

'But we have found that all the early toxicology results are different.'

This confuses me. I ask why that's significant.

'Because they all lived in the same place. Got their drugs from the same suppliers. They should have similar results.'

'So you're saying there was more than one supplier?'

'No. I'm saying that someone was cutting the drugs with different strengths, using over-the-counter meds to produce different results.'

'I'm sorry, Arnie. I'm not following you.'

'Someone was experimenting on them, Sammy. Testing what they could produce and also what they could get away with. The Project was nothing but a laboratory. Using people that no one would miss, to trial their products.'

I'm speechless. I guess Mike has already been told, but he's still pretty shaken up. He's the first to speak.

'We have to find who's responsible for this, Sammy. If you want to be looped in, it's fine with me if you okay it with your sergeant.'

'I'm in, Mike. My sergeant will be too. Whatever you guys need on this one. You'll have our full support.'

'Thanks, Sammy. We'll be meeting later in the day. I'll let you know when.'

***

Back upstairs, the conversation with Dan goes much as I predict. It upsets him, just as it has the rest of us. This needs a joint task-force approach; he doesn't care who heads it up. Homicide or Narcotics.

He tells me he'll update the Sheriff on the status of finding Mark Jason's killer and this joint task force effort simultaneously. Then repeats how sorry he is that my cousin had been caught up in all of this. I thank him and return to my cubicle, feeling as low as I have. I can't imagine the suffering these poor people were being put through. Not only had their lives fallen apart, but they had lost everything, become junkies, and then turned into lab rats for some asshole dealer. Probably Chico Vegas.

A new message on my desk tells me that Forensics have received the last cell phone back from their external consultants. I can collect it whenever I have time.

Now is as good as any, so off I go, questioning how far I walk in this building daily. Wondering whether the information this new device reveals will fit into my understanding of Pamela Wilson's retirement scheme.

I should have known it wouldn't be so easy.

25

I bring the Galaxy S8 back down to the small conference room in Homicide and enter the 0000 code, set up to allow me easy access. It's a little different to operate from my cell, so it takes me a while to figure it out, but eventually I find the video and play it.

This time, Pamela's guest is a young girl. To my eyes, she looks about sixteen with an as-yet to develop body. I'm not sure of the legality of what I'm about to witness, but I see a new aspect of Pamela Wilson. And I don't like it. Her morality, or lack of it. Anyone with a sense of decency would have refused to do what I'm now witnessing.

A few minutes in, I see this isn't the girl's first rodeo. Pamela may be the dominatrix, but this girl is in charge. That's obvious. She knows exactly what she *wants* or is it *likes*. It's hard to tell when she spends most of the time squealing. I have to fast-forward to when Pamela starts connecting Croc clips to the girl in places Croc clips shouldn't go.

I get to the end, and as before, it finishes with the young girl still cuffed to the bed iron. I freeze the last frame and scrutinize the girl. Thin, short-cropped black hair. A nose-pin with what looks like a skull on it. I can tell she has dark eyes but I can't tell the color. I would guess ninety-five pounds, five foot six. Pale skin. She doesn't look healthy.

I study her expression in that one frame. This is one I'll print and consult my favorite shrink with next week. My interpretation includes pleasure, for sure, but there's something else. Something less positive. Perhaps even dangerous. Maybe this *is* the femoral slasher?

I capture this frame and send it to the printer nearest my desk, close the Galaxy S8, and head to the printer to pick it up before taking it back to my cubicle.

I put the picture in a file I've created for Miss X and turn my attention back to the Galaxy S8. There are some documents in there I haven't yet looked at. Being me, I start with the first and work down. Orderly.

The first dozen mean nothing to me at all. Some relate to music, others to meetings she either attended or planned to attend. The only thing of interest is that the events are all from three years ago, which ties into when Pamela hung up her dominatrix outfit and retired. It also matches to the Galaxy S8 being the most recent device released. I'm now confident this was her last client.

Further down, I open a folder to find a collection of files within it. Each has a name. There are eight in total. All male.

Arden Kotnik
   Terrance Frazier
   Laurence Spencer
   Paget Vicic
   Josh Ransom
   Coleman Kaler
   Jon Smith
   Joseph Wright

I open the first. Arden Kotnik. Polish, living in West Palm Beach. Twenty-eight, single, and employed as a groundsman at the Breakers Ocean Golf Club.

Then the next. Terrance Frazier. Yugoslavian, twenty-three, single, and living in Fort Pierce on the East Coast. A waiter at the Thirsty Turtle.

And again. Laurence Spencer. Born in Florida, twenty-five, single, living up in Tallahassee. A porter at Florida State University.

I keep going, but a pattern is forming, and the rest all conform. They're all single. All are in their twenties and live and work in Florida, although widely spread from north to south.

Why would this young teenage girl have files on these men? Why would she have researched their details? Did she know them? If so, how?

I then think back to what I've seen in the video. I made her around sixteen, and if I'm right about her being Pamela's last client, she must now be around nineteen, maybe twenty. But I also remember thinking she wasn't new to the game. So, I dread what age she might have been when she picked up her previous experience. And what is it that makes her seek pain for pleasure?

There's another problem rattling around in my head. I know I can tie Pamela's other clients to her career choices. And each of her clients is senior enough to afford her blackmail charges. So where does this young girl fit in?

More questions than answers. I've been there often enough. So all I can do is start looking into these eight names. See what I can turn up.

I start with Motor Vehicle and License status. The easiest way to find both date of birth and a photo. All eight are registered. Their DOBs agree with the ages in the girl's files, as do their photos. The only odd thing I encounter is that three of their licenses have expired. But then I remember, during my time as a State Trooper, how many people drive not only with expired licenses but no licenses. Not to mention insurance. So, maybe not that odd.

Next, I try the old faithful criminal arrest records. They've prosecuted two for sexual abuse of minors. The others have accumulated a few misdemeanors, but no red flags exist. They seem primarily like regular citizens on the up-and-up.

Looking into more detail about the two sexual abuse cases, they both involved seventeen-year-old girls, and the men were barely older. Illegal, but the case files read more like boyfriends and girlfriends to me, which explains the light sentencing - community service, which I've never encountered before. They must have come before a detective's nightmare - a liberal-minded Judge.

Thinking about the rest being regular citizens makes me look into immigration status. But, again, there are only three immigrants, and they're already green-card holders, with two of those already US citizens. More evidence to say they're just regular guys.

Now it's time to get more personal. Look into the backgrounds of the eight men and their families. Births, marriages, and deaths.

I'm still working through them in the same order, so start with Arden Kotnik. He was born in Zabki on the outskirts of Warsaw, Poland, and moved to America with his parents. He was ten then. No marriage. He died four years ago.

Now I'm not expecting that. So, on one of these detective hunches, I try his name in the system and come up trumps.

Arden Kotnik. A homicide case - open for the past four years. Someone stabbed him at his Kenwood Estates, Palm Springs home.

I'm now getting a nervous, sinking feeling in the pit of my stomach.

I skip the family research on the following name and type it into our system. Up comes the answer I feared. A homicide case in Fort Pierce further north on the east coast of the State. Open for two years.

One after another, I type the names and quickly find six open homicide cases spread around Florida, all in the past six years.

All knifed to death. Either this girl collected data on knife killings from press articles, or she's a killer. I don't know which, but I know where I would put my money if I had any.

The oldest open case is for Laurence Spencer, up in Tallahassee six years ago. If my estimate of the girl as sixteen in Pamela's video is correct, she would have only been thirteen then. Fuck.

I need time to let all this sink in and am just thinking about a fresh brew when I check the time and remember my promise to attend Joey's spirit-passing with my family.

I still have no car, which would mean an expensive cab ride, so I grovel on my hands and knees in front of the duty sergeant until he takes pity on me. Of course, a patrol SUV isn't the ideal vehicle to bring to a spirit-passing ceremony, but beggars can't be choosers.

26

Joey's ceremony is taking place at my Aunt's home. Mama and Papa get a kick out of arriving in the patrol SUV. I'm tempted to put the light bar on for them, but any complaint might cause a problem if I need to borrow it again, which I probably will at some point. Still, it's an impressive enough entry.

Fortunately, our family is not large by Native American Indian standards, so we squeeze all two dozen relatives into my Aunt's modest home. The incense burning and chanting have already started when we arrive. I find Mama a seat close to her sister, and stand at the back with Papa.

Joey's elder brother tells us about some fun times they had growing up together, then his sister follows.

Listening, I don't recognize the person I'd seen the week before. In times like these, we focus on the good bits and let the rest go by.

We sing songs and speak prayers. Chant and then pass around the ceremonial pipe to inhale. I've done this before and know how to avoid choking and coughing.

It's a happy ceremony. Childhood stories. Funny moments. Joey's papa even recalled some of his son's more troublesome moments with a tinge of humor.

Overall, the family has done him proud.

It's late when I take my parents home, and I agree to stay over. After that, it will be easy to nip home early to change before going to the office.

Mama shows me to my childhood room. Other than having a larger bed, everything else is the same. It's comforting. Little do I know it's the calm before the storm.

I'm on I75 driving south by five-thirty. I'll be home by six, showered, changed, and in the office by seven. Today, I will talk about my most recent findings with Dan. We need to decide how best to approach the investigation from here on. This is going to be State-wide. Someone will have to lead, and I have a funny feeling I know who that will be.

I give Dan a five-minute brief of the highlights, and he stops me. He lifts the phone and asks if the Sheriff is free. Apparently, he is. And that's where we head next.

I've rarely seen the Sheriff from behind his desk, and today is no exception. The Under-Sheriff is already there when we arrive and nods his welcome. He's in his usual position. Couched on the arm of a sofa, giving his massive girth room to hang on either side. Dan and I get the two plastic chairs. My butt isn't pleased.

The Sheriff asks me to start from the beginning, so I jump right back to the death of one of our own. Mark Jason. I give them the full-length story and am glad when Bill Putinski asks if we can get some fresh coffee before we continue. I think I've found a kindred spirit.

Ten minutes later, we're back in the office, with everyone discussing their views.

Dan says it sounds like I've stumbled upon a Statewide serial killer.

Putinski says that it's still possible this young girl is only following the stories in the press for some reason we don't yet understand.

The Sheriff asks me if I think this girl is responsible for Pamela Wilson's death. I tell him I don't know. He then asks how old I think she was when the first victim on her list was stabbed, and I tell him thirteen plus or minus a year.

He's finding it hard to see a thirteen-year-old as a vicious serial killer.

Everyone agrees with that.

Putinski asks me if I have any theory of why the girl might act this way. I tell him I don't but intend to ask a consulting psychiatrist that same question as soon as possible.

After a few minutes of silence, the Sheriff looks at Dan and asks him how he intends to proceed. I feel a wave of relief wash over me. He has asked Dan, not me. The relief is short-lived.

Dan responds that I've gotten this far. Therefore, it seems reasonable to have me push onward.

'State-wide,' says the Sheriff.

'State-wide,' agrees Dan.

The Sheriff turns towards me. 'You haven't closed Mark Jason's case yet?'

'No, Sheriff. Without finding the stiletto, I don't think we can progress any further.'

'You're telling me we have a detective homicide that will go unproven?'

'I'll keep it under review a little longer,' I promise.

The Sheriff grunts, then asks. 'You up for this serial-killer case detective? You ain't been back in the saddle long.'

I nod, afraid he might notice the tremble in my voice if I speak.

'Okay, then. Get to it and keep me in the loop.'

In Dan's cubicle, he asks if I agree with his suggestion. What can I say? No, I can't handle it. I'm still dreaming about the baby I terminated and scared to draw my Glock in case I shoot a young child. You picked me off the floor at EJ's and drove me to a psychiatrist. I didn't say any of that.

'Sure, Dan. I'll get started.'

Instead of going to my cubicle, I head out of the building. I need to clear my mind. Mid-February around these parts is about as nice as it gets. The temperature towards midday is in the low to mid-twenties, with a light breeze blowing in over the gulf. Perfect.

We're lucky where the office is. There's Baker Park out the back, and it backs onto the inlet from Naples Bay. Across the water, there's plenty of open grass, but beyond is the constant airport drone. So if you can tune the noise out, it's a beautiful spot to think. And I've got a lot of thinking to do. This will be a big case, and I need to get my head on straight.

I sit on a bench at the waterfront. There's a dedication plaque. I read it. The bench is in loving memory of James Daly, who died too young. Doing the math, I reckon he was only twelve when he died. Just about the same age as my potential serial killer when she started on her killing spree.

I quiet my mind and try to structure my thoughts while watching the sailboats and power launches go by, their owners with not a care in the world. They should be so lucky.

First, there are still things I haven't finished while investigating the deaths of both Mark Jason and Pamela Wilson.

Then there's my commitment to Jerry to support him in finding whoever is responsible for the abomination at the Project. This isn't just a commitment to Jerry. It's also a commitment to my cousin Joey. I failed him and let him down when he came to me for help. This isn't something I can give up.

I have to figure out how to continue to follow up on the details while leading a Statewide hunt for a serial killer.

27

Knowing my day is likely to get even crazier. I head for Subway a couple of blocks away. If I'm to be busy, I need to eat.

I attack and demolish a steak and cheese sub, then walk back to the office.

My plan's simple. First, figure out how to close both the Jason and Wilson homicides, then get started on the serial killer case. But it won't happen like that with me in charge. I think not.

The System has already flagged my earlier inquiries on unsolved homicides across the entire State, and when I get back to my desk, I've questions from four other Counties already waiting for me.

It's clear I can't do this on my own and have to get some help, so I make a bee-line for Dan's office. He isn't there, but I can hear his voice in the background. I look around and spot him towards the back of the office. He's in the middle of a group of three detectives. Good detectives - I know them all. I work my way around toward him. He sees me coming.

'I was just coming to find you, Sammy. I want you to meet your new team,' he tells me, indicating the three figures beside him.

'I've asked them to hand over all current investigations to others and dedicate themselves one hundred percent to your case. I meant to discuss this with you first, but you had left for lunch.'

I'm a little wrong-footed. I've gone from pissed he has thought this out before me to feeling guilty for sitting in the park to being super-pleased at having a team to work with - all in seconds.

'No, that's great, Dan. Thanks. I was going to talk to you about something like this.'

Then turning my attention to the three newly assigned detectives, I welcome them and tell them I couldn't have chosen any better. I'm grateful they will be sharing the case with me.

We agree to a first get-together around three that afternoon in the larger conference room. That will give them time to off-load their current work and start reading up on the case. I leave with Dan feeling much better than just thirty minutes before. I've got some serious horsepower now.

With a couple of hours to spare, I do a little digging.

I want to know which homicides occurred in which County. I pull up the list of names, and this time I want to stay under the official radar until the team is up to speed. If I start talking with half a dozen other Counties, I'll personally get all their future calls. I don't want that. So this time, I use a website I've used many times before - Truth-finder. It searches Federal, State, and Local Government databases and organizes them into easy-to-read reports.

It's a website available to the public, not guaranteed to be one-hundred percent accurate, but it's a great first step when you're looking for someone. It checks online profiles, weapons permits, bankruptcies, phone numbers, court records, relatives, misdemeanors, judgments, assets, sexual offenses, felonies, traffic offenses, arrests, and addresses.

I try one of the eight names, who may still be alive. I choose the local one and typed in Jon Smith. It couldn't have been a worse name to search for. It turns out there are twenty-eight Jon Smiths. But then I look into the background detail and see there are only three in Collier County.

I note their details and keep going with the list.

Homicides
Arden Kotnik (1) - West Palm Beach - Palm Beach
Terrance Frazier (1) - Gainesville - Alachua
Laurence Spencer (1) - Tallahassee - Leon
Paget Vicic (1) - Miami - Miami-Dade
Josh Ransom (1) - Orlando - Orange
Coleman Kaler (1) - Jacksonville - Duval
Still Alive?
Jon Smith (3) - Naples - Collier
Joseph Wright (2) - Tampa - Hillsborough

By the time I've made it this far, it's time to meet with the team. When I told them I was pleased to have their support, that wasn't bullshit. If I had to pick three, I would choose each in a flash.

Jamie Samson has been here for twenty-plus years. He never made it through the promotion board, but most of us reckon he never tried. He's a solid investigator. Good at the details.

Dene Winscome is different. He joined the department around the same time as me, three years ago. More of an intuitive guy. Prone to jumping to conclusions and then trying to work backward. Not an approach recommended by district attorneys, yet he's had plenty of success with it.

Then there's Kathy Mason. The only other female in the division. Five years younger than me and smart as a whip. She is probably a little too quick to judge but popular with everyone because of her biting humor. Double-D breasts don't do her any harm, either.

They'll make an excellent team. I hope I'm up to the task of leading them.

We start with me walking through everything, as I'd done earlier with the Sheriff. After that, they ask plenty of questions before we agree on the priorities and who will do what.

* * *

1 Find and protect the two remaining people on the list who have not yet been attacked.
2 Contact all relevant County forces and gather case files for all open homicides.
3 Analyze all information to see if we can find why these people are targets?
4 See if there is any pattern to the killings - method, timing, weapon
5 Establish what connects these people?
6 Fresh review of all evidence from Pamela Wilson's home, including the videos and cell phone records.
7 Find out if Pamela Wilson had an assistant. If so, find this person.

By the time we've completed this initial list, the scale of the case is getting to us. I realize that all three are giving up cases that are probably important to them. That's how we are as detectives. We start something; we commit to seeing it through. So I feel guilty that I intend to keep two of my own involvements going. I decide to own up and take their criticism on the chin.

I explain about my cousin, Joey. And why I want to help Narcotics if I can. I don't think this will be a significant effort, but it's personal, and they all appear to accept that.

Then I tell them I want to reel in Mark Jason's two gym buddies for the assault on Pamela Wilson. They argue it's part of the same case anyway, so I should proceed. They'll handle the volume of grunt work on the serial killer basics.

It's already dark when I leave the office in a cab, heading home. I get the driver to stop at the local twenty-four-hour mart, and I buy some basics. Milk, coffee, bagels, yogurt, popcorn, Tampax, and a six-pack of Corona. I intend to pig out and watch more MASH. A girl needs downtime.

Loaded up, I'm just approaching the front of my apartment block when I see movement ahead in the shadows. I stop where I am, with both hands full and no way to get to my

Glock without dropping either the grocery bag or my Corona six-pack. It won't be the six-pack.

Chico Vegas steps out of the shadows and stands directly before me, hands casually in his pants pockets.
 'Yo, detective. See you partyin' tonight?'
 'If I am, you're not invited if that's what you're hoping for.'
 'No, man. I mean, I likes you an' all, but you're too old for me. Couldn't keep up, you know.'
 'Not a question I ever see myself having to answer. What do you want, Chico?'
 'I want to give you ma condolences, man. Joey was a screw-up, but he was okay.'
 'Next, you'll be telling me you had nothing to do with his death, right?'
 'Not me, man. I think you already dealt with the guy responsible.'
 '*The Joker*?'
 'What can I tell you, man? He was one scary dude.'
 'Rumor has it he was your right-hand enforcer, Chico? Are you losing control?'
 'You got it all wrong, Detective. I don't need no enforcer cause I ain't doing nothin' illegal.'
 I don't even respond to that one.
 'I ask you again, Chico. What do you want?'
 'I just want you leave me alone. I done nothin' wrong. Just let me be. Best for both of us, don't you think?'
 'Is there a threat in there?'
 'No, man. No threat. Just think of it as friendly advice. You know. Neighbor to neighbor.'
 'Yeah, well, thanks for that. Very thoughtful. I'll take it on board and give it some real deep thought.'
 'That's my sweet sugar. Knew you would see it my way. Job done. See you around, Detective.'

With that, he steps back into the shadows and disappears. I hate that he knows where I live. That he keeps appearing out of the shadows. But what can I do? This is home, and I can barely afford it as it is. No way can I afford to move.

By the time I change into my sweats and Blades Tee-shirt, take the popcorn from the microwave, and pop the cap on a Corona, he's already slipping from my mind.

I slump into my beanbag, notice that my butt's no longer painful for the first time, and tune into MASH only to hear a knock on my door.

Laying the Corona aside and unholstering my Glock, I reach the door and open it to find the young girl I'd given the throwaway cell phone. In the shadowy hallway, she looks small and fragile. I don't know what to say. She beats me to it.

'I want to live with you.'

I'm so surprised. I say nothing, just stare at her. Then wave her in.

She enters, looks around, then turns her sad eyes on me.

I remember what I'd found out about her background. That she'd never known her father, that her mother OD'd and never cared for her. She had been in and out of juvie court and the care system. Now, here she is, telling me she wants to live with me.

I need time to process. I don't trust myself with what to say, so I pass her the bowl of popcorn and tell her I only have coffee and bagels. Would she like either or both?

She opts for both and flops onto the beanbag. I head for the kitchen and the coffeemaker.

I set the machine up and stand watching this lost soul sitting in my beanbag, eating popcorn like fury. I suspect she hasn't eaten for some time again, and I feel guilty that I live such a frugal existence that there's nothing else but bagels in the apartment to offer her.

I think back to her words at the front door. She said she wants to *live* with me. Not visit. Not stop by. But *live*.

The childish simplicity of her request upsets me.

If only the world were so simple.

Given her background, I reckon that's quite a statement for

her to make. In one way, it makes me feel privileged that she has singled me out. But at the same time, horrified that I'm the best on offer to her. For her to trust me so much after such a short time speaks volumes about the people she has been around, living on the streets. That embarrasses me. I guess it reminds me how privileged I am to be a detective and have an apartment to live in, even in this shitty neighborhood. How there are many just like her, much less well off and living a life in a nether world ignored by almost everyone.

The coffee stops draining. I ditch my corona, pour two mugs, fish the bagels out of the toaster, and take everything into my small lounge area. I hand Trace one cup and both bagels before sitting on the two-seater. I start the conversation like a good detective would, with a question.

'How have you found me?'

'I followed you home. The night you gave me the cell phone. It was easy. I think something was distracting you.'

'I was probably thinking about you.'

'I guessed that,' she said, blowing on her coffee.

'You know you can't come and live with me. You realize that, right?'

'Why not?'

There's the faintest quiver in these two words, but I hear it, and my heart sinks. For someone so fiercely independent and used to looking after herself, it's taking a lot of courage to ask for help - and to risk trusting someone she barely knows. She sees me as the way out of her hopeless life. All I did was buy her a meal. Not charge her for attempted theft, and give her a cell phone. Yet I've become her beacon of hope.

My mind is racing. For her, this is an important moment in her life. One of these sliding-door moments. In her mind, living with me, her life will improve; otherwise, she'll be back on the streets. That realization makes me feel guilty again.

I realize I'm only thinking of how to get rid of her without hurting her.

'I'm not capable of looking after you.'

'You needn't do anything. Just let me live here, that's all.'

'I can barely afford to feed myself, never mind two of us?'
'I can help with that?'
'How?'
'I've been watching you. You shop at the 24/7 across from the apartment.'
'Watching me?'
'Sure. And you waste money shopping in the wrong place.'
'And you can do better?'
'Much. I know the cheapest place for everything. Like your Corona, for instance.'
'You buy Corona?'
'No, but you do. You pay eleven dollars, ninety-nine cents for a six-pack. I can get you the same for seven dollars, ninety-nine. That's a four-dollar saving.'
'That's just one thing,' I hear myself argue, secretly impressed.
'You use regular Tampax and buy the small packs of thirty-six for nine ninety-seven. I know where to buy the large pack of two hundred for twenty-nine, ninety-nine. So you're paying twenty-seven cents for each instead of fifteen cents.'
'How do you know I use regular Tampax?'
'I told you. I've been watching you.'
'Where did you learn math like that?'
'If I ever have money, I want to get as much as possible for it, whereas you throw money away. So if I do the shopping, we can live on what you earn.'
'It's not all about money.'
'Everything's about money.'
'No, Trace. It's not all about money. There are legal issues and your education to consider, not to mention I don't have a spare room, and maybe I don't want the responsibility. Have you thought of that?'
I feel instantly ashamed of myself again for that last sentence. I've spoken about what's on my mind, but that's where the thought should have stayed. I realize it as soon as the words come out of my mouth.
It could be my imagination, but I see a tiny spark of light

extinguish in Trace's eyes. I've doused the enthusiastic mathematical wizard with reality. Now, she's just a vulnerable twelve-year-old asking for my help. And I've potentially destroyed her dreams. I try switching tack.

'Why tonight?'

'What do you mean?'

'I mean, why have you chosen this particular night to come to me?'

She paused for a few moments before answering.

'You rounded up the friends that were helping look after me.'

'I did what?'

'You and a hundred others. You cleaned us out. I saw you come into the building and split through the back.'

'You were living in the Project?'

'With my only friends. Now they're gone.'

More guilt creeps over me. I remind myself that actions often have unintended consequences. And one of these is sitting in front of me with her heart on her sleeve, pleading for my help. I try to be positive.

'Look, before we decide anything, we have to talk everything through a lot more. Agreed?'

She nods hopefully.

I wonder if I've just given her false hope and whether this is kind or cruel. After all, it doesn't matter how much we talk. There's no way I can look after this girl.

'Right. Step at a time. I've got a sleeping bag somewhere. Why don't I look that out for you? You'll have to sleep on the floor.'

'Fine with me. I'm used to hard floors. At least it's not cold in here.'

Twenty minutes later, Trace is asleep - at least, I think she's sleeping. I'm laying in bed, wide awake, wondering how the hell I got into this mess. Puzzling over how I might get out of it. Feeling guilty again - this time about having a twelve-year-old sleeping on the floor when I'm in my nice, comfortable bed.

At the same time as I'm having all these conflicting thoughts and feelings, there's something strangely comforting in listening to her breathing and knowing that someone is prepared to trust me so much. I guess it's how I would have felt had I allowed Bossy-boots to survive.

28

When I climb out of bed, it's the first morning my entire body feels okay in a long time. As I noticed the night before, my butt is no longer painful. The even better news is that my knee doesn't hurt. I guess time does heal, after all. When I swing out of bed, I realize I can smell fresh brew. Then the events of the previous evening come back to me. I'm no longer alone.

Trace is sitting on a stool at the small breakfast bar, her hair wet, already sipping coffee, and looking at something on my laptop.

I don't have the energy to tackle her for making herself at home, so I mutter good morning and make for the shower.

I'm not exceptionally tidy, but things aren't where I left them. The hair shampoo is on the base of the shower rather than on the rack. My hair brush has moved to the wrong side of the washbasin. I see a scrunched Tampax wrapper lying on the floor in front of the bin. The shower head is still dripping, and water trails cover the glass frontage.

I'm just beginning to realize how little Trace has had in her life and how dependent she will be on me until I figure out what to do with her. She doesn't even have her hairbrush.

Realizing that, I look suspiciously at my toothbrush and decide I can survive without cleaning my teeth for one day or showering.

* * *

We don't talk much over coffee. I explain that I don't work regular hours and can't say when I'll be home. She's okay with that. I give her a spare key and twenty bucks for food.

Then, as I still don't have transport, I tell her I'll run to work.

On goes the gear, including the badge and Glock. I'll head for EJ's, then shower at work. I pack fresh underwear and a shirt in my small backpack and set off on a leisurely run: medium pace, medium length.

I arrive at EJ's forty minutes later, still pain-free. It feels good after so long. I'm not even sweating.

Breakfast that morning will have to be light and cheap. It's getting close to the end of the month, my bank balance is running on air, and I can't really afford the twenty I've given Trace. So, I order waffles and syrup, with coffee and more coffee. Top-ups are free. I love this place for that.

Thirty minutes later, I'm in the shower in the locker room when someone else comes into the next booth. We have a sign we put on the door with a man in a shower on one side, and a woman on the other, so I hope this is Kathy. It wouldn't be the first time some smart-ass has turned the sign over once I'm in there. I'm apprehensive till I hear Kathy's voice.

We talk while we scrub.

I decide not to mention Trace to anyone until I've decided what to do about her. I'm at least due her that much. So instead, I tell Kathy I'm heading up to meet with a profiler.

She tells me the team stayed till late after I left. They think they've identified the two live possible targets and have also established communications with the other Counties. She says they'll update me fully when I get back later.

When I'm toweling off, Kathy's standing in front of the washbasin, with her head hung low and hair down over her head, using a hair dryer. She's naked.

It seems I'm right. Her boobs are several sizes larger than mine, and as ridiculous as it seems, I feel inferior and suddenly self-conscious. I wrap a towel tightly around me and move beside her to use the other hair dryer.

We stand together like that, the entire female detective contingent, with one of us drying her hair and the other worrying about her boob size.

When the dryers are off, Kathy turns to me and tells me how lucky I am not to have her massive boobs. How hard it is to have any of the guys take her seriously. Whenever she enters a room or meets the guys for a drink, they look at her boobs first.

I don't know what to say. I've never thought of it like that, probably because I've never noticed guys looking at my boobs. Why would they? Nothing to see.

After that, we finish dressing in silence and go our separate ways, with me still trying to figure out if my smaller boobs are a good thing or not. It seems a strange thought to be entering a psychiatrist's office with, but, hey.

Maggie, the receptionist, isn't at her desk, so I go straight to the open door of the inner office. Del Roy is rummaging around in a file box with her back to me. She's a little older than me but still in trim shape. I know she served with the FBI for quite a few years, earning a reputation as one of the finest profilers. But, of course, you don't get any job in the FBI if you're not fit. It looks like she's still exercising regularly.

I knock on the door to get her attention. She turns and smiles.

'Good morning, detective. Good to see you again.'
'Thanks for seeing me so quickly.'
'Come in and take a seat.'
Then she says the words I always love to hear.
'I've just brewed some fresh coffee. You like yours black, I believe.'

After we're sitting, I show her the picture from the last frame of Pamela Wilson's video. I want her take on the expression on the young girl's face. I also want to understand why such a young girl would like the services of a dominatrix.

Del Roy says she would rather hear the whole story before commenting.

So, a few minutes later, I'm retelling the story again, wishing I'd made a recording the first time back at the Sheriff's office. Del Roy sits quietly, just listening, which surprises me; I thought she'd be full of questions.

I underestimated her.

When I'm finished, she tells me what she heard me say, but in psychiatrist-speak.

'It's most likely your girl has been through a psycho-sexual trauma either once in her childhood or, as is more often the case, many times throughout her life. Close family members commit over ninety percent of cases such as this. Most commonly, fathers, uncles, or even brothers. Sometimes, it can also be female members of the family who are responsible. Sometimes for sexual reasons, other times out of jealousy or a desperate need to control something in their own miserable lives.'

As she tells me this, I think how lucky I've been with my close family.

'You should check for runaways from fostering or residential care homes for the young. It would be best to look for someone who disappears from the system around twelve. If you are right, she has been killing since then without significant breaks, so she has outsmarted the system repeatedly. You have a list of at least some Counties you know she has been in. In each of these, there will be places where local law enforcement knows someone like this can hide. Unfortunately, they are often ignored because there are too many such places or because they are best left alone as long as they don't cause problems.

As she tells me this, I can't help but think of Joey, Trace, and her friends hiding out at the Project.

* * *

'I would need to see the details of each of the homicides to confirm my next statement, but I think you will find she is a quick learner, and her kills are becoming more sophisticated. She likes the knife because, for her, this is all personal. She likes to get up close and uses her age and vulnerability like a fly trap for unsuspecting male predators.'

'The hunted becomes the hunter?' I suggest.

'Exactly. She's not like most other serial killers. She does not appear to be speeding up, needing more and more, quicker and quicker action. She is not addicted to killing. This is very rare, as is her age. You asked why she would use a dominatrix?'

I nod. I'm already almost in a trance, just listening to her voice. I need to pay more attention.

'A part of her doesn't understand why she is doing what she is. A part that feels guilty and needs to be punished. I suspect not a very large part. But, another avenue you could follow would be to see if she has had these needs satisfied elsewhere.'

'You mean, she may have seen more than one dominatrix?'

'Yes. Or else she has visited your particular dominatrix more than once.'

Something I will have to follow up on.

'So what about the expression on her face? What does it tell you?'

'Absolution. She is paying her dues. But that frees her up and freshens her intent. As this picture was from the end of her session, I would say your dominatrix has delivered. She has a satisfied client.'

I'm holding the picture in my hands and studying it. She's right. I can see it now, but I would never have gotten there alone. Del Roy has more to add.

'If you note, all her kills have been men, which tells me one or more men abused her when she was a younger child. I have heard of cases where a father shares his daughter with his brothers or a brother shares his sister with his friends. It's hard for anyone to come to grips with the sexual-physical side of this type of event and the breaking of unwritten family behaviors and rules. As a result, she will probably have lost the ability to trust anyone and may be a complete loner.

As she moves through the underworld, most of us deny - where people live in doorways and abandoned buildings and addicts live - she will be virtually invisible. Although this will help her hide, she will be lonely and highly vulnerable should anyone be kind to her.

She has grown through puberty while pursuing her self-appointed task and given her lifestyle. You are looking for someone undoubtedly suffering from malnutrition, possibly with stunted growth. Underweight. Sallow complexion. Sunken eyes. You should have your police artist bring your three-year-old photograph of her, and I will help him change it.'

Luisa del Roy sits back and looks directly at me.

'One last thing, detective. Suppose you end up in front of her. Please don't talk to her like you might someone threatening suicide. This young woman does not fit any previous profile of a serial killer. She does not conform, making her unpredictable and, most likely, very dangerous.'

I nod my understanding.

'Questions?'

Del Roy has stunned me into silence. My mind is either too full of additional information or just blank. She fills the awkward gap.

'Sorry, detective. I'm a little intense when I get going.'

'I can see that.'

'It's one reason I left the FBI.'

I nod.

'Don't worry if you struggled to keep up with everything I said. I set my cell to *record* before I started talking. I'll send the recording to you, and you can share it with your team. I'll also have Maggie type it and forward it to you.'

'Thanks, doctor.'
'Luisa, please.'
'Sure.'
'And I'm still seeing you personally in a few days, right?'
'Yes, you are. I'm looking forward to it.'
With that, she stands and shakes my hand, saying that she hopes she has been helpful and that I should send her the files from each homicide as soon as possible.

I promise to do just that.

When I'm leaving, I ask her receptionist to call me a cab while I go downstairs and stand outside in the mini-mall to wait, thinking over everything I've just heard.

I need to get the team started searching records for adoption and care homes back over the years preceding the killings. This will be a massive undertaking as we're looking across the entire State. With luck, perhaps we can nail who this girl is. Then get the police artist up here to update my photograph of her. We'll also need to convince each County to go into their Projects and find out if she has been there. They won't want to do that so some persuasion will be necessary. Finally, when the case files arrive from the other Counties, get them copied and sent up here.

When the cab arrives, I reflect that Luisa del Roy is even better than I thought. And that helps me accept the more personal thing she said in my previous meeting. That there is not very much wrong with me. When she told me that, it gave me hope. And that makes me wonder what I've just done to Trace the previous evening.

29

Back in the office, I hand the recording of my conversation with Kathy into the conference room the team has sequestered, then make for my cubicle. While they work through Del Roy's comments, I intend to spend an hour making some progress with the assault on Pamela Wilson. After that, it's time I bring Xavier and Tyrone in. But to do what I have in mind, I'll need help from the District Attorney's office. I need to offer a deal and play one of these guys against the other.

I don't want to call the District Attorney directly, as he was Bossy-boot's father. That would be too weird. So, I call one of the ADAs I've worked with before. I talk him through the case and my plan, and he agrees to offer a deal and to attend meetings with me the following morning. I hang up, feeling good. These two guys are in for a shock.

First, I call Xavier Rivera and invite him at ten the following morning. He tells me he'll bring his attorney. I agree with him that it would be the wise thing to do. I actually want an attorney whispering in his ear. Attorneys are usually easier to play against each other than their clients, in my experience. They're familiar with deals and understand how to weigh the probabilities of conviction and the likely sentences. Clients are too suspicious. Attorneys are pragmatic.

I hang up and immediately called Tyrone Ross at the gym. I

have to wait while they find him, and he's breathless when he comes to the phone. I suspect I've dragged him out of the ring. I give him the same invitation. He gets stroppy. I repeat the invitation. Then he tries to tell me he doesn't see the need to talk with me any further. So, I tell him I'm sending a patrol for him within the next twenty minutes. I don't have time to see him until the following morning, so he should shower, then prepare to spend a night in the cells.

He suddenly changes his mind and tells me he will attend in the morning but will bring his attorney.

With that all setup, I book two small interview rooms downstairs for ten the following morning and check that I have all the necessary information and photographs. I'm good to go. No, I'm better than that. I'm on a white steed, delivering justice for Pamela Wilson - a woman who thrashed people for money. A blackmailer and quite probably a killer. Still, she had been abused in a most degrading fashion, and those responsible shouldn't escape punishment.

I return to the team conference room when they're discussing ordering Chinese for lunch. No way can I spring for Chinese, so I tell them I'm fine. Dene leaves to place the order, and Jamie updates me on what the team has been doing since I left the previous night. They start with the order of deaths.

The earliest was six years ago in Tallahassee in the north. Then five years ago, across on the northeast coast in Jacksonville. Four years ago, it was Gainesville to the southwest of Jacksonville. Three years ago, it was Orlando in central Florida, then two years ago, it was Fort Pierce over on the lower east coast, and finally, the last death was in Miami. So there's an unmistakable trail of death from north to south, zigzagging on the way.

The two remaining names are living here in Naples and up in Tampa, which will more or less complete her round trip of Florida.

It is excellent work and suggests where to start looking for a twelve- or thirteen-year-old girl in County records. Up in Leon County. Where everything started.

Kathy tells me they've created a list of the Counties involved and shared them, two a piece. Dene has Leon and Duval in the North. Jamie has Alachua and Orange in Central Florida, leaving Kathy with Palm Beach and Miami-Dade. Each has already contacted designated counterparts and requested the case files.

At that point, Dene returns, lunch mission accomplished. The food will arrive in thirty minutes. My stomach's rumbling at the thought of it.

I've long since burned through my waffles, and extra coffee isn't enough.

As if I'm not impressed enough by the team's achievements, Dene now explains how they've already narrowed down the two names on the list who are, as yet, believed to be still alive. Jon Smith and Joseph Wright.

There are three possible Jon Smiths in Naples but only two Joseph Wrights in Tampa. They've already contacted Hillsborough and asked someone to talk with each of the two targets in Tampa. To warn them they may be in danger.

Jamie, Dene, and Kathy have each taken a possible local target in Naples, contacted them initially by phone to give them an early warning, and arranged to meet them personally later in the afternoon. All three are coming into the office. No doubt confused and worried. By rights, one of them really should be.

I can't imagine how these people must feel having it explained that their names are on a serial killer's hit list. What are the chances?

I ask the team what they're planning on tackling next. First, they want to see if they can figure out why these particular people are being targeted. Pamela Wilson had caught the young girl on video three years before. Only three of the homicides had occurred by then. The three furthest to the north.

Yet she was in Naples visiting a dominatrix with all six homicide names already on her list. Then she goes north again to Orlando to the first of three more kills before presumably returning to Naples for kill number seven. This doesn't fit the orderly flow we mapped out for her, moving gradually from north to south.

I shudder to think she had this whole State-wide killing spree planned from the age of twelve.

It seems she's left us a clue somewhere in her route, but we can't figure out what it is.

After some inconclusive discussion, we're moving on just as they send the food up from reception.

Suddenly, the energy level in the room shoots up as they start opening boxes and sharing food around. I'm preparing to make some feeble excuse to duck out when Kathy says there's too much for the three of them and that I should help myself. Boy, I'm conflicted, but not for long. Hunger wins out.

I tell myself I'll pay everyone back if I ever get out of this financial hole. But they have about as much chance as my Papa has. Easy to make these promises. Much harder to keep them. Which is why I remain silent.

We continue talking as we eat but move nothing on. When we finish, I thank everyone for sharing lunch. Kathy jokingly says that lunch will be on me next time. I try a laugh it off, but it's a struggle.

We break up after that, with them each heading to meet with their respective Jon Smiths and me intending to get on with my prep for the next morning's sessions with Mark's gym buddies.

I haven't even sat down when Jerry arrives.

'Fancy a coffee upstairs?'

On the way up, I ask him how he's doing after his fall through the floor at the Project. He shrugs it off, saying a few painkillers, and he's more than ready to catch some bad guys. I can relate to that. His mentioning painkillers makes me realize, for the first time, I haven't taken any all day. Another first. On the way, I also tell him about my late-night conversation with Chico. But I don't get the response I'm expecting. He grins. No *'be careful'* or *'watch your back.'* Just a stupid grin. What am I supposed to make of that?

Shortly afterward, we're sitting in the conference room in Narcs. Jerry's entire team is present. Something's about to happen, and I'm getting a sinking feeling in my gut. It's something big, and I don't need anything else on my plate right now.

Jerry kicks off the discussion.

'I heard from Dade County this morning. They busted a dealer in the south side of Miami yesterday. He has a list of previous convictions and is looking at a long stretch. Longer than he fancies, apparently. He's offering a deal. He wants to walk, but that's just his starting point. He knows that's never going to happen. But he's also confident we will want what he has to offer.'

At that, he goes silent and looks around the room, from face-to-face.

'Anyone care to guess?'

No takers. He carries on.

'He wants to give us the Naples branch of the Savage City Gangsters.'

'You're kidding, Jerry?' I say, in shock.

'Nope. He says he knows where they hang out, where they cut the drugs. How and when they're supplied. How they distribute. He even hinted that something was going down in the Project.'

One guy let out a low whistle.

'Will Dade County deal with him?'

'They say it's up to us. If we want to take these guys out, they'll do a deal. What do you think?'

At that point, the meeting breaks into a noisy rabble, with everyone talking at once, each trying to shout louder than the other. I don't become involved. I'm just quietly recalling my conversation with Chico back at my apartment the previous night. How the little fucker had tried to intimidate me. I guess I'm smiling when Jerry speaks to me.
'Looks like your in, Sammy?'
'You bet your ass I am.'
Will I ever learn?

30

I'm back in my cubicle an hour later, thinking about the Serial-killer case again. I'm struggling with many small details that either don't fit or aren't yet fully understood. How did this girl develop such a Statewide plan when she was only twelve? Why was she visiting the dominatrix in Naples after three homicides - when this was way off her north-to-south route? Why did Pamela Wilson video-record the girl when she clearly didn't fit her retirement plan criteria? And why would she have kept it? Did that result in her being killed three years later? Why did the girl choose Pamela Wilson in the first place?

The more I sit thinking, the more I don't understand this whole case.

A cough behind me snaps me out of my thoughts, and I turn to find it's Jimi.
'I thought I should let you know how I'm getting on finding the guy who robbed the garage you asked about.'
Of course, I've forgotten all about the garage, but I try my best to sound enthusiastic.
He tells me he has singled out almost twenty further break-and-entries in the past six months that look like they could be by the same guy. He then says he's gathering security and street-cam details for all the locations and that he's hopeful he'll soon have a photo to work with.
I make encouraging sounds and thank him.

He's about to leave when I ask him if he can handle another task. Part of the big serial-killer case we are all working on.

He gives me that same keen puppy look again.

So, I lay out the details of the task I want fresh eyes on, and off he goes, almost skipping. His enthusiasm takes me back. Is it only three years since I joined Homicide?

I see in the conference room the others beginning to drift in, and they're carrying what looks like the homicide files from the other counties.
I make a coffee and go join in.

They each update the room about the particular Jon Smith they've met with. They haven't found any apparent reasons they might be the targets other than a feeling Dene got from the guy he talked with. He was left thinking the guy had come in expecting a different conversation. He was twitchy and nervous throughout their discussion, and Dene didn't think it was because of the Serial-killer's list. We label him JS1.

We spend the next few hours wading through the homicide files, looking for reasons these particular victims are being chosen or anything else that might tie all the cases together.

It's nearly five when we finish and start discussing what we've learned.

All cases are knife attacks, expertly and accurately executed. None targeted the femoral artery. All lethal at the scene. No witnesses. No DNA. No suspects. All single men. Only the two on the sexual offenses register. No criminal records for the rest. All died in their homes. All lived alone. All in their twenties. No pattern in their employment.

We're no closer to understanding anything and are frustrated.

So we decide to go back and review the goals we set.

1 Find and protect. This has translated into find and *warn*. Unfortunately, we don't have the budget to protect all of these individuals.
  2 Establish contact with all other Counties involved. Done.
  3 Discover how people are being targeted.

At this one, I suggest we need to be more specific. It looks like the killer already had all the names on her list when she started up in Tallahassee when she was twelve or thirteen. So we need to understand why these people were targeted - not through current eyes, but six years ago. Everyone agrees with that. After that, we carry on with the priorities.

4 Look for patterns across the killings. All we can agree is that she's an expert at killing with a knife. Kathy asks if that makes her the most likely suspect in the killing of Pamela Wilson, and in the nascence of anyone else as yet, it's hard not to agree. Still, it's another thing that doesn't fit. The video was taken three years ago when she was only halfway through killing the first six people. Why would she then suddenly come back and kill Pamela Wilson? Nobody has any suggestions for that.

5 Establish *why* these particular people?

6 A further review of evidence from Pamela Wilson's home, including the videos. I asked Dene to do this.

7 Find out if Pamela Wilson had an assistant. Jamie offers to take that one.

8 Need for a psych profile for the killer. Kathy said she would arrange for copies of all the homicide files to be sent to Luisa del Roy, the psychiatrist. I offer to follow up afterward.

After this, we all agree that if we have any spare time between individual assignments, we'll spend it trying to figure out why these people are being chosen. If we understand that, everything else will fall into place.

I explain to everyone that I will be busy the following morning with Mark Jason's gym buddies but will still be in the building if they need me ' Then, I head out of there.

Rather than take a cab - it's dark outside but an ideal temperature - I walk home. I want to pick up a couple of my favorite kebabs on the way. Also, the night air will clear my mind and give me a chance to think.

I try using the insights Luisa del Roy has given me to put myself into the shoes of a twelve-year-old girl who has perhaps been repeatedly abused from God alone knows how young, by one or more people she should have been able to trust. That's a tough ask. I have no idea how she might feel. She was just a kid. Maybe she was taken into care? Perhaps she couldn't trust anyone, and who would blame her? Did she run away? Live on the streets? How did she eat? Where did she sleep?
    Somehow against all odds, she survived. Full marks to her. I don't think I could have come through something like that. But, of course, she didn't strictly come through the experience undamaged. She came through seeking revenge.

That makes me wonder, who would she want to take revenge on? Of course, the obvious answer would be the people abusing her. So, was the first victim her abuser?

Excited by the thought, I try to go through the file for the Tallahassee Vic in my mind. If he was abusing her, he likely had been for some time, perhaps years. Then, suddenly, she snapped and stabbed him to death.

No way. It didn't happen like that. All the victims were

carefully targeted. My recollection of the Tallahassee case is the victim died from a severed carotid artery. Everything was planned with precision. If he had been a relative, she would have been found and forensically examined, which she wasn't. So he must have been a stranger. But not just any stranger. A particular stranger.

I arrive at the kebab shop, buy two, then remember Trace waiting at home and order two more. Ten minutes and six flights of stairs later, I arrive home. Trace is in my beanbag watching tv. We say hi, and I put the kebabs straight into the oven before changing into sweats and the Blades shirt, feeling strangely uncomfortable that someone else is in the room with me as I'm doing this.

When I'm ready, I make a simple salad with tossed greens with a little vinaigrette, and Trace and I sit side-by-side, enjoying the meal. She tells me how she bought a sandwich from the back of a deli for a dollar-fifty for lunch and still has eighteen dollars, fifty of my cash left. I tell her that's impressive and mean it. She's survived a day on a dollar-fifty.

Trace asks me how my day has gone. She already knows I'm a detective, but not that I'm with homicide. When she finds out, she's impressed and full of questions. At first, I'm reluctant to talk with her about work, but she has a sharp mind, and while not giving too much of the case away, I do begin to use her to help think through some of the things still worrying me.

Knowing how to buy food from the rear of a deli has already given me an idea of how the serial killer I'm looking for might have found one of her victims. If she lived off the streets the same way as Trace, maybe that's how she met him. Someone who worked in the kitchen of a small 24/7 dinette. A chef, or perhaps just someone who washed up. Maybe he gave her food? Felt sorry for her. Took her home?

* * *

No. That doesn't make sense. She's looking for revenge, not just to kill some poor guy trying to help her. It has to be more personal. Maybe he takes her home and tries to assault her? Bringing back all kinds of bad memories. So she lashes out?

No to that one either. None of the killings are random. They're carefully planned, as is her escape.

Trace nudges me out of my musings by asking what I'm thinking of doing.

I assume she's talking about my case, but she isn't. Instead, she's talking about what I intend to do about her. After figuring that out, I tell her I honestly haven't had time to think about it, but until I have, she's welcome to stay. She laughs and tells me I can take as long as I like. No problem.

As I laugh with her, I realize that this apartment has never heard the sound of laughter before other than during MASH. I suppose when people live on their own, they don't go around laughing at their own humor. But this is a nice feeling. It somehow makes the apartment feel more like a home than just somewhere to be.

When we finish eating, I introduce Trace to MASH. She gets the program immediately, and we share more laughs as Hawkeye, Hunnicutt, Frank Burns, and company work their magic while saving lives.

Later, with Trace back in her sleeping bag, I lay in bed wondering once again about my other young girl and just how she has become a serial killer. She's meticulous in planning everything. Was she just born that way, I wonder? Even if so, she wasn't born knowing the most efficient ways to kill people. She had to find that out somewhere, and it was hardly likely to have been at school.

* * *

There was another thought. Something that having talked with Trace about education helped me consider. Was this young fledging killer at school in Tallahassee? We could check the yearbooks for the couple of years she would have been there around twelve. I immediately text the thought to the team. Someone will pick it up in the morning.

For now, I need sleep. But tomorrow will be a good day with Xavier Rivera and Tyrone Ross coming in.

I don't need the bones to tell me that.

31

The six am choice for the day is Elvis singing *'Jailhouse Rock.'* It's a song I've always liked, from a period of his music I like the best. I've deliberately preset the volume to the minimum so as not to disturb Trace, which works. She's still sleeping like a lamb.

Today, the music suits what I think will happen to Tweedle Dum and Tweedle Dee, Mark Jason's gym buddies. They're going away, and I'll make sure of it.

The action is due to start at ten, so I've time for a run and breakfast at EJ's.

Trace still has cash left from the previous day, but I leave a five on the breakfast bar, anyway.

When I arrive at EJ's, I feel so guilty about the size of my tab; I pay it off using some of the cash Papa gave me for the Honda. The Honda I don't have. It's payday in two days, so I can top-up the car fund then.

An hour later, after a shower in the locker room, I'm heading upstairs when my cell rings, and I answer it to find it's Arnie Collins, the Medical Examiner. He wants to catch me before the day starts. Clever guy. He knows life usually goes to hell when we reach our desks. Until then, we're available.

I turn and go down to his office. I find him waiting and sit, he indicates, facing him. The last time I was here, he explained the experimentation that had been taking place at the Project -

and with my cousin. Hopefully, today's conversation won't be like that.

'Good morning, detective.'

I nod.

I don't communicate too well first thing.

I have to wind up gradually.

I've no idea why he wants to see me.

'Pamela Wilson. One of your cases, I believe?'

'Sure, you know that, Arnie.'

'Well, do you remember discussing whether she had ever had a child?'

'Vaguely.'

'I explained that normally it is easy to tell because of stretch marks, scarring from vaginal tears, or an enlarged cervix.'

'Fascinating.'

'Patience, detective. An exception would be if the birth occurred when the mother was very young. Much of the evidence would not be visible all these years later.'

'Are you going somewhere with this, Arnie?'

'I wasn't sure about your Pamela Wilson, and I don't like being unsure about details, as you know, so I ran an extra test.'

'Which test is that?'

'I checked for micro-chimerisms in her blood.'

'Micro what?'

'A micro-chimerism is the occurrence of small populations of cells with a different genetic background.'

'Okay, Arnie. Now you've got me interested. But you need to explain what you're talking about. Pretend I know nothing about micro-chimerisms.'

Arnie smiles. I don't think he believes I'm pretending.

'During pregnancy, fetal cells enter the maternal circulation, and maternal cells enter the fetal circulation. This happens as early as seven weeks of gestation and remains detectable in maternal blood for decades afterward.'

'So, if someone has been pregnant, they'll have some of these alien DNA cells in their blood?'

'Correct.'

'So, had Pamela Wilson been pregnant?'

'Yes, Detective. It's all been very interesting, really. I believe your victim had twins. Most likely as a naïve teenager.'

'Twins? Not two children?'

'No. These alien cells, as you call them, deteriorate with time. So, by studying the micro-chimerism density of each, I can say with ninety percent probability that they were both born at the same time.'

'Can you tell the sexes?'

'Yes, by studying the makeup of X and Y chromosomes, I would say she had a child of each sex.'

'Boy and a girl. Thanks, Arnie. Nice work.'

'But there's something else I need to remind you, detective. This woman was a long-term heavy user of cocaine. If she was already a steady user in her early teens, I think it's likely that this would have affected her children and that when they were born, they may have been seriously physically or mentally impaired.'

'Shit.'

'Quite, detective. One aspect of drug-abuse youngsters don't think about. Too busy getting high and having fun.'

On the way upstairs, I'm trying to get my head around this additional information, but I'm not thinking about Pamela Wilson.

I'm thinking about myself and Bossy-boots.

Does this mean that her microchimerisms are still in my blood? It was past seven weeks when I had the termination. It doesn't seem like I can ever escape what I've done. Maybe not for *decades*, according to Arnie.

I need a strong coffee to deal with this recent information, so go straight to the rec area. I stand there and drink a whole cup. In shock, vaguely aware of people coming and going, mumbling to me.

Armed with a second cup, I make it to my cubicle without running into anyone and sit, still struggling to get my head into this morning's game. I have two bad guys to nail. I need to focus.

I check the overnight reports, pull the file I've prepared for the morning interview with Rivera and Ross, and head to the small interview rooms at reception, where I will meet the ADA.

I'm still thinking about tiny bits of my unborn child swimming around in my bloodstream when I enter the room and stop dead in my tracks. The District Attorney, Cliff Bodie, sits at the small table sipping a coffee. Bossy-boot's father.

I'm speechless. He gives one of those quirky smiles. My insides flip. Fuck, he's still got it, whatever it is.

'The lengths I go to to see you, Sammy Greyfox,' he smiles.

I sit, still not trusting myself to say anything.

'You know I called dozens of times over the past nine months? And came round to your apartment at least twice?'

I nod. With still no idea what to say.

'I'm guessing I'm not a father?'

Now that could have sounded like an accusation, but it didn't.

But, he said it in fun.

'Guess not,' I manage. 'What are you doing here?'

'Thought I'd get my hands dirty. Deal with a proper case rather than the politics that take up most of my time.

'But why this case?'

'Don't you remember how we first met, Sammy?'

'How do you mean?'

'You landed that *cop-killer* case eighteen months ago and solved it. Now, here we are again, another cop-killer case, so it seemed appropriate, that's all.'

'But this isn't about the killing of Mark Jason. It's about bringing two guys to justice for assaulting a woman who is now dead and unable to defend herself.'

'I've read the file. Like your proposed approach. Would love to help.'

I'm flustered. I am trying to figure out the chances of finding that Bossy-boots was still circulating inside me, with meeting her father on the same day. I feel like I'm receiving a cosmic message.

I fumble with my carefully prepared details, completely thrown off track. Until finally, the duty sergeant knocks on the door and tells me he has provided drinks to both guys and shown them into separate meeting rooms.

It's time to go. I've no choice.

32

I reckon I'll go a first round with the accountant rather than the boxer. So Cliff and I enter one of the small interview rooms and sit opposite Xavier Rivera and his attorney. Naturally, it's the attorney who speaks first. Earning his salary, I suppose.

'I want to point out, Detective, that my client is here purely voluntarily to help you with your inquiries, and as you have not charged him, we are free to end this meeting at any point.'

'Good morning to you, too,' I reply. 'I'm Detective Greyfox, and this is the District Attorney, Cliff Brodie. And you are?'

'James Delaney, attorney for Mister Rivera.'

I thank Xavier for his cooperation, telling him we have a few questions he can clear up quickly for us. He nods his agreement.

I remove a photo of Pamela Wilson from my folder and place it on the table before him.

'Can I ask if you know this woman?'

'I know a lot of women. Not sure about this one, though. Maybe?'

I take the picture and lay it on one side.

'Fair enough. Let me see if I can improve your memory. I would like you to return to two nights before someone stabbed Detective Mark Jason. I formalize Mark's role rather than ID him as a friend. I also want to mention the stabbing. Keep up the tension I can detect on Xavier's face.

'At around eight-thirty, you were drinking in the *All American Sports Bar* with your friend Tyrone Ross and

Detective Jason. Is that true?'

'I'm not sure. We go there regularly. I don't remember if I was there that particular night.'

I open the folder in front of me again, careful not to let him see what else is inside, and withdraw one photo from the security camera showing him with the two others. I put it in front of him and attract his attention to the date and time stamp in the top corner.

'Yeah, I guess I was. But like I say, we were in there regularly.'

'And what about the woman in this picture? Do you remember her now?' I ask, showing him yet another security photo from the folder. This one shows Pamela Wilson talking and drinking with all three of them.

I can see he isn't as confident now. He suddenly *'remembers'* they had talked with her at the bar for a few minutes. Dipstick. He hasn't realized I have the entire security cam video for the evening.

I then lay out several photos showing them at half-hour intervals, drinking at a corner booth, laughing, and having a good time.

His confidence falls another notch. He tries lamely to excuse his terrible memory, but no one believes him. Not even his attorney.

'Let's try this then, Mister Rivera. When did you leave the bar?'

His confidence goes up a notch as he feels on safer ground. This guy is so easy to read. No subtlety at all.

'I left with Tyrone around ten-thirty.'

'And Mark stayed behind with the woman?'

'I guess. I don't know. I wasn't there, was I?' he says, trying to be smart.

Time to get him on the hop. I ask him where he lives.

'Why do you want to know that?'

'Can you please just tell me?'

He gives me his address, and I write it down carefully.

I open the magic folder again and place a copy of a street

map of downtown Naples before him.

'I'm not familiar with where that is. Would you mind just showing me?'

He looks across at his attorney but gets nothing. So, he takes the pen I offer and circles his home address.

I nod sagely and thank him before moving the map to the side.

'When you left the bar, did you drive straight home?'

'I told you, I'm not sure because one night is much the same as another.'

'Well, what would you normally do then?'

Another look to his attorney, who is doing nothing for him. I almost hope Rivera isn't paying this guy very much. Or maybe that's the problem!

I tune back into Rivera's answer.

'Usually, yeah.'

'So, let's try something different. Can you confirm the identities of the two people in this next photo for me?'

I'm showing him a security cam photo from the car park outside the sports bar.

'Not sure. It could be Mark and the woman you showed me before?'

'Yes, that's what our facial recognition systems tell us.' White lie. There isn't enough detail for the FR system to ID them. I carry on.

'Well spotted. Can you see the time stamp?'

'Sure.'

'They left five minutes after you. Is that right?'

'Didn't know that. As I said, I wasn't there.'

I lay another photo in front of him showing him leaving the car park in his car *after* Mark Jason.

'Of course. You had already left by then,' I said sarcastically. 'So perhaps you can explain this photo to me?'

Confidence severely punctured, he mumbles but can't come up with a credible answer. I let him off the hook and move on.

'Don't worry, Xavier. I understand it's hard to remember. You're there most nights, and they all blur together. Why don't you look at this next picture?' I say, showing him Mark Jason with Pamela Wilson in his car, turning into the small estate he lives in, some ten minutes after leaving the club. 'Do you recognize where that was taken?'

He says not. So I explain and say it looks like Mark had taken the woman home with him.

Xavier helpfully says that's a surprise to him. Not the brightest bulb in the box. I've made an excellent choice picking him first.

I then show him his car turning into the estate, two minutes behind Mark.

'And this would be you? Apparently, according to where you indicated on the map, not going directly home. In fact, traveling in the opposite direction from your home.'

His attorney is now advising him not to say anything more with this line of questioning.

I nod my consent and switch the topic. I pull out a picture of Pamela Wilson lying dead in her home and place it slowly and deliberately in front of him.

'What can you tell me about this?'

He hasn't seen that coming, and the color drains from his face completely. His attorney answers for him.

'My client knows nothing of this matter.'

I take another series of photos from the file during the autopsy and spread them out before him one at a time. These showed the bruises on the arms and legs and around Pamela's throat.

'What can you tell me about how these occurred, Xavier?'

'My client is not obliged to comment,' his attorney interrupts.

I gather everything up and replace it all in the folder. Then pull out another photo of Mark's most recent ex - Emily Jason.

'Do you know this woman?'

He nods and identifies Jason's recent ex.

I take the photo back and lay out another. This time Mark's previous ex - Lynda Goldway.

'And this one?'

Again, he tells me who she is.

I clear my throat and spill some other white lies into the room.

'Both women are prepared to go on file claiming your involvement in sexually abusing them, along with Tyrone and Mark Jason. You were violent with them and often left them bruised and in pain. Do you have any comment on that?'

The attorney is quick off his mark this time.

'My client has no comment to make at this time.'

After a few moments of pregnant silence, Cliff enters the conversation for the first time, addressing himself directly to Rivera.

'You may wonder why I am here personally and not one of my ADAs. It's simple. Let me explain.'

He pauses. Waiting to make sure Rivera is tuned in and receptive.

'We are talking this morning to both yourself and Tyrone Ross. One of you will undoubtedly tell us what happened on the night in question. With whoever does so first, I will not mention any previous incidents in court. I will not be offering this to both of you. We are interested in understanding what may have led to the death of a detective, and you may help us do that. For that, I am prepared to be lenient. When Detective Greyfox and I leave, we will have the same conversation with Mister Ross, and I will make him the same offer. The first to accept will get the deal. The offer is on the table until two pm this afternoon.'

After I'm certain Cliff is finished, I return all photos to the folder, rise and follow him from the room.

Outside, I ask Cliff how he thinks it has gone. He says that if his attorney is half-decent, chances are fifty-fifty, but I've given it an excellent shot.

With nothing more to say, we enter the second small interview room and repeat the whole thing with virtually the same result.

Finished by midday, Cliff asks if he can take me to lunch. Of course, this is the last thing I want, but he's so damned nice about it. I can't think of a way out.

One of the things I miss about Cliff is the guy has class. He doesn't do Subway or Mcdonalds'. I don't think I've ever seen him eat fast food.

Lunch is fifteen minutes away at Pazzo, a local Italian upmarket restaurant. A place that has highly polished silverware, three different glasses by each place setting, and neatly folded linen napkins.

I knock the place. But it has style. I'm only glad he has offered to pay.

We spend most of the walk there, discussing my main case. He seems genuinely interested. Again, it is a serial killer running amok across the whole State. What District Attorney wouldn't be?

When we arrive and are seated, we order sparkling water and stay away from wine. Cliff then orders a simple Caesar salad, but I can't pass up the opportunity to have homemade pasta, so I order the linguine-alle-vongole, made with fresh clams in white wine with garlic and lemon.

Having danced around anything serious for as long as possible, I surprise myself by telling Cliff about having Bossy boots circulating in my bloodstream. He laughs and suggests she's probably still kicking ass and in control, just as she was when I was pregnant.

It surprises me how comfortable I am talking with him about Bossy boots. I haven't spoken to anyone about her for almost nine months, and it's nice to do it with someone who understands.

He asks me how the termination procedure went, and I tell him I was early enough to take a couple of tablets. No invasive procedure at all.

I ask him if he can forgive me for how I dealt him out of the whole thing.

He says there's nothing to forgive. In his opinion, it was my decision and not an easy one. So, whatever I needed to do to get through it, was okay with him.

I ask him if he's upset that he's not a father.

He laughs and says that he hasn't given up hope yet. That one day, he was sure he would be a father when the time was right.

Then, he asks me if I think I will ever be a mother. I tell him I have no idea. How this time, I had chosen my career over Bossy-boots. But I don't know if I will make the same decision again. Part of me misses her, and now knowing something of her is still floating around inside me - makes me miss her even more.

Lunch is first-class, and we leave the restaurant having cleared conversations that should have happened months ago if I'd been brave enough. It's hard to explain, but I feel lighter as if someone has lifted a burden from my shoulders.

We walk back to the office, simply enjoying each other's company. I'm happy for the second time in just as many days. Both times in the company of others. I wonder if there's a message there for me.

33

We start again with Xavier Rivera. He begins by admitting that I was right. He and Tyrone had followed Mark back to his place that night, and things got a little out of hand when Pamela revealed she was a dominatrix. He said it was Mark's idea to let her experience what it was like to be dominated. So, naturally, he was only a virtual bystander. But, of course, he would have done nothing if it hadn't been for Mark egging him on. Classic *blame the dead guy* response.

Ten minutes later, it's as if they have conferred in the other interview room. Tyrone Ross's explanation is the same. Mark was responsible. Mark made him do things he didn't want to do. So he was innocent.

Both Xavier and Tyrone want the deal. They don't know I've been bluffing about Mark's two exes being prepared to press charges.

Afterward, I talk with Cliff in the corridor. I thank him for lunch and tell him I've enjoyed seeing him. He asks if he can see me again, and I say I'll have to think about it, then I leave him to oversee Mark's two gym buddies being charged. They will both get the same deal and be charged with the assault of Pamela Wilson.
    As I go upstairs, I should be congratulating myself for getting justice for Pamela. But, instead, I'm savoring the time

I've just spent with Cliff.

Deciding not to stop at my cubicle, I make straight for the coffee area, then the conference room we have sequestered for the team. As I arrive, they're in the middle of an intense conversation.
My arrival seems to dampen the excitement.
Jamie explains what they've found out.
'We think we've found her.'
'What? You've captured her?'
'No, we've found out who she is.'
I sit back, feeling stupid. Jamie carries on as if he hasn't noticed.
'We all worked on this one together, and we've found out a lot about her. Her name is Charline Ellis. But apparently, she goes by the name Charlie.'
Jamie hands me a printout of a picture of her in custody. She's so much younger than the sixteen-year-old I had seen in Pamela Wilson's video, but I can see the likeness.
'We were right to suppose a troubled childhood, starting as early as five years old, but probably earlier than that. She was five when her teacher at kindergarten became worried about her and reported her concerns to Child Services. They took her into custody and had her examined by a doctor who confirmed both vaginal and anal injuries consistent with sexual abuse. An investigation ultimately ended with her father being charged. We've checked. He's still serving time now.'
'And she was only five?'
'Didn't get any better for her after that,' he continues. 'She was in care for about a year before being taken in by a foster family, where she lived for two years until she was further abused. Here, the foster mother's brother was their babysitter and the culprit. After that, she spent another year in care, during which a psychiatrist assessed her as having PTSD and ADHD. In other words, they have difficulty concentrating and interacting normally with others. Her social skills were close to

zero.'

'No surprise there, then? What happened to her after that?'

'A second foster family took her in.'

'Don't tell me the same thing happened again?'

'Fraid so. This time it was the foster father renting her out to a handful of his buddies.'

'Fuck. That's awful. How could someone do that?'

'There are just some bad people in the world.'

'So by now, she was what? Eleven?'

'Yes. Only with her history they would never give her out to foster care again, so they institutionalized her. She started Junior High there. She was twelve.'

'What happened next?'

'It's not what happened next that's interesting. It's what happened when she started Junior High. Because she had such poor attendance in grades two through six, they gave her a series of aptitude tests, and she came through with flying colors. They rated her above one-thirty in the IQ tests, which was incredible given her lack of proper schooling.'

'I don't know how you all feel, but I'm not up there. I can tell you that.'

'We already admitted that to ourselves before you came in. This girl was super-smart, even at twelve years old. What was extra special is when you look at the measurements the particular IQ test was taking - use of language, ability to reason, speed of thought, visual-spatial awareness, memory, and math.'

'Math? Surely she didn't have enough classroom hours to excel at that?'

'No, she didn't. So she would have flunked out in one category yet still come out extremely high. The girl is super-super-smart.'

I'm trying to absorb the thought of someone so young being so clever, but Jamie hasn't finished.

'Then, the school she attended entered some pupils in an online game in the public domain and open to all ages. Guess who won?'

'Charlie?'

'Apparently, there were over ten-thousand entrants, and some were in their teens and twenties, spending their lives locked in bedrooms playing online games.'

'And she had no previous experience of the game?'

'None.'

'Well, that sure explains a lot.'

Dene takes over at that point and describes what they have been discussing since finding this out.

'Think of the skills they measured in her IQ test. *Ability to reason* - given her distorted view of parenting and families, it's easy to understand how she could have used this skill against family members or men in particular.'

I nod my agreement.

'*Speed of thought.* She escaped shortly after this and has evaded being recaptured. She has also survived as a twelve-year-old girl on the streets, where she must have had to escape some tricky situations. Quick thinking would be essential, and she would need the ability to adapt to different situations.'

'What do you make of her winning that online game?'

Kathy answers. 'I've played the game she won a few years back. I tell you, it's difficult. First, you need an overall strategy, then you plan your tactics but change whenever you have to. So, strategy, planning, and flexibility. You also need to be single-minded and dedicated. Part-timers don't do well.'

'So, even at twelve, this girl is brilliant with computers and has all the skills she would need to become the serial killer we're looking for?'

'And,' added Kathy. 'Plenty of motivation.'

I sit back and summarize what we've found out.

'So we know who she is. We think we can understand why she has become the way she is. We know she has the skills to plan and execute these killings. Have I missed anything?'

Jamie adds one more item.

'Remember in her assessment. They rated her highly on visual-spatial awareness.'

'Sure, I remember.'

'Think of the six homicides. Clean single strikes delivered with deadly accuracy. She knew exactly where to strike and executed each time perfectly.'

'Okay. What about why she has chosen her particular victims? Any ideas?'

Blank expressions are the only answer I get. Unperturbed, I congratulate them on making such fast progress before turning to what we need to do next.

'Obviously, we should figure out how she is targeting her victims. Have we got the updated artist's impression of what she looks like now as a nineteen-year-old?'

'Yes. We can get that circulated along with her name,' said Jamie.

'Let's communicate what we have with the other Counties. Keep them onside.'

Kathy asks what I think about Pamela Wilson's death and argues that we should add her to the list of Charlie's victims. The weapon used doesn't match, but the placement accuracy of the deadly strikes does. I'm unsure, but I find the logic hard to argue with.

While we're all thinking that over, I tell them I've asked Jimi to give us some fresh eyes on all the evidence from Pamela Wilson's home and that I'll follow up on that with him. Maybe he can provide us with something new to work with.

I quickly update them that the District Attorney is charging Mark Jason's two cohorts with the assault of Pamela Wilson. Everyone's pleased with that.

We agree to meet the following morning again.

It's been a long but productive day, and I'm ready to head home. This time, I'm going to do some online research with Trace. It's time she realizes how unrealistic her request to live with me is. On reflection, I probably need the same advice. I'm noticing that I look forward to going home at night. Even my internal dialogue is changing. I would typically think about going back to the apartment, not *home*.

34

I save cab fare again and walk home. Everything's still going around in my head, and I don't even make it all the way when I text the team with a new question. *What ages was each of Charlie's abusers?*

I'm in my apartment making cheese on toast for Trace and myself when the answer comes back from Jamie. *Twenty-five, twenty-nine, and twenty-seven.*

Before I can even process the information, another text from Jamie follows. *'All the victims were in their twenties or early thirties.'*

Trace and I take our cheese on toast, me with a Corona, Trace with a Diet Coke, into the lounge area. Trace collapses onto my beanbag, now her default seat, and I sit on the two-seater.

I take a first bite, then ask Trace if she would like to help me look into future options for her. She asks if that includes living with me.

Not wishing to burst her bubble, I tell her it should include all options. We agree to finish eating, power up the laptop and see what we can find.

Before we finish eating, I receive another message from Jamie. *'backdated the vics ages to the time Charlie put them on the list, and they were all in their twenties.'*

It looks to me like Charlie is exacting revenge on people the same age as those who had abused her. That they were not

211

personally responsible doesn't seem to matter to her. At least maybe we're beginning to understand what she's up to and why.

When we finish our cheese on toast, Trace takes control of the laptop. Again, I can't help but see how comfortable she is working with an unfamiliar laptop without an education. This is precisely how my serial killer must be.

When I ask her about it, she explains that her formal education is non-existent, but she is street-smart, and technology's a way of life.

I don't ask, but I guess a lot of stolen cell phones and laptops would pass around her former community all the time.

She pulls up several relevant websites one after another, and we consider their content through different lenses. I confess I focus my lens on the difficulties, responsibilities, and costs. Her lens only sees the possibilities. She writes off my concerns with her positive need to succeed.

I read her a passage. *As a single parent, there is typically no break or relief—parenting is a 24-hour job. As a single parent, the individual will not only have to provide an income that can support two lives, but the individual must also tangibly care for the child to provide the youth with all the essentials to secure and maintain a productive life.*

Trace explains everything away by saying that she's no ordinary youth. That she's not only self-sufficient but can help me run my home life more cost-effectively. And she can clean and learn to cook, so I will live more hygienically and eat better.

I try a different paragraph. *When undertaking single-child adoption, you must understand the costs associated with the endeavor. Because of agency fees, national fees, traveling fees, and the costs associated with caring for a child, the single-parent adoption process is exorbitantly expensive.*

Her take here is that I don't need to adopt her. That she wants somewhere to live and someone to share her life with. Hearing the raw innocence of her thoughts expressed like that, my guilt floods me all over again.

Here I am, arguing complexity, expense, and legal issues. But what else can I do? I can't just have her live here, can I?

As we keep looking, we find another site that tells us that single adults of either gender can adopt children of either gender. But prospective parents of children above five should be between fifty and fifty-five. When we read this, without saying anything, we mutually agree to switch the laptop off and MASH on, which is how we spend the rest of our time together. Each silently wondering what we are going to do.

Later, in bed, I start thinking about Charlie again. She's far too intelligent and focused to be killing random twenty-something-year-old men. There has to be more to it than that. But then, I remember that two of them were guilty of child abuse involving seventeen-year-olds. That would be an excellent motivation for her in those two cases, but it doesn't explain the rest; something to think more about tomorrow.

That night, I have the best sleep in a long time and awaken to the Black-Eyed Peas singing about how *people killin', people dyin', children hurt, and can you hear them cryin'* on the lowest volume.

It makes me think of Bossy-boots again, but Trace and Charlie are also there this time. Life's becoming more complicated with all these kids to think about.

Stepping into the shower after my conversation with Cliff, I feel like Bossy-boots has finally forgiven me, and I'm now seriously considering seeing him again. If I do, we'll sleep together, and I don't think I'm ready for that, but I won't rule it out either. I wonder what he would say about me sharing my apartment with a street urchin?

After the shower, I again consult my body in front of the mirror. Butt ok, check. Knee okay, check. Boobs are still smaller than Kathy's - check. Everything's fine, so I select a turquoise shirt, trusty jeans, dress, badge, and Glock-up, ready to walk to the office. I'm just wondering why I haven't done more of this before when I remember that I struggled with my crocked knee for the best part of the last year. Then just when I'd recovered from that, it was my fractured butt, and before either of these, I had my trusty late Chevy.

This may be the new me. A walker.

I check Trace, but she's still sound asleep. Hard floor or not, I suspect she's enjoying the relative safety of the apartment. I can't imagine how frightening some places she'd slept in before must have felt. Places like the Project. I leave another five on the breakfast bar and head out.

My decision to walk is a good one. It's still cool, but the sky is clear, and the sun is on its way up when I arrive at EJ's. It certainly feels different not being soaked in sweat. I haven't considered it before, but my sweat and dry skin must be all over my booth. I know it would all be my own, but somehow sliding in still gives me the creeps.

I'm just about to order when Cliff slides in opposite me. I imagine the look on my face must be funny. But it gets a laugh from him.

I'm too surprised to be tactful.

'What are you doing here?'

'Well, that's not a friendly welcome, Detective. We ate out in one style yesterday, so I thought I would see how the real world lives today. Can you pass a menu?'

I'm still in shock. I tell myself again; he doesn't do fast food. He shouldn't be in here.

The waitress pours us some coffee and asks if we are ready to order. He orders the full breakfast fry. I go for the cheaper option of waffles and hope he isn't expecting me to pay.

Sipping his coffee, he says that he hoped to find me here. That yesterday, he'd forgotten to ask how I was doing after the shooting almost a year ago.

I've been so busy since returning to work; I admit this is almost the first time I've thought about it. I plan to discuss it with Luisa del Roy later in the day.

When I don't reply, Cliff gently reminds me that his office carried out the independent review and provided recommendations back to the Sheriff that he had followed the review closely.

Again, he asks me how I am.

What can I say? As long as I am busy, I'm fine. Or, You're the first person to bring it up again. Thanks for that. But again, I surprise myself with the answer I give - the truth. That I honestly don't know.

He has this habit of being able to get me to open up to him like this. It's annoying, but also something I like about him. He's easy to talk with.

We talk all through breakfast, and like the true gentleman he is, he pays, then tells me he hopes I'll be in touch soon.

Ten minutes later, I'm at work, wondering what just happened. I watched him eat a full-fried breakfast and enjoy it. I've told him things I've never told anyone about the shooting. We laughed about quite a few things. Shit. Now I'm in a good mood and happy again. That's now three times in so many days.

I grab a coffee and head into the conference room to meet with the team. They're checking off the objectives we agreed on a few days before.

It seems like we're now left with two immediate objectives. To review the killing of Pamela Wilson and decide whether she was one of Charlie's victims or not. Then, to track down Pamela's assistant and bring him in for questioning.

I add a further aim. Figure out Charlie's next step and catch her.

After that, it's time to check in with Jerry in Narcs and see how he's getting on with bringing down Chico Vegas.

As I approach the Narcs conference room upstairs, I can hear the sound of raised voices. There are two other people in the room with Jerry, and I recognize one of them as his Lieutenant.

I don't know the other.

I look for his team and find them huddled at the rear of the room, drinking coffee and talking in whispers.

'What's up in there?' I ask, indicating the conference room.

'Fucking DEA.'

'What do they want?'

'We're only guessing from what we've heard, but it sounds like they don't want Miami allowing us to use their mole to wrap up the Savage City Gang here in Naples.'

'Why would they want to stop us doing that? That makes no sense.'

'It does if you think the alternative may be to let the guy buy his way out with information about the supply chain leading *into* Miami instead so they can cut that off.'

'So, Chico Vegas and his guys just find a new supplier and keep experimenting on people?'

'It seems.'

'Well, not on my shift, they won't. Can you guys somehow make sure they stay here for twenty minutes?'

'Sure. What have you in mind?'

'I'm going for the cavalry.'

With that, I head back downstairs.

Twenty minutes later, I'm back with the cavalry right behind me. Well, a *cavalry individual,* to be specific. But a very good one.

I knock on the conference room door and enter with Arnie Collins behind me.

The lieutenant immediately tries to tell me to leave, but I jump into the conversation feet first.

'It seems like you're struggling with a simple choice, gentlemen. To round up the Savage City Gang here in Naples or cut the supply chain feeding Miami? Which, by the way, will be replaced within days if not hours.'

'And who exactly are you?' asks the DEA agent.

'Just a concerned detective. Concerned how the Savage City Gangsters have used one-hundred thirty-four people most horrifically. This is our head Medical Examiner, and before you decide anything, I would like you to listen to what he has to say.'

Giving no one a chance to respond, Arnie quietly explains how the Project was a laboratory. How it was used to test various combinations of drugs on a population, nobody cared about. He then goes into the details of how badly affected people were. How much suffering the victims had gone through because of the uncontrolled experimentation, and the number of deaths had now climbed to nineteen and would probably go much higher.

One of the great things about Arnie is he naturally commands respect. It's not just that he's an expert in his field, which he is. It's more about his manner and how he speaks to people, drawing them in. In addition, his age adds a gravitas that no one else in the room can match, so he's on a winner with that.

I observe their faces throughout his explanation. I know where Jerry's coming from. That's a no-brainer. The DEA agent will obviously have his own agenda, and I guess I must respect that. But the lieutenant's on the fence. He'll probably want to support his team as any leader should, but he's also being forced to get involved in inter-departmental politics. If he has to have a career ahead of him, he must carefully consider which side to come down on. I don't know this lieutenant personally, but I do know that Jerry and his team don't rate him.

Arnie finishes what he has to say. Then asks if there are questions before thanking everyone for allowing him to speak and explains he has work to get back to.

When he leaves, I see from the lieutenant's expression that he is pissed at me and on the wrong side of this thing. But, at least I've taken my best shot.

Sure enough, he speaks first. Directing his comments directly at me.

'Well, detective. Thank you for attending a meeting to which you had no invite and for dragging the ME away from a busy workload to attend a meeting *he* was not invited to either, to tell us what we already know. I'm sure this will stand out on your performance review, although perhaps not in the way you might have intended.'

Jerry tries his best to support me, but it's useless. The damage has been done. The lieutenant has already decided. At least, that's what I think until the Agent from the DEA speaks up.

'First, Detective. I believe you are Detective Greyfox. Am I correct?'

'Yes, sir.'

'Then I would extend my condolences on losing your cousin. I was sorry to hear about that.

I believe he was just about to help bring in a dangerous man. A man we tried to prosecute many times and failed thanks to expensive attorneys.'

'Yes, he was.'

'As you rightly point out, cutting a supply line isn't a permanent fix. We're lucky if it has any noticeable effect on the streets at all before they establish a new one. As the lieutenant here has said, I was already aware of the damage caused by the SCG in the Project. But being aware of their despicable acts and the longer-term consequences of an experiment such as the one at the Project are very different. I appreciate you bringing your ME in to share that with me, and I will take on board everything he said when I go back to speak with my superiors.'

Then he finishes with a sentence I'm not expecting.

'I'll be recommending that we form a joint task force to bring down the SCG here in Naples at the earliest date. Thank you, Detective.'

I don't think my lower jaw hits the floor, but I'm not sure. What I *am* aware of is that I've made an enemy out of the lieutenant and need to make sure I come across as trite and thankful instead of smug the way I feel. I do my best, but he'll be the only one who will know if I succeed. Besides, I don't work in Narcs.

I doubt he'll make an alternative *positive* contribution to my performance appraisal.

Now it's time for a change of gear. I have a psychiatrist to see.

Jerry gives me a wink on my way out the door.

35

Maggie welcomes me and ensures I have a cup of fresh brew before I see Luisa del Roy for my second personal session. Since talking about the shooting with Cliff over breakfast, I'm strangely unconcerned about any further probing discussion with this woman. That I left here feeling so positive the last time was also helping.

This time, she spends quite some time explaining PTSD to me. I've heard the term many times in past years and always took for granted that I know what it is without stopping to understand it in any detail.

The way she describes it is so simple.

It explains many things about how I've felt in the past year. Why I've been so emotional - sad, angry, depressed? Why do I feel so guilty or hopeless and out of control? Why I've been behaving irrationally much of the time and have been finding concentrating and doing my job ten times harder than before? And most interestingly, why I've lost confidence and have such a low opinion of myself.

I've been going through these without understanding why. Just accepting them. It's clear to me now that I've been allowing all of these symptoms to change how I lead my life, not just at work but also in my personal life.

But now, once she has explained why I've allowed this to happen, it's easy to understand how she helps people recover. I don't think I've ever had such a meaningful conversation. It explains everything to me.

I feel armed with this new understanding of myself, and I know I'll now look at other people differently. I'll be more able to recognize people struggling emotionally and empathize better.

So, I'm already feeling better before we even run what she calls her simple little process. Knowledge can do that to you. It changes the way you think.

Thirty minutes later, I'm back in a cab heading downtown. The process del Roy used involved her relaxing me and having me recall troublesome times in my life in a specific and very unusual way. This, she explained, would help to calm down my past distressing memories and free my mind up to deal with my current life.

Based on how I'm already feeling, I think I believe her.

As I reach the Homicide Department, I can already feel a buzz in the air and know something is happening. I see both Dan and the Under-Sheriff in the conference room with the rest of my team. I head straight there.

As I enter, they stop talking, and Kathy updates me.

'There's another victim.'

'Jon Smith, here in Naples?'

'No. Joe Wright is up in Tampa. One of two we had warned about being on the kill list.'

'I don't understand. Surely they would have taken extra precautions?'

'Yes, if they *had* both received the message.'

'He wasn't told?'

'Officers knocked on the door of his apartment twice yesterday without getting an answer. They only found the body today because the downstairs neighbor complained about a stain on the ceiling.'

'A stain?'

'Turned out to be a mix of bodily fluids. According to the Medical Examiner at the scene, Joe Wright has been dead for six to ten weeks.'

'And nobody noticed?'

'He was single and unemployed, and his neighbors describe him as a real loner.'

As I'm absorbing this latest twist, the Under-Sheriff asks about the implications for our investigation. I have no answer for him. But Jamie does.

'Our killer is still active. Either the killer has substituted Pamela Wilson instead of Jon Smith here in Naples, or Jon Smith is next. But if it's the latter, we still don't know which of the three Jon Smiths is the most likely target.'

'Then get protection arranged for all three,' said Dan. 'We have no choice.'

I nod to Kathy, who leaves the room to arrange that.

'You think you've identified the killer, right?' asks the Under-Sheriff.

I explain our thoughts on it being Charline Ellis. Who she is. How the whole thing started, and why we think she's doing what she is. What I'm not able to tell him is *where* she is. Yet, that's obviously what he wants to know.

A little later, when Dan and the Under-Sheriff have left and Kathy's back, we sit trying to work out our new priorities.

When each of the three has taken two Counties to liaise with, Hillsborough isn't on the list. So Jamie volunteers to head up there and bring the detectives up to speed with everything we know.

Before he leaves, I ask everyone what they think about all of Charlie's victims being in their twenties, and Dene interrupts.

'I'm sorry, but with this fresh case in Tampa, I haven't told you yet.'

'Told me what?' I ask.

'Well, when you got us to understand that all of her victims were in their twenties, that made some sense, but it still didn't feel specific enough. And why are eight victims on the list? Why not three or eleven?'

'So?' I prompt.

'I went back through her history, and if you add up the number of people responsible for abusing her, I think it was eight.'

'So she's seeking revenge for eight assaults on eight random people? That doesn't sound right.'

'It's more personal than that,' says Kathy. 'It has to be.'

'We're missing something and need to figure it out,' I say. 'Unless anyone knows how to find her, let's make answering this question our number one task.'

With that, I leave them to it and head for my cubicle. I haven't checked for messages or gone through my emails for too long and feel out of touch.

I've been catching up for a few hours when Jimi stops by with an update. He sits, and I listen. Then, dragging him behind me, I head back into the conference room.

'You got to listen to this,' I announce, nudging Jimi to talk.

He's nervous at first but fine once he gets started.

'Detective Greyfox asked me to look into a question bothering her; how your serial killer found Pamela Wilson. I found her business cards with her pseudo-name in the evidence locker. She called herself Lady Jane. The card had an address and email. But it also had a web address at the bottom.'

'She has a website?' asks Jamie.

'Yes, and no. To be accurate, she *had* a website but appeared to have taken it down three years ago.'

'When she retired,' I add.

'Damn. At least that explains how our killer found Pamela Wilson,' said Jamie.

'Yes, but that's not all Jimi discovered,' I say. 'Go on, Jimi. Tell them.'

'I noticed we had her laptop in the evidence locker, so I signed it out. I know you have all been through it for mail and social media activity, but I gave it to one of the cyber-techs to look at. He managed to find where her website had been hosted and reconstructed it. When I went through the website contact history, I found the dialogue between Lady Jane and someone who identified themselves as Charlie Brown - the owner of Snoopy.'

'That's her,' interrupted Jamie. 'When I looked through her childhood, there was a particular picture of her when she was with one of her step-parents. She was holding a Snoopy rag doll.'

'Well spotted, Jamie.' I congratulate him.

Jimi has more to tell.

'That's what I discovered also. So, once I thought I had the killer's email, I started checking for other dominatrix sites around the State. I didn't know there were so many. This is big business, apparently.'

'How many?' asked Jamie.

'Too many to count. There were many pages of listings. But that's not what's important. I looked for dominatrixes in the locations of each of your victims.'

'Don't tell me,' said Dene. 'She visited others?'

'Correct. In fact, with help from cyber-tech, we found her email address in three other locations. Orlando, Palm Beach, and Miami.'

'Not Tallahassee, Jacksonville of Gainesville?'

'No.'

'But,' I add. 'Stop and think about it for a moment. When Charlie started on her killing spree, she was only thirteen. By the time she contacted her first dominatrix, she was sixteen and had already been killing for three years.'

'So she was too young to visit a dominatrix when she was thirteen to fifteen,' said Jamie. 'So, Pamela Wilson was her first? But she doesn't act like that on the video?'

'She must have been finding some other way to punish herself before discovering how a dominatrix could help her,' I suggest.

'Too young for a dominatrix, but not too young to kill in cold blood,' Jamie adds. 'This is fantastic work, Jimi. Well done.'

Pleased with the praise, Jimi leaves the room, and once again, we regroup.

'So, we're back to where we were before. Trying to figure out why our killer is targeting these specific people. If we can do that, maybe we will understand which of the three Jon Smiths to focus on protecting,' I say.

As if by divine intervention, my cell rings, and seeing it's Luisa del Roy, I tell the group and step outside to take the call.

'Doctor?'

'I hope I'm not interrupting anything important, detective?'

'No, not at all. How can I help?'

'It's the other way round, Detective. Or at least it may be.'

'I'm all ears. We need all the help we can get.'

'I've been reviewing all the case records you sent me and your current notes about Charline Ellis. First, I congratulate you and your team on what you have discovered. Well done.'

'Thanks, Doctor. I'll pass that along.'

'Okay. Now I see you have figured out that the number eight is significant?'

'The number of people who abused her as a child.'

'Yes. You also say you realize it's more personal than her randomly choosing eight names all these years ago, then methodically killing them one by one.'

'Sure. Have you figured out why she's choosing these names?'

'Not exactly. But let me ask you a question first. They took her into Junior High when she was twelve, but she didn't run away until she was thirteen. Why did she wait?'

I think about that for a moment, but nothing comes to mind.

'I don't know, Doctor. Tell me.'

'I think she was using the year to prepare. She was already intelligent and computer literate. At Junior High, I bet she had access to a school library and computers.'

'She was planning?'

'That's what I think. You realize that although still very

young, she was a clear thinker and strategist. She used that year to find the most suitable eight names for her revenge.'

'What criteria did she pick?'

'It would surprise me if it isn't something to do with abuse of other children.'

'But only two of the names on the list have ever been on the sex offenders register?'

'You know better than I, Detective.

Unfortunately, many more never get officially charged or put on trial.

'So, you think we should look for the fish that got away?'

'Precisely. And concentrate on news reporting for the year your suspect was at Junior High.'

After that, I thank Del Roy and head back to the conference room to update the team. Jamie has already left for Tampa, but the others are keen to hear everything.

When I leave, they're already starting to search news articles for that particular year. So it feels like we're finally getting a handle on the case. This is maybe going to be the breakthrough we need.

36

The walk back to my apartment on a balmy evening allows me to think back through the case and reassure myself that our priorities are correct. That we're truly getting close to understanding our killer. We need to ID which Jon Smith is on her list.

The other concern is whether we can justify using him as bait. A question I would never discuss with anyone else. I'm not even sure I want to discuss this question with myself. But everyone knows if you're going to catch a fish, you use bait.

If del Roy's other assumption is correct, then whichever Jon Smith is the one, he's had some involvement with child abuse, and it has to have been in the news. That's something specific I can look into when I get home.

When I open the apartment door, the first thing I notice is the smell. Someone's cooking and the smell is great.

I recognize Taylor Swift singing *'Shake it off'* on Alexa.

Trace is in the kitchen and opens our conversation with a reprimand.

'You must start letting me know when you're on the way home, detective. You're lucky tonight. I guessed right.'

'You've cooked?'

'I hope you like pasta?'

'I do.'

'Right, sit down,' she tells me, handing me a Corona from the fridge.

I do as I'm told and sit watching this twelve-year-old wonder open the oven and remove a casserole with a bubbling cheese topping.

'Cheesy pasta from a box. But I cooked it,' she tells me, laughing.

'It smells delicious, Trace. Thank you.'

As we eat, she asks me how my case is going, and I tell her we have three possible next victims and can't decide which would be the most likely. Perhaps one of them has been accused of child abuse, but he has no record as he wasn't charged.

Now, although, as far as I can remember, I haven't told her much about the case, she's brighter than I imagine. That becomes obvious when she mentions that if the killer had targeted one of these three people six years ago, she wouldn't have been using news streaming back then.

When she says this, my mind seizes up. How the hell did she figure that out? I don't remember telling her the killer created a kill list six years ago. But before I even ask, she explains her theory a little more, that the killer was probably accessing local press articles, or maybe she had online access to their archives.

When I hear that, I stop worrying about how Trace has figured this out and realize that what she says would agree with what Luisa del Roy told me. The killer was doing her research six years ago when she was in Junior High.

Trace pushes her empty plate aside, opens the laptop, and suggests we look at which newspapers were likely to have covered stories about child abuse story six years ago.

To my dismay, we find fifty possibilities in circulation within Florida alone. I'm about to focus just on the smaller number that has State-wide distribution when Trace suggests if we're only looking for reports of *possible* abuse, local press would be the most likely to cover the stories, whereas convictions would be by State-wide press.

At this point, I'm beginning to wonder which of us is the detective.

I log onto the Sheriff's office network and look back through our online notes on the case to check past locations for the three Jon Smiths. One of them has always been a resident of Naples. Another has been living in Arkansas until he moved here five years ago. The third was born and raised outside Panama City Beach and moved to Naples six years ago.

It looks to me like we can rule the Arkansas Smith out of the equation. It's unlikely that the press would cover a *possible* Arkansas abuse case in Florida. So, I'm down to two.

The one who lived in Panama City Beach six years ago would have been on her list there, but most likely, she would have killed him in the earlier stages when she was up in Tallahassee. Making a giant leap, I discard Panama Smith - number two.

That now leaves us with one to concentrate on, and I also know that he's a lifelong Naples resident, so I can easily single out the local Press. There are only two.

The Naples Daily News and the News-Herald.

Unfortunately, at that point, we run into a brick wall. Neither offers online research facilities for back issues.

Unable to get any further, I tell Trace I'll gain archive access through the office the next day, and we mutually agreed to stop thinking about it and enjoy a couple of episodes of MASH.

The following morning starts strangely with Alexa choosing to wake me to an old single by the Rolling Stones - *Lady Jane* of all tracks. I keep Alexa on a low volume to allow Trace to sleep.

I lay in bed listening to Mick Jagger sing the words - *My sweet Lady Jane, When I see you again, Your servant am I, and will humbly remain.*

I can't help but wonder if Pamela Wilson - AKA Lady Jane, is going to find peace and happiness in the afterlife. I guess I feel halfway to helping her achieve whatever might be possible, with two of her abusers being arraigned, but I still need to catch her killer to complete the job. That may bring her peace, but I doubt it will deliver happiness. If she killed Jason, it will haunt her forever.

With my body still feeling good, I quietly slip on the running gear, check that Trace is okay, leave ten dollars on the breakfast bar, and set off for one of my longer routes. As I run, I break my habit of not thinking. I don't mean to. It just happens.

In my thoughts, I'm back at Luisa del Roy's. She'd gone through a relaxation exercise with me. My eyes were closed, but I can still hear her voice guiding me through my past.

When she explained the process to me, I wasn't sure what to expect. Even now, having gone through the process, I'm still not quite sure what I think of it all.

Sure, the past events I thought about included the moment I shot and killed a two-year-old girl by accident, as well as my decision to terminate Bossy-boots, but these were all mixed up with other things that happened to me in the past, some even from childhood.

Thinking back now, it's strange the way my unconscious mind didn't seem to prioritize any one memory over another, regardless of how I thought it should.

In some way, I find that reassuring. I think the whole process has shifted the balance of how I view my past decisions or actions in a positive way.

Even now, as I run, I can sense my mind clearing. If not exactly razor-sharp, at least thinking more clearly than it has been for a long time. Del Roy said that I would feel different after a good night's sleep, and although, at the time, I didn't want to be skeptical, I was.

But here I am. Feeling better than I have in almost a year.

It's only when I finally slow down, entering the car park at the rear of the Sheriff's office, that I even realize I've been thinking all the way.

Fifty minutes. Odd. Never done that before.

Showered, changed, and when pouring coffee, I bump into Dan. After a few friendly exchanges, he asks me about the incident - his word, not mine - upstairs in the Narcs conference room. I give him my update. He gets it. I can see it in his eyes. He gives me a telling-off for interfering and for not respecting the lieutenant when he asked me to leave. I take it like a man. Well, as like a man as I can, given the obvious difficulties I have with the thought.

Dutifully contrite, tail between my legs, I head for the conference room to join the team.

First up, Jamie tells us about the victim up in Tampa. Joe Wright.

It fits our killer's profile perfectly. He was found naked on the floor in his lounge. He'd suffered one puncture wound to the carotid artery in his neck. It looked like he'd clamped his hand over the wound and staggered as far as his main lounge before collapsing and dying. There was no sign of anyone else being present in the apartment at the time of his death, which is obviously impossible. Because he had died so many weeks before, the body was in a state of advanced decomposition before it was discovered. The stain in the downstairs apartment ceiling was confirmed as decomposing body fluids. A mix of blood, urine, and decaying flesh.

I can't imagine how the downstairs neighbor might feel when they explain that to him. Creepy.

Determining a precise date of death was impossible, so the door-to-door visits hadn't turned up anything of specific use. The usual story, no one had seen or heard anything.

Other than that, Jamie has brought the Hillsborough homicide folks up-to-date on our investigation and offered to act as their liaison down here.

Dene and Kathy are about to explain what they've been doing, trying to find press articles that will help us understand how Charlie has put her kill list together when I interrupt and tell everyone how I have thought through the three Jon Smiths the previous evening. I don't mention that a twelve-year-old runaway, who's sleeping on the floor of my apartment, has done most of the work. Everyone agreed with the logic, and Kathy takes the action item to dig into the individual we're now calling JS3.

Next, Dene promises he will talk with several of the local Press agencies and get access to their archives. He plans to start his research as soon as we finish the meeting. Jamie offers to help.

I feel I've nothing else to add, so leave them to it.

Back in my cubicle, the macaroni and cheese from the night before has worn off, and my stomach's rumbling. So much so that Dan comes across from his cubicle and asks if I'm hungry. Yes, it embarrasses me, but he smooths it over by telling me he had little the previous night and is heading out for a sub. I tag along.

Half an hour later, we're sitting under an umbrella, enjoying two subway specials - his treat. I'm wondering if Dan has figured out how hard I'm finding it to get by month-on-month. He has turkey breast with all the fillings; I have a B.L.T. Two 7Ups, and we're all set.

I expect Dan to ask for an update on the case, but he doesn't. Instead, he asks how I'm doing with his ex - Luisa del R0y. He clarifies that he isn't asking about my treatment or anything personal. He's just wondering how she was to work with professionally.

I think I shock him with my positive response. To be honest, I shock myself. I didn't realize therapy can be so effective so quickly. It wasn't what I was expecting at all.

Dan seems pleased.

I suppose he feels responsible as he had taken me there from EJ's.

I tell him I've met Cliff for lunch and again for breakfast.

He just grins. I hate it when people do that.

I can see what he's thinking, so I correct him by explaining that we met *at* breakfast, not after waking up together.

He nods sagely and gives me a wink.

Unwilling to spend any more time under his inquisition, I turn the tables and ask him how his own love life is going.

He nearly chokes on some turkey but keeps chewing, choosing to ignore my question.

Not one to give up easily, I offer to give him a couple of introductions.

Nope. No interest. I swear the guy should join a monastery or something.

Back in the office, a message on my desk tells me to go see Jerry upstairs.

37

Jerry is in the conference room with his team and the DEA guy from the previous meeting. I knock and enter.

The DEA guy stops talking and turns towards me.

'Welcome, Detective. How does it feel to come into a meeting when you're actually invited?'

I don't know what I expected from the guy, but humor wouldn't be high on my guess list. I'm not one for lying down, though.

'Actually, I've got an open invite to this conference room, and am always welcome. How about you?'

'Touché, Detective. How about we start with an introduction? My name's Bond. James Bond.'

There's a strange pregnant silence in the room. Hard to explain, really, but I can feel the intensity of seven pairs of eyes burning into me. It's like a single moment in time, drawn out.

I stick out my hand and say I'm pleased to meet him.

As he takes my hand, I can sense the disappointment in the room when I don't come out with the line they're expecting.

I take one of the spare chairs and sit.

Jerry quickly brings me up to speed.

'We have the location of the SCG factory. It's in a small industrial estate on the outskirts of town. We've been told they use nearly fifty locals to cut and package the drugs. Although what these people are doing is illegal, they are innocents. We suspect many are illegal immigrants, but that's a different problem. So we have been discussing how to avoid these people being caught in a crossfire.'

Bond chips in.

'Based on many similar operations we've been involved in, they will protect the factory strongly. We can expect electrified fences, a gun emplacement, and they may have mined the approach from the rear.'

Jerry and his team go very quiet, and I end up in a one-on-one Q&A season with 007 himself.

'What's at the rear?'

'Until last year, it was swampland. But a construction company has the approval to build more industrial units there, so they have been infilling with sand and concrete for the past twelve months. The work is almost complete, but it needs to settle for a good while before they can build. They will probably start next year.'

'So, in the disruption, you think they've placed mines?'

'It's possible.'

'So, front entry then?'

'Front entry and by air is what we were debating when you arrived. The problem with air access is....'

'Rocket launchers?' I suggest.

'Excellent, Detective. Yes, that would be my fear. We've come across that before.'

'Any access from underneath. Sewage, maybe?'

'We've looked at that, but they aren't hooked up to the main waste management system. Instead, they use a large septic tank.'

'Can we cut off the power?'

'Yes, as long as we aren't counting on the element of surprise.'

'Do we know how many we will face?'

'Again, only from previous experience. There's likely to be at least twenty and possibly a few more.'

'And they'll be heavily armed?'

'Sub-machine guns at a minimum. The last place we took down was in Wichita. I brought these pictures to show you what we will likely be against.'

At that, 007 spreads a range of twenty or more photographs of the armaments they had captured. I don't recognize many guns, but I see a Sig Sauer long-range Sig50 sniper rifle. If they have even one of those and someone who knows how to use it, that could cause a problem. I also single out a Remington 870 Shotgun, usually sold for home defense. I wouldn't want to be caught in someone's house if they had one of these things. Beyond that, there's an AK-47, and would you believe a Browning? When I see that, I ask if he's serious about one of these being lined up against us.

'M1919 chain-belt bullet-feed-stacks around five-hundred rounds per minute. Been around since 1919. But it's still a timeless classic and deadly.'

Having browsed the photographs, the room has gone quiet again. Everyone undoubtedly thinks much the same as me. Fuck.

007 continues. 'Questions?'

As usual, I have.

'You say you've taken down places like this before? How did you do it, and can we copy that?'

'We have, but previously we've had someone helping from inside, even if it was just giving us the layout and an idea of the numbers and armaments we would be up against.'

'But we don't have that in this case?'

'Nope.'

'How about aerial surveillance? Can we get a drone over there?'

007 thought about that for a moment before saying we could, but it would likely give the show away if spotted.

Jerry suggests we use one of the newer drones with night-vision and infrared heat detectors.

Something we all quickly agree is a good idea.

007 then suggests that we get set up for a fly-over that night and reconvene the following day to review what we learn.

As the meeting wraps up, 007 asks me if I want to join him for coffee. I assume he means for us to use Jerry's coffee machine, but he means to *go out for a coffee*.

Having stumbled through not knowing what he meant, hopefully without looking too thoughtless, we head for the Fifth Avenue Coffee Company. A place where I know we can sit outside under an umbrella and watch the world go by.

007 is a good four or five inches taller than me but about the same age, mid-thirties. I can see he's probably clean-shaven every morning, but by mid-afternoon, his dark growth is prominent, leaving a strangely clean-cut line between dark growth and fresh skin down either side of his face. Dark eyes, almost black. Dark hair cut not quite crewcut level, but he would still pass morning inspection in the ranks.

I think he would pass most *women's* inspections with flying colors. So maybe James Bond isn't such a bad name for him after all.

When we have our coffees and are settled outside, we swap some everyday stuff about our personal lives. I confirm for him that I'm Native American and raised on the reservation up beside Fort Myers. I studied criminal psychology and started my career in the Miami Sheriff's Office.

In turn, he tells me he's Boston, born and raised in a small town to the West called Acton. He studied law and passed his bar exams, only to decide he didn't want to practice law.

Instead, he wants to enforce it.

So he joined the DEA ten years ago and is working out of the Atlanta division, but he is considering applying for a change.

Neither of us mentions that we're both single and unattached. I suspect he's as aware of the assumption as I am.

Inevitably, we start talking about the upcoming conflict with the SCG. He admits that it's quite a daunting prospect. He went up, in my opinion. In my experience, guys rarely reveal their fears. Stupid. Everybody has them. Why wouldn't you admit it?

Checking the time, I see it's virtually five. We've talked for the best part of two hours and haven't noticed. I've enjoyed that, and on the way back to the office, when he asks if I would like to have dinner with him the following night, this time, I don't hesitate.

At the car park, he heads off, leaving me to skip up the stairs wondering why life is suddenly so much more fun.

38

Having had extra playtime, I'm feeling guilty, so I make for the conference room to catch up with the team. I have another couple of thoughts about the case and need to follow up with the case files.

Jamie and Dene have moved the investigation on in my absence. I think there's more to this delegation thing than I've previously realized.

It's Jamie who explains their findings.

'We looked through the articles for who was in the press for that one-year timeframe when Charlie was in Junior High. We found all eight of the victims. The first is Laurence Spencer up in Tallahassee. As we already know, he was a porter at Cedar Ridge Academy. We didn't know that this is an all-girls boarding school for troubled teens.'

'And is where Charlie spent her first year?'

'Exactly. While she was there, the local Sheriff took him in when two girls made complaints against him over separate incidents. They didn't charge him as both accusations ended up with the - *he said, she said* - problem, and there were no independent witnesses. Charlie disappeared from the school at the end of the third term just after they found Spencer dead in his on-campus apartment.'

'Victim number one?'

'Looks that way. After that, we found similar accusations against all the people on Charlie's kill list, with only two convictions. The rest all failed to even reach trial, usually on technicalities.'

'So,' I said. 'We now know why she picked these particular men?'

'Looks like it.'

'Outstanding work, Dene. You too, Jamie.'

Turning to Kathy, I ask for confirmation that she has our local Jon Smiths safely protected for now.

'All three,' she assures me.

'But now, thanks to Dene and Jamie's excellent work, we know which one is at risk, right?'

'Sure do,' said Dene. 'We can take the protection details from the other two.'

'I'll do that now,' says Kathy, leaving the room.

'So, I would like to look at another detail,' I say. 'The knife being used. What do we know about that?'

Jamie answers. 'Got that one covered, Sammy. It's always been the same. The Medical Examiners all describe it as a Stanley knife or blade. Thin and razor-sharp.'

'It would have to be,' adds Dene.

'Why's that?' I ask.

'Think about how she gets close to her victims. Initially, she would use innocence in her early teens and allow them to think they were in charge. Then, they would entice her back to their apartments and start sexual advances. Finally, they might talk her into stripping, if not naked, at least to her underwear....'

'...she would have nowhere to hide a knife!' I finish. 'Brilliant, Dene. I think you're probably right. Although the same problem exists, even if it's a Stanley Knife. She still must conceal a naked blade somehow.'

Dene keeps going. 'I think that *innocence* approach makes sense for her earlier victims, but I am not sure it works so well as she ages.'

Then Jamie points out that if you consider the poor nutrition she's been suffering while living on the streets, combined with the under-developed body we saw in Pamela Wilson's video, she would still look young enough to be innocent, even at

fifteen or even eighteen.'
'And that innocence is her bait?' I conclude.
'Exactly.'
'We need to show her picture to Jon Smith.'
'I'll do that. I'm the one who spoke with this particular Jon Smith a few days ago,' Dene replies.

'So, we now know who the killer is, why she's killing. Why she has chosen her victims and how she kills them. As well as the identity of her remaining target. All we need to do now is find her. Any ideas, anyone?'

'We have an update on the artist's impression, aged to look nineteen. We plan to release that to every law enforcement agency in the County today.'

'Good. Anything else?'

'How about a public appeal?' suggests Jamie. 'You know - *Have you seen this girl? If so, contact us immediately.*'

'What are you thinking? Press or television?' I ask.

'How about both?' said Dene. 'We don't have any leads, so we need all the help we can get.'

'We would need to staff up to receive calls,' I say.

'Some lads will be more than happy with the overtime if you can approve it,' answers Dene.

'Okay,' I agree. 'I'll take it to the Sheriff. In the meantime, can you communicate our findings to each of the Counties involved? I want them kept with us on this entire case.'

'Another couple of things,' adds Dene. 'First, the fact that Charlie uses a naked Stanley blade should rule her out for the Pamela Wilson killing. In that case, the killer used a standard kitchen knife and left it at the scene.'

'Good thinking, Dene,' I tell him. 'You said a couple of things. What else?'

'You'll like this one. After Jimi's success going back through Pamela Wilson's computer, I thought having another look through all the evidence we took from her apartment might be worthwhile. So looking through her dominatrix outfits, I noticed a hollow tubular fold of material at the back of the nurse's uniform. It was roughly around eight inches long and an inch in diameter. I checked her other outfits on a hunch, and they all had the same. All empty until I looked at her faux-leather catsuit. And guess what I found?'

At this, he holds up a clear plastic evidence bag with a knife. A stiletto knife.

'The murder weapon used to kill Mark Jason?' I ask.

'That would be my guess. I wanted to show you first, but now I'll take it to Forensics and ask them to confirm Mark's blood is present.'

'So. She carried the stiletto for protection while doing her dominatrix thing?' I suggest.

'Yes. And if you recall, eBay sold this stiletto nearly ten years ago, which ties into when we think her dominatrix career started.'

'Well done again, Dene. More excellent work. I need to tell the Sheriff. He'll want to know that we've found who killed Detective Mark Jason. As soon as you have confirmation from Forensics, let me know.'

After this, I call the Sheriff's secretary, who tells me he's out of town for the afternoon, and make an appointment for the following day at nine sharp. That will give me time to prepare my case for involving the press and the public in the hunt for Charline Ellis. I don't think I'll have trouble convincing him, but it always pays to go there prepared. I'll also use Dan as a testing ground beforehand.

I can tell him about the stiletto at the same time. That should close Mark Jason's case. No prosecution. No further costs. A budget saver.

Checking the time, I decide to quit for the night. Another walk home in the dark. At least this time, I'm not hungry. As well as afternoon coffee, 007 had sprung for a Cannoli - made the traditional Sicilian way. Fried pastry tubes filled with ricotta cheese, mixed peel, and chocolate. Very rich and very filling. Before I leave, I remember that Trace has asked me to call and tell her when I'm about to head home, so I do just that. I ask if she's cooking again, and she tells me she's hoping I will order in. I ask what she wants and take her order for a pizza with chorizo topping.

Before leaving the office, I dial in the order and put the charge on my credit card. It will be delivered in thirty minutes. Time for me to get home, so I can at least join Trace for a drink.

It's nearly eight-thirty before I get to the apartment, and the pizza still hasn't arrived. I decide on coffee rather than a Corona, only to find I'm out of filters. Now I have a significant decision: instant or a trip to the 7-eleven. I choose the latter. Trace offers to get them at half-price - but when I decide I need my coffee, I'll pay any price. I tell her to start with her pizza if I'm not back and throw on my lightweight jacket.

Walking through the dark car park, there's no one in sight, but I still have that prickly feeling that someone's there somewhere. I halt suddenly, and whoever is following me is quick but not quick enough to prevent me from hearing one extra footstep.

I pull my Glock, whirl around and scan everywhere.

Nothing. Maybe Trace is following me. I already know she's good, but then I doubt she would leave the apartment when her pizza's about to arrive.

One more check before re-holstering my gun and continuing the journey.

At the store, I buy the filters and a six-pack of Corona - hearing Trace reprimand me in my head for wasting another four dollars - and start for home.

I only make it across the street when I find Chico Vegas leaning casually against a parked car at the curbside.

'Evening, Detective.'

'Are you following me, Vegas?'

'I'm just standin' here, mindin' my business, man. That's what I'm doin'. Ain't no law against that? You know. Passin' time.'

'Good. Cause if I thought you were following me, I wouldn't be happy about it.'

'Don't get riled, man. This is my hood too.'

I'm getting frustrated now.

'What do you want, Vegas?'

'You know, detective, Every time I see you, you carrying beer.'

'And every time I see you, I get a pain in my butt. So tell me what you want?'

'I was just wonderin' if you remembered our last conversation?'

'About leaving you alone? Can I point out you're the one who's following me around? I do not need to see you again, ever! Am I clear, Vegas?'

'But what about your friends? You gotta long list of friends.'

'If you mean the entire Sheriff's department? Yes, I have a lot of friends. And if any of them are interested in going after you for as much as dropping a cigarette butt, I'll cheer them on.'

'I don't smoke.'

'Not tobacco anyway, Vegas? You're not telling me you're weed-free?'

'Never touch the stuff, detective. It's illegal.'

'Look, Vegas. It's been nice talking with you, and if you wanted to remind me to leave you alone, consider your message delivered. Now, I've got a coffee percolator I would rather spend my time with.'

With that, I push past him, feeling his eyes penetrating my back. At least, I hope it's my back and not my butt. I don't want to think about him being close to my butt. It's had enough trauma recently.

39

I meet with the Sheriff at nine o'clock in the morning sharp as planned. I start with the highlight. The discovery of the stiletto.

I'm disappointed.

Not only does he already know, but he's also received confirmation from Forensics. *He* ended up telling *me* it was the murder weapon. Regardless, he congratulates me on solving the case. I point out that it has been a team effort. He grunts. I guess he's heard that line before.

Moving on to the serial-killer case, as I hoped, he had no problem agreeing to involve the Press and find the overtime budget.

I make my way back to the team, pass on the message of congratulations, give them the news that we are going to the Press, then leave them to take care of the detailed planning. They need me upstairs. The results are back from the drone night flights over the SCG drug location, and I want to keep up to date.

I'm late to the meeting, and we're crowded in the room this time. I can see Jerry and his guys and recognize one or two others from past cases, but most faces are unknown. I reckon they're DEA agents. 007 is on his feet explaining what they now know about the compound we're planning to take down.

'The compound has three buildings. The main one is approximately twenty-thousand square feet, where the drug packaging operation occurs. From heat signatures, we estimate that there are about a hundred people on site in total. Around sixty of these workers are most likely a mix of illegals and others who are being coerced. The remaining forty, we have to assume, will be armed members of the SCG.

'The two remaining buildings are smaller, with one a dosshouse for SCG members, the other a kitchen where food is prepared and served every six hours.'

I ask a dumb question. 'Where do the workers sleep?'

The initial silence tells me how dumb it was, and I catch a hint of amusement on 007's face as he answers.

'They don't need a doss house because they don't sleep. From observing during the past few days, we think they work twenty-four-hour shifts. There are two workforces, and they rotate every day. They're bussed in and out in the middle of the night.'

'Where are they taken?'

'Good question, detective. At this moment, we don't know the answer to that.'

'Isn't it critical?'

'How do you mean?'

'Well, if we find where they're taking them, we might get some of them to talk to us. Confirm the number of SCG guards and their locations, for instance.'

'Good thinking, detective. The changeover is due tonight, and we plan to follow the buses. Until we know where they are going, planning beyond that is impossible.

'There can't be many places you can sleep sixty people?'

'What are you thinking?'

'Abandoned motel maybe?'

'And you know of such a place?'

'I think a couple are not too far off Rte 41 up East of Fort Myers. When they built the I75 extension in the early 80s, they abandoned them. It was like the death of Rte 66 but for Rte 41 motels.'

'Okay, we'll have someone check them out.'

* * *

After this, 007 returns to his main presentation.

'The aerial recon shows two gun emplacements, most likely armed with heavy-duty Brownings and rocket launchers. These are operated 24/7. At least ten armed guards patrol the perimeter constantly, with probably another ten inside controlling the operation.'

'We can take out the gun emplacements and the external guards easily enough, but our concern is still how to avoid the innocents inside being caught in the crossfire. Any ideas, anyone?'

The room is quiet for a few moments, then Jerry chips in.

'Can we infiltrate some of our guys on the next buses?'

'If the detective is right, and we find where the off-duty shift is staying, that would work.'

'Can I ask how you will take out the gun emplacements so easily?' I ask.

'Technology. We use remote-controlled robots to deliver a variety of charges, both lethal and non-lethal. Against this level of firepower, we will use lethal force.'

'And the perimeter guards?'

'Our attack will be at night. Two experienced snipers will paraglide in and land on the roof of the principal building. Ten men, ten shots, minimum fuss. We will coordinate this operation with destroying the gun emplacements and the primary force crashing through the front gates.'

'With a little luck, the entire operation will be over in less than five minutes.'

With nothing else to add, 007 addresses the whole room. 'You will not talk to anyone outside this room about anything you have just heard. Surprise is key to a successful operation and to protecting lives. We will run the operation tonight if we can find where the next shift is being accommodated rather than wait to watch the buses. We'll decide the exact timing after we assess whether we can get people inside the operation.'

007 asks for any final questions and, when the room remains quiet, invites Jerry and a couple of others to stay behind for

detailed planning. I'm apparently excused. I try not to feel put out. But I am. Fuck. I'd just helped them figure out how to get people inside the operation. You think I would have at least earned a place at the planning table.

Later, back downstairs, I'm minding my own business when 007 appears beside me and sits down.

'Thanks for your input today. They were helpful. I've been struggling with the same questions you came up with but would never have known about those two motels.'

'Have you checked them out?'

'Yes. You were right. There are armed guards at both, with buses parked at the rear out of sight.'

'What's the next step?'

'It's already happening as we speak.'

'You don't hang around, do you?'

'Life's too short, Sammy.'

I'm left wondering if there's an implied innuendo for me.

'So, what's happening.'

'We're jamming cell phones and taking out all the armed guards. Once that's done, we talk to the motel's occupants, explain the operation, and ask for their cooperation.'

'And if they don't want to help?'

'We will replace some with our men anyway and promise all illegals citizenship. That should about get us the number we need. I doubt the SCG will notice a few missing.'

'Who will drive the buses?'

'We'll negotiate deals with some of the guards. If they play along, we'll offer them reduced sentences or maybe even possibly avoid prosecution altogether, depending on their degree of involvement. Once they realize we're going in with serious firepower, they will most likely play along.'

'So, we're all systems go for tonight?'

'Yes, but that's why I stopped by. I hadn't expected this to move so quickly. I'm afraid we won't be having dinner as I promised.'

'Let down on a first date. That's not much of a start to a

relationship, Mister Bond.'

'True. But wait till you hear what I have in mind for a second date!'

'Promises, promises,' I laugh. 'I can hardly wait.'

After that update, I'm restless. Besides the public appeal, little is happening in my serial-killer case, and that's worrying me. We have answered all the questions we set out with but still have no idea how to catch our killer.

I need to talk with Dan. I know he's a keen fisherman. I wonder if *he* has ever used human bait.

40

It's a quiet afternoon in Homicide. The office is virtually empty. Everyone is out catching killers, apart from me. I've told the team to take the rest of the day and go home. They've earned it.

This leaves me alone and thinking and thinking not about how to catch my serial killer but about what's wrong with 007's plan to take down the drug operation. He's highly experienced and moved quickly when I gave him the suggestion about the disused motels up by my parent's place. So, why am I feeling we're all missing something?

Mulling this over, I look for a coffee and find Kathy doing the same.

'I thought you were taking off?'

'Nowhere to take off to, Sammy. Or, more precisely, *no one* to take off with.'

'So, coffee for two,' I smile.

We sit together, chatting about nothing and everything for a while, then she asks me what's going on with the DEA in the house. I swear her to secrecy, then update her on the plan for the middle of the night and tell her I'm worried everyone is missing something.

She suggests we return to the conference room and review the detailed plan.

It's gone eight before we figure out what's worrying me. I

asked what was at the rear of the building and was told it was a landfill site, zoned for more small commercial properties.

The thing that's been bothering me is that if I were in a compound with a drug operation, I would never have one way in and out.

I would worry about becoming trapped.

But the only other way out would be over the landfill, which 007 explained is probably mined as a precaution.

This is what's niggling at me.

Recently I watched a MASH rerun where the Vietcong could run through a minefield because they knew where the mines were. Our troops couldn't follow.

If I were Chico Vegas and wanted to protect the rear of the compound with mines, I would arrange with the landfill company to ensure an escape route.

The problem is, I can't see 007 being convinced of this, so I call Jerry and tell him I think he has more than enough tactical support for the takedown, so I'll skip the take-down and concentrate on my serial-killer case instead.

After that, Kathy and I both head home to get some rest, knowing it will be a late night.

I explain to Trace that I'll leave extra early the following morning, so I want to get to bed by ten. She's okay with that and asks if we have time to watch some tv first. When I agree, she asks if I've ever watched a series she likes called Supernatural. I say no, but I am happy to try it. This pleases her. She gives me the run-in. It's a story that follows two brothers - Sam and Dean Winchester - as they hunt demons, ghosts, monsters, and other supernatural beings. Not something I would ever choose, but it doesn't seem fair to inflict non-stop MASH on her. So, we give it a go.

I'm firmly hooked by ten-forty-five; we're three episodes into the first series. I liked the look of Sam or the one I call the handsome one. But Dean is more my kind of guy. A man of few words and lots of action. He also gets into trouble quickly, which I connect with.

We could have been on an all-night bender if I hadn't planned the early morning start. As it is, I ask Trace to wrap it up, and we both hit the sack.

I set Alexa for twelve-thirty and sleep well until then. An hour and a half will have to do. I can catch up the following night.

Showered, dressed, and ready by one. I go downstairs and find Kathy already waiting for me in an unmarked. We head out to the landfill site.

The contractors have fenced off the entire site and secured the gate with a simple chain and padlock. It takes two seconds with the bolt-cutters, and we're inside looking for the best place to park. We want line-of-sight but not to be too visible to anyone hurrying out of the targeted yard.

The landfill is mostly barren, but we partially obscure the car behind some scrub that has survived, which is more than any indigenous life forms have done. I hate that we're slowly covering the whole of Florida in concrete.

We both have night-vision glasses, and Kathy has brought a flask of strong black coffee. So we're good to go.

The buses are due at two am. The strike force will then hit the compound as soon as the change-over of workers is complete and the buses have left. I reckon around two-thirty. I've no fear we will miss the action. Noise travels at night, and 007 plans to make plenty of that. By my watch, we have less than an hour to wait. I pour two coffees and make myself comfortable.

The first thing we hear are two quick explosions, one immediately on top of the other. I realize that will be the gun emplacements being destroyed. Then a loud crash tells us the heavily armed vehicles are through the gates and heading for the doss-house and canteen. After that, there's a lot of shooting. Mostly automatic.

Throughout this, Kathy and I are monitoring the action. I'm

feeling a little guilty for not telling 007 what we're up to, but not when I see the figure appear out of the rear of the doss house and make its way to the fence. It's a man, but we can't make out anymore at that distance.

When he reaches the fence, we watch as he lifts one post out of the ground, moves it aside, slips through, and then replaces it, leaving no trace of his exit. The shadowy figure then starts across the landfill precisely as we thought. He's following a carefully pre-determined path, zig-zagging his way toward us.

As soon as he starts to run straight, he's through the minefield and coming our way. We wait until he's close enough, then switch on the headlights and throw open the doors.

'Armed police. Throw down your weapons. You're surrounded!'

No point telling him there's only the two of us.

He stops, frozen like a deer in headlights.

'Hands on your head!'

He obeys.

'Down on your knees!'

He obeys again. I'm guessing the guy doesn't want to die.

We walk towards him. It *is* Chico Vegas, just as I expected. He's saving his ass while his men go down in the compound. Sounds about right to me.

Kathy grabs one of his arms and twists it behind his back, ready to apply a tie wrap, when he recognizes me.

'Detective. What a surprise.'

'Hello, Chico. It seems we keep bumping into each other.'

'Always good to see you. Though not sure about right now.'

'Maybe you aren't, but I am. This is exactly where I was hoping we would meet. And after this, I don't think we'll be meeting again for a long time.'

'Maybe you shouldn't be too hasty, detective.'

'Oh, I don't think I'm being hasty, Chico. I've wanted to put you away for quite some time.'

'Nah. You don't get me, man.'

'What are you talking about?'

'I mean, I got a trade for you. You're gonna' want to take.'
'I don't think so, Chico. You're not getting out of this one.'
'But what if I can give you something you *really* want?'
'You trying to bribe me?'
'Nah. I'm offering to give you something. Something special.'
'Cut the crap, Chico. You've nothing special I would want.'
'How about I give you what you're spending all your time looking for?'
'Oh, you mean world peace?'
'I always like that about you. You're funny, man.'
'It's good to laugh. Don't you know?'
'Is it also good to catch serial killers?'

Now, this isn't exactly where I think this conversation is going. I'm expecting some considerable cash pay-off proposal. I could pay my papa back his four hundred and buy a Rolls Royce. It wouldn't look at all obvious in the car park at the Sheriff's office.

'What are you talking about, Chico?'
'I can give you the serial killer you're looking for. You let me go.'
'What makes you think I'm looking for a serial killer?'
'Come on, Detective. I tol' you about blue-cover before. I got inside folks who tell me things.'
'And what are they telling you about my serial killer?'
'It's a girl, and she's young.'

I catch the look of surprise on Kathy's face and guess my expression will be the same. How the hell does he know this?

'I know where she is if you want her.'
'Why should I believe you?'
'Cause she's planning to kill the last on her list real soon, and you won't want that?'
'List? What list?'
'The list she drew up in detention school. The list of the eight men she's killing for revenge.'

Kathy and I exchange another glance. We're both thinking the same thing. There's no way he can know all this information. We've only been learning it in the past couple of days. Yet, here he is. Spouting off the facts, it has taken us so much time and effort to have discovered.

I've no choice but to believe he knows about Charlie. But it's a much more significant jump to think he can tell me where she is. There again. If he knows this much, why would he not? I need more proof.

'So, assuming we believe you. If you know so much, do you know her name?'

'Sure, detective. But before I say's anything else. If you take me in, I'll refuse to talk, and my attorney will have me out in no time. Your girl will be long gone by then. So, we need to have a deal right now. You cut me loose. I tell you her name and where you can find her. Deal or no deal?'

I can't believe I'm even considering what this slimeball is suggesting. Yet, I am. My mind is furiously weighing up the pros and cons.

His drug operation is a bust, so it's not like he will be up and running again anytime soon. Also, whoever supplies him will want to be paid, and I suspect that will be a problem for him after tonight's raid. He might not even survive.

I also have to consider Jon Smith. His life is in the balance, and although we've given him round-the-clock protection, this girl is a very accomplished killer, and if I were him, I wouldn't feel safe with an army around me.

How could I ever explain letting the head man in this drug bust go free to 007 or Jerry? Fuck.

I know that time is ticking. Eventually, someone will come around the back of the compound and see us. I look at Kathy but can't tell what she's thinking. I need to decide.

'Name first. If you're right, we have a deal. You give me the location, and we will leave you here. After that, you can make your own way to town.'

'Okay with me. Her name is Charline, but she calls herself Charlie. You believe me now, man?'

I give Kathy another glance. This time a shrug of her shoulders tells me she's not there. That she's at home in bed, and this whole thing is a figment of my imagination.

It's my call.

The following words come out of my mouth before I finish thinking of what to say.

'Okay, Chico. We have a deal. But if this is a double-cross, I will hunt you down. You hear me?'

'Sure, detective. But this is good info. You've already got her.'

'What do you mean, we've already got her? Don't fuck with me, Chico.'

'I mean it, Detective. You already got her. She's in the hospital.'

'What the fuck are you saying?'

'She was in the Project when you rounded everyone up.'

I feel sick in the depths of my stomach. Disgusted that I've just made a deal with this slippery eel. That we already have Charlie and don't know it. But most of all, as the man responsible for Joey's death walks away, I'm letting my cousin down. Not to mention my parents, who asked me to help him.

I nod to Kathy, who hauls Chico to his feet and shoves him towards town, then watches as first he stumbles and then runs.

'What have I just done, Kathy?'

'What you had to do. Nothing more. Let's go pick up a serial killer.'

41

It only takes twenty minutes for us to pull to a halt right outside the main entrance to NCH and rush inside. It being the middle of the night, Reception is unstaffed, so I run straight to the security guard.

'Where are the people from the Project being treated?'

The guard looks momentarily shocked by the question, but then I figure he's likely been dozing with his eyes open when we walked in.

'East wing,' he tells me, pointing to my right.

I turn and head that way when he shouts after us.

'But some of them just left.'

That stops us short. I turn back and ask what he means.

'Some left with the GFT bus a couple of hours back.'

'GFT?'

'Yeah. The Growers' Foundation Trust.'

'Pretend I don't know what you're talking about and explain that to me.'

'They're a Charity that takes homeless people off the streets and gives them a roof over their heads and food in their bellies in exchange for crop-picking.'

'So they heard about what went down at the Project and took the people from here to where?'

'They only took some. There are always some who don't want to go. And there's a lot don't stay when they get there. They don't enjoy working for a living. So mostly they transport them up to farms in Polk County.'

'So, there are still some here?'

'Sure. As I said. They're in the east wing.'

Kathy asks a question I should have thought about.

'Why are GFT picking up in the middle of the night?'

'Have you seen how busy we are during the day? The place can get chaotic around here.'

'So, nothing to do with homeless people not being seen by people paying for their treatment, then?' she suggests.

'Hey, I'm just a security guard. Politics are not my thing.'

Leaving him, we follow the signage for the east wing. This time, when we arrive, there's an administrator at the reception desk. We show our badges and ask if she has a record of the people recently admitted from the raid on the Project.

She takes a few minutes rifling in a cabinet but eventually produces what she has. Together, Kathy and I scan through the information. The names are in alphabetical order of surnames. We look for Ellis. Nothing. We check all the names for Charlie, Charles, or Charline. Still nothing. Then Kathy suggests we try the age column.

This works.

There's only one person vaguely close to their late teens. She had given her name as Jessie Wells. Charlie Ellis, Jessie Wells. Close enough. This is her, I'm sure of it. I turn back to the administrator.

'Can you tell us which people left on the GFT bus a couple of hours ago?'

This time the list we need is on the desk before her.

One bus. Thirty people and Jessie Wells is one of them.

I throw the list down and start running with Kathy on my heels. I feel so close. So very close. Polk County is about two-and-a-half hours north. We need to shift.

Back in the car, I drive while Kathy calls the State Police. We have her if we can stop the bus before it gets to its destination.

Once we make it across onto the interstate, it's empty, and with blue flashing lights, I push up close to a hundred all the way. We're only halfway there when Kathy gets a call back from the State Police. They pulled over the bus and secured the occupants before it left the interstate just south of Tampa. The bus is being held forty miles north of our current location.

I run the math just for fun.

Twenty-four minutes and we'll have her.

I push the car above the hundred.

Now we're *really* shifting.

Just over twenty minutes later, we fly over a rise in the road and can see two State patrol cars with their light bars flashing beside a bus - all pulled over on the shoulder.

We screech to a halt, the tires throwing gravel in the air, and jump out. Identifying ourselves immediately, I ask who's in charge. The two patrol officers look at each other, and I could kick myself right then. This isn't a crime scene. This is just two State-troopers pulling over a vehicle. There's no one in charge. I should know better.

'Sorry, guys. Got myself a bit confused there. Have either of you been on board?'

One says he has and has spoken with the driver. That was all. I ask if he had noticed a young teenage girl.

He hadn't.

Kathy and I both draw our weapons and climb onboard. I nod to the driver, who looks on the verge of panic. Kathy stays beside him at the entrance, and I start down the central aisle, looking carefully at every face.

I can feel the tension rise as I get closer and closer to the rear seat. She would keep low, far away from everyone else.

I'm wrong. She isn't there.

I can't believe it.

Walking backward, I recheck everyone on the way until I get back to Kathy. She isn't on the goddam bus. Where is she?

Behind me, I can hear Kathy ask the bus driver if he had seen a young teenage girl getting on the bus at the NCH.

'You mean the one that said she would throw up?'

I immediately turn to pay full attention.

'She got off almost as soon as we left, way back at Golden Gate Parkway. I didn't want her spilling her guts on the bus. I thought she would throw up and get back on, but she just ran away.'

'So you kept going?' I ask.

'Hey, I work with these homeless people all the time. You can't mother them. They make their own choices.'

'What's she wearing?'

'I didn't pay much attention. It was dark trousers, jeans maybe, and a light gray hoodie.'

Frustrated, Kathy and I step off the bus, tell him to get going, then watch as the bus pulls back onto the highway and heads north.

I thank the two troopers and explain that our suspect has jumped the bus back in Naples. They tip their hats and head back to their vehicles, pulling out one after another and leaving Kathy and me to our miseries.

'So close,' I say.

'Yeah, but let's not give up now. We know what she's wearing and that she's on foot in Naples. Let's get a BOLO out on her. The day shift will start soon. We can get her picture in front of everyone. They probably have an up-to-date picture at NCH. We can circulate that. We'll find her this time.'

'We know one other thing, Kathy. We know where she's going?'

'To kill Jon Smith.'

'Exactly.'

42

It's gone five before Kathy, and I get back to the station. I send Kathy home and talk with the duty sergeant. I ask him to have someone take over the artist's sketch of Charlie and show it to the security guard and the administrator to check the likeness and ask if they have a recent photo.

I want to ensure they hand out the best possible information at the morning briefing. Specifically, the updated artist's sketch of what a nineteen-year-old Charlie should look like or the real thing. I also add the clothing details we have, then as I can't think of anything to do, I go home and creep in, setting Alexa for eight-thirty.

The following day I feel like crap when I open my eyes. My head is aching, and my fully recovered knee is not fully recovered after all. It's sore. I pop a couple of painkillers and take a shower.

After drying off, I put on underwear and glimpse myself in the mirror. An unsolicited thought runs through my head.

I'm wondering if I would stack up to 007's other conquests. He's single, mid-thirties, and most definitely attractive. He'll have had many, I assume.

Then I remember how I've probably screwed up his mission to take down Chico Vegas the night before and decide that if he finds out, the only thing he would stack me up against might be a firing wall.

That makes me realize I haven't decided whether to tell

anyone about my deal with Vegas yet. Kathy clarified that she intends to say nothing and would leave it to me to decide.

If I tell anyone, it won't be 007 or Jerry. It will be Dan.

I try to get into his shoes. If I were him and one of my direct reports told me they'd blown a hole in a critical mission, what would I say to them?

Fuck. I know exactly what he will say.

Make your mind up and live with the consequences either way.

That means I have to figure out what the consequences are first. So that will be my starting point.

If I admit what I've done, there will surely be a stink. I'm not sure it would be a terminal stink regarding my career, but it may be a suspension, or I might lose my second-grade promotion. So none of these things worry me. But, if they think I've made a poor call, that will.

But have I?

Given that I don't have my suspect in custody, I'm unsure what to think. There again, that's using the wisdom of hindsight.

If I don't admit it, life will go on much as before. Everyone would assume Vegas wasn't on site when the raid went down. They would feel good about shutting down the operation and settle for that. No harm done.

But then I remember how Vegas tried to blackmail me once before. I only avoided that by pleading guilty directly to the Sheriff. If I keep quiet, I might give him another opportunity to do the same again, and there will only be a limited number of times I can use the Sheriff to escape his web.

Very limited. Probably once - and I've already used that.

As soon as I realize that, I text Kathy to avoid her being blind-sided and finish dressing. I look over at Trace, but she seems able to sleep through whatever noise I make. She has slept in noisier places than this often enough before.

I leave another ten dollars on the breakfast bar, and as I've got a growing sense of urgency about the day ahead, rather than walk, I take a cab to the office and head straight for Dan Weissman's cubicle. For once, I'm lucky. He's there.

* * *

I ask to speak with him in the small conference room, away from prying ears, so he follows me and closes the door behind him.

I lay it all out for him, then wait for his response. It isn't what I expect.

'Have you figured out how Vegas knew about the serial killer case?'

Wrong-footed, I say I haven't had time to think about it.

'More significantly, Sammy. How did he know *you* were working the case?'

Another thing I haven't considered. I've been so consumed with worry about justifying my decision I haven't stopped to ask myself these obvious questions. I think fast.

'I don't know either of these things, Dan. But I can understand why he knew she was at the Project.'

'*The Joker*?' he suggests.

'That would be my guess. But that still won't answer the other questions.'

'Who knew you were working the case other than in this office?'

'Nobody. Well, other than Jerry and 007.'

'Who?'

'The DEA guy that led the raid last night. His name's….'

'James Bond?'

'Right.'

'How about outside the force? Friends you've been drinking with? Press you might have spoken to? Family?'

I was on the point of saying no to these suggestions when I think of Joey.

'My second cousin.'

'Say more.'

'If you remember, we had him in to finger *The Joker*, but he skipped out on us.'

'So?'

'He was in my cubicle, looking for me.'

'So, he might have seen something or overheard

something?'
'It's possible.'
'If we assume you're right.'
'He headed straight for the Project when he ran from here.'
'Because that's where he had been hanging out before. Where he was getting his drugs?'
'Yeah.'
'And that's where your serial killer was hiding to prepare for her next kill?'
'They talked?'
'And then Joey exchanged the information with *The Joker* in payment for his next fix. And he told Vegas.'
'You're right, Dan. That makes sense.'
'It just so happens that you caught Vegas sneaking out the back of the compound last night. If it had been anyone else, he would have used the information to negotiate his way out of being charged.
'Would you have traded?'
'No doubt, Sammy. I would have accepted in a heartbeat to take a serial killer out of play, especially knowing she is about to strike for an eighth time.'
Hearing Dan say this had a hugely positive effect on me. All the worry I've been carrying lifts, and the world feels better again. I need to tell Jerry and 007.

Upstairs, in the Narcs conference room, my confession doesn't go down so well. I wish I'd accepted Dan's offer to accompany me, but it's too late. I feel like a target on the range, with two semi-automatics shredding me.
When they stop firing, Jerry storms out of the room. I get it. Vegas is the major supplier in this entire area, and he's been after him for a long time.
When he's out of range, 007 chuckles.
I'm confused. This is another reaction I'm not expecting.
'Smart thinking, Detective.'
'You think? After all the shouting?'
'Pity you didn't get your serial killer.'

'Tell me about it. We were so close.'

'You could have told me about your theory for a rear escape route. I would have listened.'

'I wasn't sure you would.'

'I guess you don't know me well enough. Still, you covered it, just in case. That was a good call, and it paid off.'

'So you're not pissed off?'

'Oh, I'm pissed off all right. But not at you. These operations are about taking off the head of the snake, and in this case, he got away.'

'Thanks to me.'

'No, Detective. Thanks to *me*. I overlooked the rear escape plan. You might have shared your thoughts with me if I had involved you more. Instead, I closed you out. It's all on me.'

'You weren't to know how brilliant I am,' I smile.

'Nice try, Sammy. But when you accept the responsibility of leadership, you own the results. No ifs or buts.'

'So, does that mean we're still on for dinner?'

43

As I return downstairs, there's a message from Jimi asking me to call.

Before I can, Kathy grabs me and pulls me toward the conference room where Jamie and Dene are waiting.

They ask how it has gone upstairs, and I tell them everything's okay. I see Kathy take a deep breath. I appreciate she would back me up with whatever I decided.

Last night, when I let Chico Vegas walk, I crossed a line, and she crossed with me. I already had respect for her as a detective. Now I also respect her as someone I can depend on and trust.

After that, Dene updates me on what is happening with our serial killer case.

'We look more closely at JS3.'

'He's under 24/7 protection, right?'

'Yes and no, Sammy. We have a car outside his home whenever he's there. But if he's at work, he's on his own. He refuses to take leave. Says his students need him.'

'Students?'

'Yeah. He's a schoolteacher at Golden Gate High School, teaching Social Studies.'

'Teacher!'

'Yeah, figure that. Surrounded by eighteen-hundred kids between the age of fifteen and eighteen.'

'A happy hunting ground?'

'That's where he ran into trouble six years ago. He was a new teacher, just started at the school, and one senior girl accused him of touching her up.'
'Was it reported to the Department?'
'Yes. And followed up. But do you know how many people make accusations like these every year?'
'No.'
'Recently, a study showed over two and a half thousand teachers had their license denied, suspended, or revoked because of sexual misconduct across the Country. In one year.'
'Shit.'
'But only one in ten end up being prosecuted, and even then, very few receive a sentence.'
'So, our killer may be onto something?'
'Perhaps. Who knows why she singled out these specific eight cases? This is happening virtually every day.'
Jamie joins in.
'But, my personal experience of teenagers tells me that a newbie teacher like JS3 was back then would be a prime target for what they would describe as harmless fun.'
'Not so harmless for the guy's career,' I reply. 'So, what happened in Jon Smith's case?'
'They dismissed the case against him?' said Dene. 'But unfortunately, some bright reporter got wind of it and reported it in the Press.'
'Which is where Charlie saw it?' I suggest.
Without saying anything, we all know we have just added another brick in the wall.
One more question answered.
After that, it's Kathy who breaks the silence. 'There's something else we have learned. Charlie was quick to get off the bus last night. I think she knows we're after her.'
'She might have seen some of the early press releases this morning with her picture.'
'You think that'll affect how she operates?' I ask.
'I think she will want to get this finished and disappear.'
'Okay, Kathy. Assuming you're right. Let's assume she'll

already know we have JS3 under protection at home, which only leaves the school as an option for her.'

'And where better for a teenage killer to hide than in plain sight amidst eighteen-hundred teenagers,' says Dene.

At that point, the conference door opens, and one of the other detectives says there's an urgent call for me on my extension.

Back in my cubicle, I take the call. A patrol officer has eyes on Charlie at the Coastland Mall downtown. I thank him and ask him to keep her in sight but not approach until we arrive.

After rushing back to the conference room to tell the team what's happening, we all make for the car park.

It takes longer to get out of the building and into Kathy's car than the Coastland Center car park trip.

As we rush in, I call the officer to ask if he still has eyes on the girl.

He doesn't. He lost her when she entered Dillards and ducked out of another exit.

Although disappointed, this doesn't surprise me. The girl's sharp.

We split up. There are four main entrances, and we take one each. The plan is not to do anything until we get more officers here. Just make sure she doesn't leave the complex.

Within twenty minutes, we have two dozen officers on site, all with a copy of the artist's impression of Charlie, searching each store one at a time. Leaving an officer at my entrance, I start wandering the mall and use my time to ask some shopkeepers if they had seen her.

I don't get any hits until H&M, where an assistant says she remembers the girl because she'd run off with some clothes without paying. An alarm went off at the entrance, and she called security, but the girl was out of sight by then.

She confirms that the girl is wearing jeans and a gray

hoodie.

It's Charlie.

I ask her if she knows which clothes the girl has taken. She thinks about it for a moment, then tells me that she can only show me where the girl was just before she ran off.

I ask her to do that but quickly realize there are too many articles on each rack. She could have got away with almost anything.

Two hours later, I call off the search, gather the team, and suggest we grab something to eat while in the mall. There's a food court, so there should be something for everyone.

Our combined nourishment for a late lunch includes meatballs from Villa Italian Kitchen, a double Whopper from Burger King, and two sandwiches from Subway. We won't win a fitness award for this lot. Still, needs must.

As we eat, we're all frustrated at getting so close, but with her slipping through our fingers again. Something she's proving to be very good at doing, and we're all worried about that.

Kathy says that the fact Charlie is clothes shopping confirms that she is still committed to her kill list and that we're correct to assume she will go after JS3 at the school.

We spend the rest of our meal debating what else we can do to keep him safe. But other than keeping him locked in his home, we don't come up with anything.

On the bright side, he knows she's looking for him, which none of the other victims did. He also knows what she looks like.

He also has total protection outside school hours, but I have no idea what to do when he's teaching.

We need to warn him that Charlie will likely try to get to him at school. Kathy offers to call him and let him know.

It's time to head back to the office. I feel deflated and rudderless. I know the target and the killer but can't connect the dots.

* * *

It's in the car that Jamie remembers to tell us he's followed up on Pamela Wilson's cell phone record to track down her possible accomplice and has come up with a name. Kyle Sinclair is an ex-wrestler who lives on the same street as Pamela. Just four doors down. Minor record for brawling in a bar. But that was ten years ago. Nothing since.

It seems so long ago that I last discussed Pamela Wilson, yet it's only a few days. So much has happened since. Having found her stiletto knife, we know she's responsible for killing Jason, but we're still nowhere in trying to figure out who killed *her*. Maybe Kyle Sinclair can help with that?

When we get to the office, we drop Jamie and Dene, then Kathy and I set off to see what we can wrestle out of Mister Sinclair.

When he answers the knock at his door, he fills the door frame.

Even if I didn't know he's a former wrestler, I could probably guess. He's one big man. I would estimate two-forty, primarily muscle. He must still spend a lot of time keeping fit.

'Yeah?'

We show our badges.

'Mister Sinclair?'

'That's me.'

'Mind if we come in? We have questions about your relationship with Pamela Wilson, your late neighbor from a few doors along.'

'Don't know the woman. No point coming in.'

I give him one of my steely-eyed stares before trying again.

'So, I guess there must be some mistake with Ms. Wilson's call records. You and she spoke regularly.'

'Don't recall.'

'Have you ever been to her apartment?'

'I told you. I don't know the woman. Why would I go to her apartment?'

Time for a white lie.

'To leave us your fingerprints, dumb-ass.'

He takes a moment to give us his considered response. 'Fuck.'

'Remember your bar-fight some years back? You gave us them then. Very kind. It shows you never know when something will come in useful, do you?'

I can see I've punctured his bravado.

He stands aside and waves us in.

The home is almost identical in layout to Pamela Wilson's, but the content couldn't be more different.

The lounge area is a gymnasium. There's equipment everywhere. Stepping machine, rower, weights, everything you could want to keep a two-hundred and forty-pound body in physical shape.

'Quite a gym you have here, Kyle. Not cheap this lot?'

'Been buying it over the years, you know. Bit at a time.'

Looking around, I realize there's nowhere to sit. He sees the problem and leads us to what would have been Pamela's professional bedroom. Here, it's his lounge area. There's only a two-person sofa, an enormous television screen, and an X-box with cables trailing over the floor.

He points to the seat. I have a picture of his sweaty butt sitting, playing games, and elect to stand.

'So, Kyle. Why don't you walk us through how you helped Ms. Wilson with her business? Her dominatrix business.'

'What do you want to know?'

'Were you ever there when she performed her various services?'

'No. Not into that stuff myself. Not interested.'

'So, when were you there?'

'Am I in trouble? Do I need an attorney?'

Time to turn on the smooth charm.

'We're not charging you with anything, Kyle. As you know, someone killed Ms. Wilson, and we're trying to find that person. You are not a suspect. But we would appreciate your help in understanding what happened.'

'Yeah. I get that.'

'Okay. Why don't you tell us what you did for her in your own words?'

He thinks about that and makes his decision.

'When she finished a session, she would call me, and I would go round.'

'Where was the client when you arrived?'

'Handcuffed to the bed. Christ knows why people get off on that, but everyone to their own.'

'So, you released them, is that correct.'

'Yeah. I unlocked them and made sure they left the house.'

'So, you were like her personal protector.'

'Something like that. After they drove off, Pam would slip me some cash, and I would come home.'

'Did you ever see her take a video of a client?'

'No. Never.'

'How about, did you ever see her put anything in her safe?'

'What safe?'

His response doesn't surprise me. I carry on.

'Were her clients' men?'

'Mostly. I think there might have been a woman or two.'

'Were they always cooperative when you released them?'

'Mostly.'

'When weren't they?'

'Just from time to time. Rarely.'

'Say, what? Once a year?'

'Yeah, sounds about right.'

'Any difficult clients? Maybe one that you considered dangerous?'

That gets him thinking, and it's like watching cogs slowly turning on a rusty old machine.

'There was one. She scared the shit out of me a few years back. I uncuffed her, and she attacked me with a blade. Scratched the fuck out of my arm.'

As he says this, he opens out his left forearm and shows us three parallel thin scars several inches long.

'What did you do?'

'I stomped on the little bitch and threw her out on her ear.

Fucking cuts. I bled like a pig.'

'If she was handcuffed to the bed and naked, where did she get the blade from?'

'She had a necklace. Funny-looking thing with beads and what looked like a big flat shell in the middle.'

'She kept that on?'

'Yeah. She had a blade hidden in there, behind the shell.'

I clock that we've just solved another part of the puzzle, then remove the folded picture of Charlie from my pocket, open it, and show it to him.

'Is this the girl?'

'Yeah. That's her. But I think she was a little younger. Why? Did she kill Pam?'

'We're not sure yet, Kyle. We're looking into all possibilities.'

I put the picture back in my pocket and thank him for his time.

We're just leaving the front door when he asks if we've checked out Pamela's kids.

I turn, and my confusion must be evident. So, he clarifies for me.

'She didn't talk about them to anyone. Fuckin' weirdos if you ask me.'

'Do you know how we can contact them, Kyle?'

'No idea. Only ever seen them twice.'

I thank him again and walk towards the car, trying to figure out why I'm not as surprised as I should be.

By the time we return to the office, it'll be too late to accomplish much, so Kathy drops me at my apartment instead and heads home.

After watching her drive off, I call and ask Trace if she likes spicy wings.

Fifteen minutes later, we enter the Rusty Nail.

Before I get to my favorite stool, the barman has a Corona on the bar. He nods his recognition at Trace and, without asking, puts a glass of Diet Coke in front of her. Then, he skips the greeting and utters the phrase he thinks I want to hear. He's right. 'Hot Spicy Wings for two?'

I'm tempted to ask Trace how she's known in my favorite drinking haunt, but I guess I already know the answer. Street smarts.

Twenty minutes later, I've fed a dozen quarters into the antique jukebox, and we're sitting in my corner booth, tucking into wings, listening to *Living in a Ghost Town*. This track is an early release of a promised new album, delayed by the epidemic, and strangely appropriate to the lock-down experiences we've all just lived through. I guess that's why they released it early.

I'm a big fan of the Stones, and although I grew up on some of their more recent releases, I prefer their older tracks. Trace doesn't know much about this entire generation of Rock music. So, I decide to work on her education as we eat. I talk her through many of the big names, not from my generation but from my parent's generation. Explain the British Invasion, Woodstock, and flower power. I expect her to be bored, but she isn't. She soaks it all up, asking questions all the time.

Good music, a relaxed atmosphere, and spicy food, and Trace is surprisingly good company. She has a lot going for her. She deserves a beautiful home and caring folks to help her grow up. And most of all, a proper education. The girl is like a sponge and intelligent. She should have a promising career ahead of her, and I can't give her any of these things. I can solve complex homicide cases but don't know what to do with Trace.

During our conversation, she asks if I've ever wanted kids of my own, and I surprise myself by telling her I've already lost one.

She looks puzzled, and I immediately regret telling her but feel I might as well finish the story. So I tell her about Bossy-boots and the tough decision I made.

She goes quiet after that, which worries me. I can't figure

out what she's thinking. Then she tells me in a whisper, with tears in her eyes, and I didn't see it coming.

'If that's how you treat your flesh and blood, what chance do I have?'

If I feel low about my decision to terminate Bossy-boots - which I do - that's nothing to how I feel right at that moment. Yes, Bossy-boots depended on me, but she wasn't here. But Trace is sitting opposite me, sharing my food and living in my apartment. Making me laugh and now cry - yes, my eyes are welling up.

We sit like that. Each is watching the other cry. Neither sure what's happening, but feeling a new bond form. A bond made from powerful stuff. A bond made of love. No one was more surprised than me at the thought, but it's true. I love this annoyingly wonderful young woman. And from the expression on her face, the feeling is mutual.

I reach across the table, take her hand in mine and make one of the most ridiculous promises of all time. I tell her she'll be alright. That somehow, I'll look after her.

The relief on her face magnifies the stupidity of my promise. I'm left wondering how vulnerable I feel. It should be Trace feeling like this, not me.

Unable to process any more of what just happened, I switch back to talking about Bossy-boots. Trace seems more than happy to follow my lead. I explain what Arnie Collins told me about micro-chimerisms and how Bossy-boots is still in my bloodstream. In response, she asks another one of these bright questions she seems to come up with so easily.

'I don't understand. Why was your Medical Examiner talking with you about the unborn child you terminated?'

'He wasn't.' But as I deny it, only then do I realize it was me who applied what Arnie said to Bossy-boots. He was talking about Pamela Wilson, and I was so wrapped up in my grief that I completely missed it.

I tell this to Trace.

'So, exactly what did he say?' she asks.

I have to think for a few moments.

'I think he said that the victim had most likely had a child early in her teens. But, no, that's not right. He had looked at her DNA and found that she had twins. A boy and a girl.'

'Have you spoken to them?'

'No. A witness just told us about them today, but I hadn't connected it to what the ME said.

'You need to find them.'

'Yes, Trace. I do.'

On returning to the apartment, I put an arm through Traces.

At that moment, I feel closer to someone than I have in a long time.

As we walk, I can't help wondering about Pamela Wilson's relationship with the children she abandoned at birth. At least she allowed them to go the entire term, which is more than I did.

44

Having enjoyed the Stones on the jukebox the previous night at the Rusty Nail with Trace, I ask Alexa to wake me with a few of my favorite early tracks. Trace asks me to leave the volume up so she can wake up at the same time. She wants to spend the day on the laptop looking for home-learning classes.

So, the first up is *'19th Nervous Breakdown.'*

Then I boogie in the shower to *Jumping Jack Flash* and dry myself, accompanied by *'I can't get no satisfaction.'* I swear these guys wrote their music with me in mind, even though I wasn't even a twinkle in Papa's eye back then.

When I come out of the shower, Trace heads in.

Trace has switched the music to Ariana Grande, and I can hear her singing along to the song she recorded with Lady Gaga - *'Rain on Me.'* I wonder if she's boogying the same way I had to the Stones. Listening to her, she's obviously tone deaf, but no way am I telling her. She's happy, and that's fine with me.

As I'm lifting my badge and taking my Glock from the drawer in the bedside unit, where I've started concealing it, I notice the small box containing Papa's bones. Maybe I will introduce Trace to them that night.

I leave five dollars on the breakfast bar - the best I can offer at this time of the month.

When I hit the office, I'm in a good mood. I assume that will change, but I don't realize how quickly.

There are two messages on my desk. The first is a reminder from Jimi to call or stop by. I'd forgotten all about his message the previous day. The second is from 007, telling me I hadn't given him my cell number, so he hoped I would pick up this message. He had booked a table at Mediterrano for eight. He hoped I would be there.

Fuck and double fuck. I'd missed him the previous night.

First, I'd been looking forward to getting together with him. For food and, well, who knows what else. Second, I love the food at the Mediterrano - a mix of Italian and Greek.

I realize I don't have his cell either, so call Jerry. From his tone, he's not yet over me letting Vegas escape, but he gives me 007's number.

I call. He answers. I explain. He says he understands. I ask if we can try again. He's at the airport flying back to Atlanta. We talk a little more, then hang up. Now my good mood has completely evaporated.

My extension rings. It's Kathy to say the team is in the conference room with donuts and coffee. The prospect cheers me a little. I head their way.

We spend the first twenty minutes joshing around, with me arm-wrestling Kathy for the double chocolate donut. I lose. She shares. I like Kathy even more.

After we clear the mess, we start talking about work. Jamie confirms that as the following day is a Saturday, officers will be with JS3 around the clock. There will also be one present inside his home. We're taking no chances.

Kathy updates everyone on our visit to Pamela Wilson's neighbor, and I finish with my thoughts about Pamela having twins in their mid-twenties.

Jamie and Dene offer to track them down.

Kathy says she wants to look more carefully into the accusations filed against JS3.

That leaves me with time on my hands.

I go looking for Jimi and find him in the coffee rec area. I grab a fresh brew and sit with him at a small table that looks out over the rear car park. It isn't much of a view, but at least it's a glimpse of daylight. I ask him what he has for me.

'I reviewed all the evidence from Pamela Wilson's case as you asked. A fresh pair of eyes. Do you remember?'

'Yes,' I lie. Smoothly, I hope.

'Well, a statement from a neighbor who saw a vehicle intrigued me. She said it was parked close to the victim's home around the time of her death.'

'I think I remember. She was walking her dog, right?'

'Exactly. She didn't know what kind of car it was, but what she said made me wonder.'

'What was that?'

'She described it as unusual, with a disability badge.'

Hearing the word disability is triggering something, but I'm unsure what. However, my interest level has just gone up a notch, and I encourage him to continue.

'I took our vehicle identification manual and the police sketch artist with me and went to see her. We surprised her with the visit, but I think she was pleased with the attention. She made us tea, and we first looked through the vehicle manual until she picked out the nearest she could find. Then, the artist took over, asking questions and changing her chosen vehicle with some of her observations. She remembered a lot more detail than she thought she had.'

'And?' I'm getting impatient, but try to reel it in, remembering that working on a first homicide case is a big deal for Jimi.

'We came up with a vehicle. It was wheelchair accessible. A silver Ford Freedom. It has a tailgate and ramp to allow wheelchair access, but from her description, it was adapted for a disabled driver.'

'So, potentially, someone had two disabled visitors that night? One in a wheelchair.'

'Yes. So, I returned to the victim's address and canvassed the neighbors.'

'To see if they had a visit from two disabled folks?'

'Exactly. They hadn't. And no one recognized the Ford Freedom.'

'So, you reckon they *were* visiting Pamela Wilson?'

'Yes. That's what I think.'

'Outstanding work, Jimi. I've completely overlooked the significance of that witness statement.'

'But that's not all,' he says, struggling to hide his excitement. 'I asked for all traffic cam footage from the surrounding area for a couple of hours around the estimated time of death.'

'And?'

'Found a vehicle matching the description. We have the plate and the owner's address. I wasn't sure what to do next, so I left you a message.'

Kicking myself for not responding the previous day, I thank him again, follow him to his cubicle to collect the information and return to the conference room to give it to Jamie and Dene.

After all the work they've put in over the past week, I think they should pick up our two newest suspects in the death of Pamela Wilson.

Now, I feel strangely lost with everything at least reasonably in control. This is my first free time since returning when Dan asked me if I wanted to dive straight in. Little did I know what I would be diving into. But that's what life in Homicide is like, and I enjoy it.

I spend the next couple of hours reading routine reports and emails until Dene buzzes me to let me know they have our two new suspects in an interview room downstairs. Given that they know I'll be interested, they've chosen the room with the one-way mirrored wall. Again, they're spot on, and ten minutes later, I'm assessing the twins.

The one in the wheelchair suffers from the most significant physical disabilities. Her spine has collapsed under her weight, leaving her crumpled and in a wheelchair. Although only in her mid-twenties, she looks old. From what I can see of her arms and hands, they seem relatively okay.

Her hair is already gray and hanging listlessly to shoulder length. She's wearing glasses with a heavy dark frame and thick lenses; all I can see is a pair of gigantic eyes peering out.

I know I should feel sorry for her, but there's something creepy in those eyes.

Her sister is physically the opposite. I would guess the best part of six feet, with a flat chest and broad shoulders. However, where her sister lacks make-up, this woman excels. In fact, over-excels. I don't want to seem cruel, but she looks more like a mannequin or a circus clown.

Her face is strong, with a square jawline and a slightly bulbous nose.

They look nothing alike.

Dene and Jamie are sitting with their backs to me, facing the twins.

Jamie starts the interview by telling them it is being recorded, then confirms their names and home address and that they own the vehicle found parked in their driveway.

It's the woman in the chair who gives the confirmation.

Then Jamie asks them to name their mother.

That's when the evasion starts.

The next half-hour is spent with her explaining how difficult their past lives have been. Separated at birth. They'd grown up in a combination of hospitals and care homes, and in one case, she - the woman in the wheelchair - had been living with foster parents. But, unfortunately, that hadn't worked out.

She goes on to explain how she had found out about her sister, eventually tracked her down, and arranged for her to come live with her. The sister suffered neurological damage when she was born and is deaf and vocally impaired.

As I listen, I recall some details Arnie Collins had told me. First, a warning that cocaine users often produce children with various physical and mental challenges, and second, that the twins were male and female. Not what's in front of me. I suspect this last mystery will be resolved before too long.

I don't know precisely when Pamela Wilson's past caught up with her, but I can't imagine how she felt when it did. It would be terrible to see the damage your drug use has caused, but also to know you abandoned them to such a cruel fate must have been truly awful.

As the interrogation continues, Jamie puts a traffic-cam picture of their vehicle on the table before her and asks if she can confirm visiting Pamela Wilson on the night of her death.

I suspect that, just like me, he's expecting a denial. But instead, she confirms that she was there. Then casually reveals what happened that night.

They first visited Pamela Wilson at her home several weeks before. Told her who they were and asked for money. Pamela didn't believe them and had virtually thrown them out.

Back home, she was furious at the refusal to accept who they were. She tried to understand how she could get revenge for her sister and herself and used YouTube to learn how to sever arteries, particularly the Femoral. Also, how to leave the knife in the wound to prevent blood spatter.

When they returned to Pamela Wilson's home for their second visit, her sister in the wheelchair concealed a regular kitchen knife in her lap. She had wheeled her up to the front door, and when Pamela Wilson opened it, forced the wheelchair into the hallway, bringing their target within easy reach. The rest is history.

I leave the interview room shortly after, trying to decide who to feel sorry for, or is it, who to blame.

A detective who was a serial abuser - stabbed to death.

The victim of horrific sexual abuse by that police officer and his two friends, but who was also a cocaine addict, dominatrix, blackmailer, and a mother who abandoned two children at birth.

Or an assassin in a wheelchair - along with her deaf and vocally impaired sister, who in reality is her brother - who had stabbed their mother to death?

What a strange world we live in.

* * *

Back in the office, I can finally stop thinking about Pamela Wilson and start thinking ahead. I intend to join the guard detail for JS3 on Monday at the school. But if I do that, I should know my way around the school in advance.

I call the Principal at Golden Gate High, and he agrees to stay behind with his facility manager to meet with me later that evening.

45

On the Friday night, Trace shows me some home-learning sites she found. Some are free, and she's already signed up for those. But the ones that look most useful to me require tuition fees. I can't afford these, so we quickly agree that the free sites are the best in the short term.

Over Saturday and Sunday, Trace and I pretend we're tourists. It's strange for me to find out that even though I've lived in Naples for three years, I know very little about the place. On the first day, we tackle museums and the zoo. Then on Sunday, we head down to the Glades.

We decide on a motorboat eco-tour. I show my badge and get thirty bucks knocked off the price, and twelve-and-under is free, so what's another hundred out of my new car fund?

The three-and-a-half-hour tour is brilliant. We watch dolphins play in the surrounding water while we search for manatees, alligators, sting-ray, and various birds. The swampland is so peaceful when the tour guide switches the engine off. There's only the occasional bird cry or the sound of a jumping fish to break the silence.

Sunday night, we spend back at the apartment, both squeezed onto the beanbag, sharing a bowl of popcorn and watching Sam and Dean hunt more monsters. It's so long since I've felt so relaxed and comfortable in someone else's company. And happy.

Monday morning, I arrive at JS3's home by seven-thirty as

promised.

I called him the day before and told him I would be his escort for the day.

Charlie will be keen to finish her work and move on, so I have to catch her when she makes her move.

On the drive into Golden Gate, I'm impressed with how relaxed Jon Smith is, given that he's the last name on a serial killer's list, with all others already dead. I know I wouldn't be so chilled.

We chat about various things, primarily day-to-day things. I'm deliberately keeping the conversation light. So, it surprises me when he raises the subject of being accused of assault when he first started teaching.

'It didn't just happen at the beginning of my career, detective. It happened on the very first day.'

'Day one?'

'Yep. I had just finished the last class before lunch and dismissed everyone, but one girl stayed behind to ask me a question. She was a ninth grader so she would have been around fifteen.'

'What happened?'

'She came close to me and asked her question, but in a flirty way.'

'She was giving you the eye?'

'She acted like she intended to give me more than the eye, Detective.

I was inexperienced and didn't know what to do.

I tried to answer her question.'

'But that wasn't what she wanted.'

'No. She took my hand and told me how having a young male teacher in the school was great. That, most male teachers are old and wouldn't understand teenagers, especially teenage girls.'

'What did you say?'

'I didn't say very much. I just stood there feeling helpless.'

'What happened next?'

'She lifted my hand to feel her cheek and told me she had been dreaming of me touching her throughout the class.'

'Did you stop her?'

'I should have, but I couldn't think straight. I was only twenty-one, and she was attractive. I knew it was wrong, but I was like in a trance. I think my brain had switched off.'

'Did she go any further?'

'She placed my handle gently on one of her breasts and squeezed, asking me how it felt.'

'You reacted badly?'

'You bet. I jerked my hand away and shouted at her.'

'You lost it?'

'I lost it.'

'How did she react?'

'At first, she was quiet. Like she was thinking, then stormed out of the room, angry as hell.'

'Did you go directly to your Principal?'

'No. That's where my inexperience let me down. I assumed it would all go away.'

'But it didn't?'

'No, Detective. It didn't.'

After that, we finish the drive in silence, each deep in our thoughts. I suspect he is reliving his nightmare; I'm trying to decide whether I believe him.

I come up with - possibly.

It's the best I can offer.

The school is a complex of red-brick rectangular structures with a central walkway leading to the reception hall. From there, different corridors lead to various departments. I can see Media Services, PE, Math, and many others all signposted. He explains that first, we're making for the common room. A fellow coffee addict needs his fix, and that's just fine with me.

I always pay attention to how people treat others. I credit most other folks for being better than me at recognizing a good guy. As a detective, I recognize bad guys.

The fellow staff members that speak to him are friendly and

seem supportive. A few ask how he's coping while eyeing me suspiciously as if I'm the root of his problem rather than a protector.

I take a moment aside to check the radio I'm carrying is working. We have a patrol car out front, another round at the rear entrance, and officers stationed at both matching faces against our artist's impression. The radio works fine.

As we move on, he explains that the Principal has altered the daily routine of his classes to allow him to lecture in one theater all day. This is a sign of how supportive the school is being. I know this must mean changing not just other teachers' schedules but also that of many students. I'm impressed.

The theater we arrive in will hold around a hundred-fifty. It has banked rows of seats with an unobstructed view of the platform at the front, where Jon Smith is already preparing his notes.

I look around for the best place to spend my time and decide that there's no point in hiding my presence as all the students already know what's going on, so I elect to pull up a single plastic chair to the edge of the platform where I can get to Smith quickly if required.

Knowing I'll likely spend a lot of time sitting, I stand and wait until the last minute before sitting down.

The double doors behind me swing open, and students arrive and take their seats. I'm unsure whether they have pre-arranged seating, but the back rows seemed to fill up quickly, so I guess not. I remember always wanting to be as far back as possible. Out of sight, out of mind. That was my motto.

Nine on the dot, and Jon Smith starts his class. I'm impressed that there's not a single student late for class, which tells me something else about him as a lecturer.

I've taken some Social Science classes at University, so I realize that what I'm about to hear could come from a wide range of topics. Economics, history, public health, and many others. This day, the issue is jurisprudence. I wonder if Jon Smith has chosen this deliberately.

He talks. I listen.

He explains jurisprudence as being the science or philosophy of law. Then starts a debate by asking the class why they think the country has so many lawmakers, attorneys, courts, and judges.

He's skillful with the class; I have to give him that. He coaxes students to voice their opinions and encourages active debate between students to run without his interference before bringing them back to his crucial point of principle - of how facts should be the basis for all judgments.

Again, he asks the room what they think might be the problem with his premise, and another active discussion starts.

I'm in for a treat if the entire day is like this. I've forgotten how infectious a learning environment can be. This is fun.

Eventually, he throws out a few simple examples and discusses how facts are often not as black or white as they might initially seem. That the world in which we live is very much a gray world, where black and white merely represent the extreme ends of a broad spectrum of behaviors.

I'm almost at the point of joining in when my radio squawks, and I tune in. A male voice is shouting that *'she's in the basement. Down by the generators.'*

Within seconds, I'm out of the door and rushing down the empty corridor, shouting in my radio that one of the front-door officers should take my place in the conference room with Jon Smith.

I'm breathing heavily by the time I'm at the end. I turn past the doors to the gymnasium and head along another corridor, following the signs for the kitchen. Having studied the detailed plans the previous week, I know access to the boiler room is from the landing bays at the rear of the kitchen.

I barge through the kitchen, passing confused staff already preparing the lunches, through another set of double doors, and into the loading bay. A truck is there with more people busily unloading the day's supplies. I turn right and run to the door straight up ahead, marked Maintenance.

* * *

Moments later, I stop halfway down the metal staircase to look into the gloom. Kicking myself, I realize I've missed the light switches at the top of the stairs. I take a moment to decide. Go back, or go on. Although dim, I can still see mostly, so I descend to the bottom, my Glock leading the way.

I stand stock-still and shout.

'*Armed police. If there's anyone down here, show yourselves and come out with your arms raised above your head.*'

Nothing. No sound. Nada.

I start cautiously checking around, keeping my Glock up. Finally, my eyes have adjusted, so I'm seeing everything.

The basement area is vast. Not the size of the entire school or anything, but it sprawls under the majority.

I pass the two generators themselves, massive things. One is always in use, and the other is prepared to kick in automatically if the first fails or there's a power outage.

I swear someone with a twisted sense of space and time planned the basement, and I'm losing patience with the search when a voice speaks behind me. It isn't a young girl. It's a man.

'Gun on the ground, detective.'

It isn't a request.

Parting with my gun is a big deal. Of course, it's a big deal to any police officer but a tremendous deal to me. My gun and my badge make me who I am.

I bend and carefully drop my Glock the last few inches to the ground, then stand up again.

'Kick it, man.'

I do as he asks, wondering why the voice sounds so familiar.

'Now turn your sorry ass round.'

I know who it is before I see him. Chico Vegas. This time, he doesn't look so friendly. Nor does the gun he holds in his hand. I try humor as a first approach.

'Hi, Chico. Missed our chats.'

'Not a problem. I see you suffering again, bitch.'

'Hey, I let you go, Chico. What's your beef?'

'My beef is you fucked up my complete business, man. Now Miami is after my ass, and if I'm goin' down, I'm sure as hell takin' you with me.'

'Maybe I can help with your problem, Chico. You know. Bring down the Miami mob with your help?'

'The only thing you're getting from me is lead.'

With that, a loud explosion echoes around the basement repeatedly. I feel a searing pain in my chest and just have time to regret wearing a stab vest that morning and not a ballistic. Then everything goes dark.

46

I hear noises, but they're fuddled and confusing. Someone is speaking, but I can't make out what they're saying.

Everything is quiet again and dark. Nothing can hurt me here. I doubt anyone can find me here. I'm safe.

Then there's some light, but it's blurry and indistinct. The noises are back. Someone is talking to me. I still can't make it out. Wait, yes, I can. Someone's saying my name. Just my first name, over and over, disturbing my peace. I don't want my peace disturbed. I'm safe here. I want to shout. To tell whoever it is to go away and leave me alone. I can't.

Why can't I shout?

At last, it's quiet again. I can relax. I wonder who was saying my name. It was a man's voice. I'm almost sure. He sounded worried.

I'm having trouble understanding something, but don't know what. Time seems to pass, but nothing is happening. The confusing lights come and go. The voice returns, repeating my name over and over. I need it to stop. I need to tell him to stop. I HAVE TO TELL HIM TO STOP!

Suddenly, I'm blinded by a blaze of light. Everywhere is so bright, I can't see. I'm only dimly aware of the paradox. I close my eyes, and the brightness recedes. Almost immediately, my need to look once more takes over.

This time, as bright as the light is, I can make out vague shapes around me. Some are moving, and others are not.

I'm no longer feeling safe. I can feel anxiety coursing through my veins. I'm scared of what's happening to me.

Slowly, one of the shapes takes form. It's a face. It looks familiar, but I can't quite place it.

There's another face looking closely into mine now. I don't know this person. They're looking into my eyes. Fuck, they're shining more light. What are they doing?

Then the extra light's gone, and the details of a room slowly come into shape. I struggle to speak. My mouth's dry. My lips are stuck together,

The face I recognize uses a small cotton bud to wet my lips, then offers me a straw to drink from.

I take a couple of sips and struggle to swallow.

I close my eyes and try to remember. What happened? Where am I? But don't come up with any answers that make sense. I open my eyes a second time. This time the room is in focus straight away. Concealed lighting covers the entire ceiling. I reckon that's what I saw before. The familiar voice speaks my name, and I turn and recognize Dan Weissman. He's speaking to me.

'Sammy.'

I mumble his name, but even I don't understand it. He helps me take a few more sips from a straw. This time, I manage to swallow.

'Dan?'

'Who did you expect? The Great White Spirit?'

I attempt to smile. My cheek muscles fail to respond.

'Welcome back, Sammy. We've been a little worried for a while.'

'Me too.' My attempt at humor. 'Where am I?'

'You're in Recovery at NCH. You've been shot, but the surgery went well, and you're expected to make a full recovery.'

'That's good. I mean that I recover, not that someone shot me.'

Dan smiled. 'If your crazy sense of humor is coming back, I would agree with your surgeon. Why don't you rest for a while? I'll come back later, and we can talk a little.'

The next time I open my eyes, Dan's sitting at my bedside, flicking through a magazine. I'm much more awake this time. I raise my hand to attract attention, and he stands up and leans over.

'How you doing now?'

'Better. Can I have some water?'

He let me sip from a straw again, then lays the cup aside and asks if I want to know what happened.

I nod.

'All I can tell you, Sammy, is what we have pieced together. Chico Vegas somehow figured out where you would be. He used a police radio to get you down into the basement, where he shot you. Unfortunately for him, the very person you were there to catch killed him. She slit his throat and left him to bleed out.'

'Charlie?'

'Charline Ellis. Probably saved your life. If Vegas had seen that you were still alive, he would probably have shot you a second time.'

'How did I survive?'

'It seems a student saw you slipping into the Maintenance doorway, and wondered what you were doing, so followed you into the basement. She didn't realize you were a detective.'

'Is she okay? Did Charlie hurt her?'

'No, she's fine. I think Kathy wants to bring her in to meet you, so I'll leave the rest of the story for them to tell you.'

'What about Charlie? Did we catch her?'

'No, she escaped before anyone else arrived. Jon Smith's fine too. We don't know why, but she seems to have changed her mind about him. We have an alert out on her, but I suspect she's long gone.'

'But she saved me?'

'Looks that way.'

I close my eyes for a moment to consider what Dan has told me. I can't think why she would do that. Why would she save the person who is trying to hunt her down? It doesn't make any sense.

When I open my eyes again, time must have passed. Dan's no longer there, and they've dimmed the lights. I assume it's nighttime.

I try to sit up but have no strength in my arms. I find a cable with a button attached and try pressing it. The head of the bed begins to rise. I stop when I'm high enough to look around.

Judging from the number of tubes and wires that connect me to various machines, I'm still in recovery.

My head is slowly clearing now. I can see someone else in a similar bed in another area opposite me. She's still unconscious. There's a man with a worried frown pacing back and forth just outside the door. I assume it will be her partner or spouse. I'm watching him go back and forward when a nurse enters and comes across to check on me. She lifts my chart and asks me how I'm feeling.

I tell her I have a headache, but other than that, I'm fine. She says she'll get me something for that. Checks my blood pressure and temperature, scribbles detail onto my chart, fiddles with the ECG monitor, then leaves, telling me she'll be right back.

Two minutes later, she's true to her word. She watches me swallow a couple of tablets, then tells me there are visitors to see me, but because there are two of them, they can only stay five minutes. Not six, she tells me. Five.

Moments later, Kathy comes to the bedside with a young girl in tow. 'Glad to see you awake, Sammy. We all thought we had lost you.'

I nod. My eyes riveted on the girl.

She would be in her late teens somewhere. Medium height,

skinny as a rake. She's wearing her dark hair cut in one of those fashionable styles, shaved at the sides and combed across to the one side on top. An amateur job. Her eyes are bright and intelligent, but her skin is pallid and drawn a little too tight. She looks like she could do with a good meal. She dresses like hundreds of teenagers with jeans and a gray hoodie.

'This is the girl who saved your life,' said Kathy. 'She followed you down into the basement, staying in the shadows, and was there when Vegas shot you. Before she could react, another girl sprang out of the darkness and sliced a knife across his throat, then ran for the stairs.

She knew you were in trouble when she saw the blood pumping from your chest, so stuck her finger into the bullet hole and sealed the leak. Something she had seen in a tv program.

She was still there when our officers found you and called for paramedics. They all agreed that it would be best if she keep her finger in place, so she traveled here to the hospital with you, never once removing her finger. All the way.

Only when you were in the Accident unit was she allowed to remove it. The doctor explained that the bullet had nicked a major artery close to your heart, and if she hadn't acted when she did, you would have died in the basement.'

All the time Kathy is telling me this, I can't take my eyes off the girl. In particular, the nose pin she's wearing. It's silver with a skull on the end. I've seen the skull before.

The girl stares mostly at the floor, only occasionally glancing my way.

'I thought you might like to thank her, Sammy?' Kathy prompts.

I look at Kathy and find her expression hard to read. Nervous? Apprehensive? I feel like she's asking for my approval, but I'm not sure for what. I turn back to the young girl.

Still not sure what to make of either Kathy or the girl. I can't somehow give the words the depth of feeling they should probably have when thanking someone for saving my life. But I thank her anyway.

At that point, true to her word, the nurse returns and shepherds my visitors away, with Kathy promising to return the following day.

After they leave, I try to make sense of what I've just seen and heard. Quite a few details are bothering me, but most of all, it's Kathy's discomfort.

Then there's the nose pin.

Unable to make any progress, I'm about to lower my bed when I hear my cell vibrate. The noise is coming from a drawer in the unit by the bed. I stretch out and tug it towards me, open the drawer, and remove my cell.

I realize then when I see there are dozens of unanswered calls that I've no idea how long I've been in here. Scanning through them, I quickly realize they're mostly from one number. If I were able, I would kick myself. They're all from Trace. She must be in a state of complete panic by now.

I'm about to call her when I stop to think about what I'm going to say. Health-wise, I can say I've been shot but am recovering and will be fine. That bit's easy. But how will she manage without me? She'll need cash and food.

I need help. But no one knows about Trace. It would need to be someone I can trust. My first thought is Kathy, but I still haven't figured out what exactly her involvement is with the girl from the High School. That whole visit left me feeling really uncomfortable. Something was going on there, and I don't know what. Until I do, I'm no longer as certain about her.

The only other choice I have is my parents. Only when I have that thought do I realize that they probably don't even know I've been shot, either. I call them first.

47

Two days later, they move me to a small private room, and I'm doing something I hardly ever make time for; I'm reading a book. A crime thriller, naturally. I reckon I have it solved by the second chapter, but will have to read on if only to prove myself correct.

I'm only just starting the third chapter when I'm told my parents are waiting to see me. A nurse brings them to me, and true to form, Mama's eyes are full of tears, and Papa is as stoic as ever. We talk for a while, with me reassuring them I'm fine. They already explained on my call the previous evening, that Dan Weissman had told them about the shooting and was calling them daily with an update, so I needn't have worried.

After we catch up, Papa leaves the room and returns moments later with Trace.

At first, she stands a couple of yards away, shocked by my appearance. I realize then that she may never have seen someone in a hospital like this before. If that's the case, the shock only lasts twenty seconds before she rushes to close the gap and throws her arms around my neck, sobbing.

I put my arms gently around her and hug her back. We stay like that until I can feel her gently pull away. She stands back and examines me more closely.

'You need some mac and cheese,' she tells me.

I laugh out loud.

'I need out of here. That's what I need.'

She's still clinging tightly to my hand, making me realize how frightened she has probably been. I have become a major player in her life, and she had nearly lost me. I squeeze her hand.

'How are you getting on with my parents?'

She looks at them and smiles.

'They're okay, I suppose!'

Mama gives her a mock scolding, and I see a grin spread on Papa's face. She's in safe hands for now, and I feel so grateful to my parents. I'm sure they can see it, but I tell them anyway.

They stay for a good hour after that and leave, promising to return in two days' time.

I tell Trace to be good. I don't know why, but it's something a parent's supposed to say.

After that, a variety of people come to see me. Joey's mama, all the members of the team I had been working with, Dan several times, and an unexpected visit from the Sheriff himself - again, as he points out. I'm almost feeling popular.

Then I have a genuine surprise when Jimi drops by one day. I would never have expected it, but he's really sweet. He adds his bunch of flowers to the many already on display around the room, then asks if I want to hear how he's getting on with tracking down the guy who knocked me on my butt at the garage.

I feel bad for him. I'd forgotten all about asking him to do this. Doubly bad because my motivation is nothing to do with getting a bad guy off the street. It's about getting a new car. Although by now, my new car fund is so depleted I can't afford to run it even if they give it to me for free.

I listen as he explains how he watched hours of traffic cam and security-cam footage until eventually finding a picture of the person responsible. It turns out to be a fifteen-year-old who's supporting a sick mother and three siblings. He hasn't charged him yet and wants to know what I think he should do.

I tell him that, sad as the case is, they should send him to Juvie Court, where they would take everything into consideration. I tell him not to worry. His family will be fine. He would likely be back on the street doing the same again in next to no time.

After Jimi has gone, I reflect on the inconsistency of the advice I've just given relative to the way I treated Trace when I caught her stealing a handbag. The conclusion I come to is that, like most interactions in life, human beings aren't consistent. You take different people, different behaviors, and different circumstances, and you get unique solutions. I guess it's true for detectives as well as anyone else.

One other person has already been to see me three times, armed with flowers, chocolates, and even a smuggled cold kebab one night. The District Attorney, Bossy-boots' father.
    Cliff said he had been really worried and seemed genuinely pleased at my rate of recovery, promising me top-notch after-care in the spare room at his place if I want it. I haven't yet decided what I want to do about that one. They'll release me in two days' time, so I need to decide soon.
    I considered telling Cliff about Trace but decide against it. I'm not sure his offer will extend to the two of us, and I'm already sure that somehow, Trace and I are going to be together for the long haul. I just don't yet understand how to make it happen.

The day before my release, Kathy drops by again. Since she brought the school girl who had saved my life to see me, this is the first time she's been on her own. Every other time, she had one or another of the team with her. Call me suspicious, but I don't think this visit on her own is an accident.
    We have a few minutes of the usual - checking up on each other - before she's finally ready to tell me why she's here.
    'We had a call from the Park Rangers down in the Glades the other day. A young woman rented a canoe for the day and didn't return it. She said she would be bird watching.'

'Something suspicious happen?'

'Not sure. They brought quite a few of us in to help with a search the following day. You know what it's like down there, thousands of small inlets and creeks. It took a couple of days to find the canoe. There was no sign of the person who rented it.'

'But?'

'They found her backpack. It only had a small portable tape recorder and a stack of used tapes inside.'

'The Park Rangers have these?'

'No. I have them here,' she says, holding up a small backpack.

'You've listened to them?'

'All of them. There are eight in total.'

'What's on them?'

'Interviews.'

'What sort of interviews?'

'Young girls sharing secrets.'

'What sort of secrets?'

'Maybe you should hear for yourself?' says Kathy, removing the small portable recorder from her bag and laying it beside me. 'I've already loaded the most recent tape recorded three years ago.'

I look at it, not sure if I want to know what is on it or not, then press play to hear two young girls talking casually. You can easily assume they are friends, although with one asking a lot of questions and the other answering, it's obviously an interview.

'So, what really happened then?'

'It started as a prank. A few of us girls always like to have fun with a new teacher. And it was my turn.'

'Weren't you scared?'

'Actually, it was a bit of a turn-on. It was exciting.'

'How do you mean?'

'I stayed behind in class to ask him a question.'

'What happened next?'

'I got so close. I was way inside his personal space and making him squirm. I could see he was uncomfortable. He tried to step back, but I followed him.'

'Cool. I bet you enjoyed that?'

'Dead right. But then I took his hand and used it to stroke my cheek.'

'What did he say?'

'Nothing. It was like he was frozen.'

'What did you do next?'

'I slipped his hand down to cup my breast.'

'Never! You didn't?'

'I did. And the bulge in his trousers told me he wanted me for sure. He was getting really horny.'

'What happened after that?'

'Nothing. I left him frustrated and walked away.'

'Seriously?'

'The rest of the girls were waiting outside in the corridor, and we had a real laugh.'

'So that was it?'

'Originally, that was all we were going to do, but I wanted to have a little more fun with him.'

'You went back into the classroom?'

'No. I went to the Principal and complained.'

'But he had done nothing wrong?'

'Yes, he had. He'd felt up my boob.'

Then there was laughter, and the tape clicks off.

Kathy just takes the recorder and puts it back in her bag.

'There were eight tapes in total. The first seven tell very detailed stories of real sexual abuse, some of which are unimaginable for girls so young. They're told in the same manner, as if the interviewer had somehow become their friend and they were unburdening themselves. No adult would ever have been able to get these details from the girls. Not an attorney, for sure.'

I look directly at Kathy as I comment on what I've just heard…

'The girl doing the interviewing is very skillful. She knew exactly what she was doing. Almost like taking confessions. And eight is an interesting number.'

'Yes, it is,' Kathy agrees. 'And with each interview, she was incredibly thorough. She wanted to get all the details right. It was very important to her. Seven horrible cases of sexual abuse with very young children and one false accusation. It must have taken a lot of research to find these eight girls and build sufficient trust with them. Careful, painstaking work over some time, I would think.'

'Years, even,' I suggest. 'And the interviewer is the girl who has disappeared in the Glades?'

'I'm afraid so, replies Kathy. 'I doubt anyone will ever find her now. I fear her interviewing days are over.'

'Gators?'

After Kathy leaves, I feel the weight of the unspoken agreement we've reached. Charlie will live a normal life somewhere far from here. But for Kathy and I, we've sworn to respect and defend a line we have just willingly and knowingly stepped over.

It may take some time, but there will be consequences for sure.

MORE SAMMY GREYFOX

Follow Sammy as she comes to accept her shortfalls in motherhood and caring for friends while solving, by far, her most difficult case to date. A case from which there may be no way back.

Author Direct

HUGH MACNAB

AUTHOR DIRECT TO READER

Thank you for your purchase.

If you enjoyed the book and would like to find out what else is available, I would love to have you to visit my book store at

hughmacnab.com

If you find something you like, you can apply the following discount code to recieve 20% reduction on any book you choose.

Discount code : **Offer 20**

I am also interested in any feedbaclk you have on my books and would appreciate you letting me know your thoughts.

You can contact me at

Hugh@hughmacnab.com

Sammy Greyfox Thrillers

No Way Back

When a private detective is killed, Sammy must not only solve the case,

but race against time to save someone she loves from a painful death.

Head of the Snake

It is a strange case that even the combined skills of
Sherlock Holmes and
Hercule Poirot would struggle to solve.

* * *

Lost Souls

Sammy travels the length and breadth of the country, seeking twelve lost souls.
Some she will save. Some she will not.

All available at Hughmacnab.com

D.S. Eli Ross series

A veteran Brooklyn homicide cop, a recovering addict, and a teenage boy with an IQ in the top one percent of the world hunt serial Killers.

Available at Hughmacnab.com

Self-help series

These books will not only help you understand why you feel, think, and behave the way you do when you are at your worst but will also explain the most likely cause for all of this - and it may surprise you.

The books also include access to nine half-hour videos that will help you overcome your symptoms using a simple step-by-step process. These videos, combined with the book, form the three-week recovery program.

No program will work for everyone, but over 1200 people have successfully used these programs.

The programs start from the premise that perhaps there's really not very much wrong - and that's likely to be so different from how you feel.

All availabale at Hughmacnab.com

Printed in Great Britain
by Amazon